PENGUIN ME
WHEN ONLY LOVE REMAINS

Durjoy Datta was born in New Delhi, India, and completed a degree in engineering and business management before embarking on a writing career. His first book—*Of Course I Love You!*—was published when he was twenty-one years old and was an instant bestseller. His successive novels—*Now That You're Rich!*; *She Broke Up, I Didn't!*; *Oh Yes, I Am Single!*; *If It's Not Forever*; *Till the Last Breath*; *Someone Like You*; *Hold My Hand*—have also found prominence on various bestseller lists, making him one of the highest-selling authors in India.

Durjoy also has to his credit two television shows, *Sadda Haq* (Channel V) and *Veera* (Star Plus), both of which have done exceedingly well on Indian television.

Durjoy lives in New Delhi, loves dogs and is an active Crossfitter. For more updates, you can follow him on Facebook (www.facebook.com/durjoydatta1) or Twitter (@durjoydatta).

Also by Durjoy Datta

Hold My Hand

★

Someone Like You
(With Nikita Singh)

★

Till the Last Breath . . .

★

If It's Not Forever
It's Not Love
(With Nikita Singh)

★

You Were My Crush
Till You Said You Love Me!
(With Orvana Ghai)

★

Oh Yes, I'm Single!
And So Is My Girlfriend!
(With Neeti Rustagi)

★

She Broke Up, I Didn't!
I Just Kissed Someone Else!

★

Now That You're Rich
(With Maanvi Ahuja)

★

Of Course I Love You
Till I Find Someone Better
(With Maanvi Ahuja)

DURJOY DATTA

When Only Love Remains

Penguin
metro reads

METRO READS

USA | Canada | UK | Ireland | Australia
New Zealand | India | South Africa | China

Metro Reads is part of the Penguin Random House group of companies
whose addresses can be found at global.penguinrandomhouse.com

Published by Penguin Random House Group
7th Floor, Infinity Tower C, DLF Cyber City,
Gurgaon 122 002, Haryana, India

First published in Penguin Metro Reads by Penguin Books India 2014

ISBN 9780143422648

Typeset in Bembo Roman by Ram Das Lal, New Delhi
Printed at Thomson Press India Ltd, New Delhi

www.penguin.co.in

To the month of February 2014; to new beginnings;
and to my nephew, Reyhan

Some of this actually happened . . .

ONE

avanti

She measures each step, small and deliberate, and looks at her watch hoping time would stretch out indefinitely, locking her in the moment. Delhi University buses, the U-Specials as they are called, screech to a halt at the bus stops nearby and kids pour out, chattering, shouting, complaining and cursing. Music and strained guitar riffs blare from her pink Skullcandy earphones and yet she can't concentrate on Devrat's painful, screeching voice. She makes a mental note to get those noise cancellation earphones at half-price from an online retailer. But they don't come in fluorescent pink or orange. Then she thinks that maybe it's not the earphones, and attributes the sound to the decrepit studio in Kolkata in which Devrat must have recorded his music.

'The Endless Road'.

It's her favourite Devrat song and she listens to it on a loop every few days, staring in the distance while she does so, imagining herself to be playing a complex, interesting woman in a movie. She often scribbles down the lyrics on the margins of the books and notebooks she uses, but the words seem empty without Devrat's broken voice and his imperfect guitar riffs. Devrat never does covers of songs sung by others; all his songs are fresh compositions and most of them are recorded on cell phones. He has been uploading his videos for the last five years.

She reaches the gates of her college to collect the receipt of her admission in a correspondence course. It's her third day in Delhi and she already doesn't like it. Going back home to a reserved, stammering, absent-minded father isn't really her idea of fun.

Avanti can't wait for her job to start at Indiago Airlines as a flight attendant. Attending college, taking down notes, running after college professors and getting notes photocopied was never her calling. She was too pretty to score well and be confined to a cubicle.

There was a time she wanted to go to Xavier's in Mumbai or Symbiosis in Pune. Back in Dehradun, where she grew up with her grandmother, she had heard great things about both the institutes. She wanted to be the one who zips around in a little pink scooter with her face wrapped like a terrorist or take an auto at three in the morning without the fear of getting raped. Being in Delhi and staying with her father was the last thing she ever wanted to do. But her grandmother forced her to shift out of her house in Dehradun where she had lived for the last twelve years, to move in with her father.

'He needs you,' she had insisted and she can seldom turn her grandmother down. Avanti hadn't seen her father in a decade. She had grown up with her grandmother in Dehradun after her mother died in an accident when she was really young.

She spots a few guys looking in her direction and she shrugs it off. She turns up the volume on her iPod and Devrat's voice blares into her ears. Devrat, the reclusive young singer, has always been Avanti's saviour, right from the first song he uploaded.

Avanti had a troubled childhood. She was only three when her mother passed away, and all of five years when she was put into a girl's boarding school, a place her unsuspecting grandmother thought would be safe for her. Little did her grandmother know what would happen. The first few months were the worst. Little and lonely Avanti would be woken up by Warden Aunty and taken to the back alley of the library, every night for weeks at an end. She would be stripped and touched all over, and she would cry, she would wail, and the warden would ask her to stay shut or she would be caned the next day. Avanti, scared and crying, would bear everything.

And then after a few months it suddenly stopped. The warden preyed on someone else. For years, she stayed shut. The few girls she talked to about it would brush it away. The warden eventually left the school and disappeared. It's said that her deeds had come out in the open and she was thrown out, but there was no case against her because the school wanted to uphold its image as a safe, friendly school.

'Big deal! It happened three years back, naa? Forget it now. Move on,' her best friends would tell her.

But it was hard for Avanti. It wasn't as if she hadn't tried. She tried the hardest she could. She was still the most talkative, ebullient kid in school who participated in everything, but when alone, she used to be a scared little girl fighting with those images of being naked with the warden, her rough fingers on her body, her voice telling her to shut up, telling her that what was being done to her was nothing unusual, and every new kid goes through the same. The more she talked, the less she was reminded of those long, torturous nights. So Avanti hasn't stopped talking since then . . .

There were years when she wouldn't sleep in the night with the lights off. And if any roommate would switch them off, she would curl up in the corner of the room, and cry herself to sleep, scared. She had even tried to cut herself a few times over the years. She doesn't do that anymore, but the scars remain.

It took eight years for her to sleep without fear. It wasn't until the time she was thirteen that she got a grip on the situation. It wasn't therapy or her grandmother's love, who knew nothing about what had happened, that gave her a fresh lease of life. It was the songs of a fifteen-year-old boy, Devrat, singing in his modest house in Kolkata that gave her the strength. She had stumbled on those songs on a networking site and had downloaded them on her iPod. The boy had floppy hair, puppy-like eyes and a strange voice. And since that day, it was as if this boy was singing to her. And since that day, whenever Avanti is down and out, scared, or crying, she just listens to his songs and suddenly, everything is better. It was Devrat's songs that drew Avanti out of her fears and gave her another chance at life.

The boys are still looking at her. Avanti has been through the entire lifecycle of being the cute, chubby toddler to the adorable adolescent to now—a very attractive young girl. She's wearing a T-shirt three sizes too big, her shorts barely visible from under the T-shirt. A school bag hangs loosely across her shoulder and her thick curly hair is a careful mess that took two hours, a curler, hairspray and unwavering patience.

'You're a dream,' a boy in the fifth standard had said and she remembers it like yesterday.

She used to look at television actresses and wonder if she were better-looking than them, and she still does. She has a face fit for television but acting never held any charm for her. 'It must be exhausting to be someone else,' she thinks.

She was smart enough to know that she wasn't going to win the Nobel Prize for physics or find a cure for AIDS, and so when she heard that Indiago was looking for flight attendants, she took the bait. It was either that or staying with Dad and doing college full-time, neither of which were acceptable.

As soon as she passed her twelfth boards, she took the interview for the airlines and sailed through it. The interviewer had asked her why she wanted to be a flight attendant and she had smiled—it had always worked—and told the interviewer that she had always wanted to travel, ever since she was a little girl. *I just want to run.*

'Why are you doing this? I was sending you to Delhi to spend a little more time with your father, not this!' her grandmother had said angrily.

'Nani, I really want to do this. And my base is still Delhi, and I will still live with him,' she had answered.

'But you will fly most of the time! When will you get the time to spend with him? He's your father, Avanti,' Nani had protested.

'I will also see him.'

'Avanti, your father needs you now. He's getting old.'

'So are you! And if he needed me, he could have come and told me that,' she had snapped angrily.

'You can't be angry at him. I told you how he is.'

'Nani, you know that I really don't mind him. I'm not really angry at him; I never was. I just don't know who he is. He's a stranger to me, Nani. And moreover, I just don't want to study. I want to work and I know I will love this.' Avanti draws her breath and calms down before she continues, 'And I will be staying with him as much as I can and I will take care of him, I promise!' That had been the end of the discussion.

She's at the counter to collect the receipt of her admission into the correspondence course when her phone rings. It's her grandmother.

'Hi, Nani!' she greets her.

'Beta? Reached college? You ate something before you left? What will you do for lunch? When will you go home? Give me a call when you reach home, okay?' Her grandmother pauses for breath to throw more questions at her.

'I am okay, Nani. Don't worry about me,' she says and hopes it will be an umbrella answer to all her questions. She loves her grandmother to bits and beyond, but no one likes too many questions. It was cute at times, but right now . . .

'How's Rajiv? He is taking care of you, right?' she asks and coughs. Her grandmother has been on the verge of death for over a decade, legs dangling precariously over her grave—but she hangs on stubbornly, for now. There is no other way that Avanti remembers her grandmother other than being old and sick, coughing and wheezing but still convincing everyone that she has another thousand years to live.

'Yes, Nani, he is,' she lies. 'I will call you when I get back home. I love you. Bye!'

She disconnects the call and imagines her distraught, sick Nani on the other side of the phone. She must be looking at her cell phone wistfully, wondering how Avanti was just a child a heartbeat ago. Avanti misses her grandmother's wrinkled fingers on her face, her repetitive questions, and her undeniably fattening food. She hates the thought that she would be gone in a few years, but she tries not to think about it. She's standing in the long line to collect the receipts for admissions when a voice from behind says, 'You're from Dehradun?' It's a boy. He's drooling and he's not even trying to hide that he's hitting on her.

'I live in Delhi with my father. My mother died when I was three. And I have cut my hands a few times because I was raped when I was five. Also I have a boyfriend,' says Avanti, coldly, and shows the boy the little scars on her hands. These tricks are really old, but they never fail to work. Conversation dries up. The death of a sibling, of a mother, rape, failed suicide attempts, a terminal disease etc. are certified conversation killers. It's assumed that anyone who has gone through any of these must be under continual and unending trauma. The boy says nothing, a little confused whether Avanti is joking, and even if she isn't, he doesn't want to take the chance.

Avanti misses Dehradun. She misses the idyllic surroundings, the blue Vikrams, autorickshaw-like vehicles, she never boarded, the handful of quaint cafés, the drive to Mussoorie and Landsdowne, the house parties of her friends, the quietude of the little town, and the raging gossip circles—where even the men were as interested as the women.

Just as she is about the leave, her phone rings and it's Shekhar Malhotra, the most handsome and unnaturally ripped off boys in Dehradun. A walking piece of muscle and a perpetual protein shake guzzler. She'd started dating him when she was fifteen, and he was eighteen, a college boy. It all started when one day he forcefully made her drink at a small party. He kissed her that day, and she, drunk, had regretfully kissed him back. The news spread like wildfire in her school and his college and since Avanti didn't want to be called a slut, she started dating him. She dated him for two long, torturous years before they broke up last year.

For those two years, Avanti was nothing more than a piece of furniture to him, something that he owned and could be territorial about. Now that Avanti thinks of her relationship with Shekhar she can't find a single reason why she was with him. Yes, he was the quintessential possessive boyfriend. He never allowed anyone near Avanti, which at times was comforting. He was also very connected (his father was an IAS officer or something), so when Avanti had told him about the warden and her molestation, he and his friends in the police had hunted the woman down and she was beaten in Avanti's presence. Ever since Shekhar had done that for her, she was indebted to him somehow, and she didn't know how to pay back that debt. So she stayed with him and put up with Shekhar's abusive behaviour, his anger problem and his highly chauvinistic attitude.

Most often he would get angry whenever Avanti refused to get intimate with him. In the two years that they were together, Avanti hadn't kissed him more than twice and she got slapped quite a few times for her resistance. But she just couldn't free herself of him.

'Everyone's doing it, why can't you fucking do it as well?' he used to shout. Avanti used to break down into tears and tell him that she wasn't comfortable doing it. 'Oh c'mon! Just because you were molested when you were five, you can't continue being depressed and never do anything! SHE WAS A WOMAN AND SHE FORCED YOU! I'M NOT RAPING YOU!' And then he would grab her by her arm and shake her. And strangely, his touch reminded her of the warden's.

'TELL ME!' he used to shout.

Avanti used to cry and beg him to leave her and he would. She never gave into Shekhar and eventually they broke up.

Shekhar has had a few flings since then. But till date, Shekhar acts like he owns Avanti, and though Avanti is an extrovert, a happy girl, she still gets scared and apprehensive and guarded whenever Shekhar calls. She's not sure if he's any less scary than the warden who had molested her.

'Hi Shekhar,' she says.

'Where are you? I called you yesterday and you didn't answer. You were in college, right?' he asks in a tone that only steady boyfriends and parents can use.

'I'm sorry. It was just that Dad was around,' she answers.

'You could have called back.'

Avanti can already sense his anger on the phone so she apologizes again. 'Let me send you a phone from here so that I can call you on that number. You can use it just to reach me. How about that? Can we do that? The new iPhone just came out. It's awesome and it's only for seventy thousand.'

'I don't need a phone, Shekhar. My phone works just fine. I would have called you. You just got to be a little patient with me. It's just that Dad and the college formalities and . . .' she pleads, her voice imitating a small puppy's. There's nothing to sort out between her and her father; it's a dead relationship, but she's hoping Shekhar will withdraw.

'Okay, okay! Fine. Next time, pick up my call on time,' he grumbles. 'If you need anything, a friend of mine studies in the same college. I will ask him to keep an eye out for you. He is connected. And next time I call, pick it up at once.'

'Fine.'

She wants to shout and ask him to fuck off, but somehow her voice fails.

Avanti disconnects the line and plugs in the earphones again. She can't wait to start being a flight attendant and fly out of

Delhi and she thinks it's not entirely because of her father or
her not wanting to study anymore. It's also because she doesn't
want to be around Shekhar anymore. She wants to run away
from him. She hopes that with time, Shekhar will stop treating
her like a piece of property and will forget her.

She watches Devrat sing in the small video, his eyes always
slightly watery, wide-open, like they are searching for something,
like a little pug's eyes. She feels better all of a sudden. And just
like that she's no longer scared. She sends Devrat a mail from
one of the twenty fake accounts she has created to thank him
for his songs.

'Fuck you, Shekhar,' she mutters.

TWO

devrat

It's a dark room, filled with the stench of cigarettes and alcohol; the windows are closed. Devrat has changed five apartments in the last seven months and he doesn't think he will last in this one for very long either. Sooner or later, the landlord will discover the filth, the drugs, and his sloth-like living standards and throw him out, with all of his six T-shirts, two pairs of jeans, his guitars and his harmonica. And again he would lose himself amongst the many others in the streets of Kolkata. The city is crumbling, like him, like the people walking with him; there is no hope.

He thinks of ordering food but after the rent and the security, he is left with just over six hundred rupees. But that's not the worst part. The worst part is that he is out of cigarettes and without a smoke, words don't come to him and without his words, he's incomplete.

But what's the difference? No one listens to his songs anyway.

He lights the last cigarette, takes long drags, and keeps the smoke inside him till only a small sliver of smoke pours out of his nose. He crushes the butt and runs his finger on the strings idly. Melody has always come easy to him; it's the words that are the problem.

It's been five months since he has uploaded any videos of his songs on his YouTube channel, which has all of two hundred subscribers, most of them accidental. But some of them, and he remembers them by name, are regular followers and have asked time and again as to when they can expect his new song. They even converse between themselves if the singer, Devrat, has left the singing business and is working now as an engineer or worse, dead. A few of them mail Devrat regularly, thanking him for his music, but apart from that he doesn't really command a huge following. He replies to them whenever he's in a mood to do so.

He has not been busy for the last few months. He's been depressed, drunk and defeated . . . in love. In love that was true and undying and defying and strange and senseless and passionate and stupid, like every love is. He thought Arundhati was the one he would flee this city with, but like all great love stories it wasn't to be. Like many others, and like him, Arundhati was always confused, the confusion rising from insecurity about what the future might hold rather than acceptance of what he really was. Like in all Bollywood movies, she was too rich for him, or he was too poor for her. And it still mattered even though they were only twenty-one-year olds.

Three months back, Arundhati got engaged to a nice Bengali guy whom her parents chose for her and she gladly accepted him. The guy is diametrically opposed to what he is. He is an investment banker, belongs to a family of doctors, lives in a palatial house in Salt Lake and has never been in an apartment that has a washroom smaller than the entire flat Devrat has to himself.

Devrat contemplates if he should get himself another pack of cigarettes or if he should sleep but the phone rings and it takes him an eternity to find the damned instrument under the mess. He's surprised how much he could dirty his room even with his limited belongings. It's his manager on the other line. Actually, he is the manager of fifty other acts like him and it's his responsibility to get them gigs, possibly paid gigs in Kolkata and around. But since music is something you do because you love to do it, quite like writing, or journalism, you don't expect to get paid. And moreover, electronica is in. Female DJs are in. Real live music is out. David Guetta is in. Stereophonics is out. Despite the fading fortune of small-time musicians like Devrat, Sumit, his manager, works steadfastly to get these musicians an odd gig a month. After all, till the time he signs a big band or a label, which doesn't seem like a possibility, his income is tied to theirs.

'Hey! Where are you? Thatplace Else today, 8 p.m. I sent you ten reminders. Don't you check your phone or what? They have put big posters and shit, man. They are looking forward to your performance! The crowd is going to be insane!' Sumit shrieks. His energy is unbelievable and it's hard to imagine that he is thirty-five. He makes money off it but there is no denying that he loves music and tries to promote good music in the best way he can. He never signs a bad musician. Never.

The worst part about the Kolkata music scene is that it has too much talent for any one city to nurture and pay for, especially a poor city like this.

'I didn't get your reminders. I don't think I am going to make it today,' he sighs.

'FUCK YOU, man. It's ten thousand bucks for four hours. You're not going to get this anywhere else in Kolkata! You got to come. And this is *Thatplace Else*, the mecca of good music. Do you have any idea how rarely they bring in someone to perform solo here? The crowd is so you. They love you here. Who knows, you might even find yourself a girlfriend here! You should see the girls there, man.'

'You're married, Sumit.'

'That's why I'm banking on you, Dev,' says Sumit. 'You're twenty-one. Stop behaving like you're already a star on your way down. Get laid tonight. Do what fuck-all failed musicians do! Do your gig and then get someone home.'

'I'm not into that, and you know that. Anyway, I will be there,' he says and disconnects the call.

Sumit texts him that he would be there to pick him up at seven and would appreciate it if he took a bath and put on some rockstar-like clothes. It's still eight hours to go and he realizes it would be difficult to power through the day without another pack of cigarettes. He picks himself up, drags his body to the shower and stands listlessly under the pouring hot water. Despite repeated pleas that turned into threats, Devrat has not managed to switch off the geyser for a single minute since the time he has moved in.

He dries himself off and puts on a T-shirt with the washed-out graphic of his favourite band, The Stereophonics. They were the ones who had inspired his hobby into a compulsion, a passion into a career which wasn't the most promising but satisfying. In retrospect, Devrat wasn't only in love with the band and their rusty, jagged music but also the enigmatic yet boyish, never-ageing lead singer and guitarist, Kelly Jones.

When he was thirteen, he still remembers, girls used to crowd around him as he imitated Kelly Jones's whisky vocals. He basked in the attention of girls in short skirts with pink cheeks and felt like he had arrived. Devrat Roy was the barometer of coolness in general.

The streets were empty when he left his flat to get some cigarettes. Kolkata shuts down in the afternoon for a nap of a few hours after it has had its elaborate rice and fish meal. Of all the things that have held back this city, laziness is at the forefront. The city loves to argue, loves raging political discussions, holds on steadfastly to its culture and its numerous heroes, and is ridiculously proud of its rich past and dismissive of its dark future. Under the garb of intellectualism, Kolkata is full of people with crushed ambitions, diminished hopes and no business sense. The city bears a defeated look.

He buys two packets of Wills Navy Cut, a brand he has smoked since the twelfth standard. For the year he was with Arundhati, he had stopped smoking, but now he's back to the habit with a vengeance, thinking of it as a quiet rebellion against the break-up. After smoking five in a row, he drifts off to sleep.

It's seven when he wakes up and checks his phone which is flooded with missed calls and texts from Sumit. He calls back and Sumit replies with the choicest abuses in three languages he knows and asks him to get ready in fifteen minutes.

He shaves, puts on his shoes, chooses between three T-shirts and waits for Sumit outside his apartment building. Fifteen minutes later, Sumit and Devrat are negotiating the traffic to Thatplace Else, Park Street, Kolkata. Sumit is on the phone handing down a verbal spanking to a new band, which got too drunk on a gig and left it halfway to join the revellers.

Sumit parks the car and leads Devrat through the back entrance of the club into the tiny office of the club manager. The manager has seen quite a few big stars in music over the last two years that the club has grown in prominence. He knows almost everyone on a first name basis. He smiles when Devrat walks in and Devrat smiles back. Earlier, Devrat used to play as a back-up singer for an act at Thatplace Else. He was a big hit amongst the girls back then, his floppy hair, his sharp nose and his big eyes were a big draw.

'All set?' the manager asks and offers him whisky which Devrat promptly accepts.

'As usual,' Devrat says, smiles back, and gulps the whisky. It's good for Devrat's nerves.

'All yours,' he says and instructs his office boy to help Devrat set up his instruments.

Devrat leaves with the boy. The pub is still relatively empty with only a handful of people drinking and chatting idly. He starts setting up his instruments and looks over his shoulder, wondering if Arundhati knows about his gig. Two years back, it was Thatplace Else where they'd first met, talked about music, and slowly fell in love.

He is sure he would see some of the familiar faces. Thatplace Else is meticulous about informing people of the schedule of the gigs and if Sumit is to be believed, there were people waiting to hear him again.

As he does his first sound check, he feels his heart split open. And then it settles. He mistook a girl for Arundhati.

'Check. Check.'

He flashes a thumbs-up to the manager who is now on the floor. He is a fan. Everyone who has ever listened to Devrat sing is a fan. Only if Devrat sang a little more.

THREE

avanti

Out of habit, Avanti checks the newspaper for gigs, hoping Devrat would land in Delhi for a performance. Nothing. She checks Devrat's Myspace and Facebook page and there are no updates there as well. His last update is quite old. It was a song he had composed which revolved around the lost city of Dwarka. The other girls in her hostel who heard the song thought nothing of it, but she thought the song was about lost love and not the lost city.

'You're just in love with a cute songwriter,' the girls used to say.

She keeps refreshing her Twitter timeline as she eats her breakfast, Kellogg's cornflakes and cold milk. The selfie she uploaded today morning on Twitter tagging it 'lazy morning' has been favourited twenty times. She doesn't upload pictures on Facebook because . . . well, Shekhar throws a tantrum. Her father is solving the crossword; he's already done with the Sudoku in the three newspapers that lay on the table. He doesn't initiate any conversation as well. She checks her mailbox to see if Devrat has replied to any of the mails she keeps sending him from her dummy accounts. He hasn't. For the past few months, there's absolutely no activity on Devrat's pages and it saddens Avanti a little. He's been like a drug to her. If he doesn't respond for long, she gets restless.

'Do ... do you need any money?' her father stammers a little later and she shakes her head. She has an ATM card that her father gave her when she first came and she hasn't really spent anything from it although she has been wanting to since the money her grandmother gave her is slowly running out.

'When's the t ... raining starting?' he asks again.

'Tomorrow,' she says, looks up and smiles.

'The maid will come at twelve,' mumbles her father, still not making eye contact.

Avanti nods. Her father is still looking into the newspaper struggling to find a five-letter word in 21 across as he eats the soggy cornflakes, his legs constantly in a nervous shiver. He smells of talcum powder and Keo Karpin hair oil and looks quintessentially middle-aged, just like a mathematics professor at a government college should look like. She is not angry at her father for driving her mother to leave him, she's just unsure of the man sitting in front of her. She hasn't seen much of him growing up. She has just heard about him from her grandmother. And in her grandmother's version he was a gentle, warm man. That was before he went slightly mad, and got consumed in his obsession with mathematics, and her mother had no option but to leave him.

Once in the room, she wishes she had continued the conversation on the dining table. She hears the door close and realizes that her father has left for college.

Bored, she walks into the living room and switches on

the television. She has started to miss Dehradun a little more now—her friends, their friends, their friends and her mutual friends, her mutual friends' boyfriends. There was no end to people she knew there, and everyone knew her. She wishes she had someone to talk to right now. Nothing deep, just talk. Her grandmother often remarked that Avanti couldn't go to sleep unless she's done with her quota of ten thousand spoken words every day.

She watches ten minutes of a soap where the main protagonist and antagonist are crying over spilled milk. No pun.

'What's wrong with these people who make soaps!'

She updates her Facebook status. Five guys respond to it. They drop names of English sitcoms they watch (in wrong grammar of course). Thirty-three guys like the status. Including Shekhar, who writes, 'Stp wtchin em, baby'. Avanti cringes. A lot of guys comment. She's half-expecting Shekhar to call and blast her for being an attention whore. But thankfully, her phone doesn't ring.

She opens the cabinet to find movies she could watch and finds none. Instead, she finds a stack of video games arranged alphabetically and cross-referenced according to their genre and their year of release. Borderline crazy, she thinks, and closes the cabinet. The next cabinet is brimming with comic books. The next one has science journals. And books on conspiracy theories. There are still around twenty to go and there are three rooms she hasn't checked yet. She wonders what her crazy father hides behind those doors. Skulls? Knives?

'Your father was a great mathematician till one unsolved question made him crazy,' her grandmother used to say.

She thinks, what if her father was more than just a crazy mathematician? What if he's like Dexter? A crime-fighting mathematician? That would be cool! Also impossible, for her father wears loose trousers with sports shoes. *Hardly an attire for a suave crime fighter!*

She walks into her father's study and it's a mess. Unlike the rest of the house, which is comparatively clean, this room looks like it has never been cleaned. There are books stacked on books, notes, journals and stray papers strewn all around, blackboards filled with numbers and letters in illegible combinations. *He's still crazy!*

She leaves the room, goes to the kitchen and cooks herself some Maggi in the microwave, the Indian snack that can replace any meal and can be had any time of the day. The noodles are a little overcooked and they drip out of the bowl. She pours bright red tomato ketchup all over the Maggi noodles.

She has just opened one of her father's comics, when her phone rings. It's Shekhar.

'Hi. Are you home?' Shekhar asks as soon she picks up the call.

'Yes, why? There were no classes to attend today so I stayed home.'

'Where is your house?' he asks.

'It's near Dhaula Kuan, why?'

'I am in Delhi and I am coming to see you. Give me your exact address and I will be there in an hour.'

She's already a little scared. When they used to date, Avanti would make sure they never met alone in a closed space. She is still apprehensive about meeting him.

'Umm . . . Dad is home and he doesn't let me go out. He's very strict. He's hovering around me as we speak. I don't think I can see you today. I'm sorry, Shekhar,' she mumbles.

'You can come out of the house for a few minutes. Just tell

him a friend is here to see you. I really need to see you. And I need to see you now,' he grumbles.

'I can't do that. He is very protective and even if I tell him, he would ask the friend to come and meet him too. And my grandmother has already told him about you, so it's better that you don't come. Also I'm down and I have cramps. I don't think I can walk down. I also have a fever,' she fibs nervously.

There's brief pause from the other side. 'Oh, okay. Take care. I will see you tomorrow, then,' he says, not giving up.

'I start work from tomorrow, Shekhar.'

'Miss it,' growls Shekhar.

'I can't!'

'Oh, sure you can. It's a shitty job. I will give you the money. Just meet me. Don't try to avoid me, Avanti. And who do you think you're uploading these pictures for? You think I haven't seen them? You think I wouldn't know just because I'm not on Twitter? You have started dating someone, haven't you? Give me your passwords.'

'I can't, Shekhar. And I haven't started dating anyone.'

'Then give the passwords to me! I want to see who you are talking to. Just give them to me, you . . .'

'I'm sorry,' says Avanti.

'I'm sure you're fucking someone, aren't you?' shouts Shekhar. 'I just knew it! I just fucking knew it. That's why Delhi, right? You're just a fucking slut, Avanti.'

'Shekhar!' Avanti has almost started to cry.

'JUST GIVE ME YOUR FUCKING ADDRESS. I WILL COME TO SEE YOU!' shouts Shekhar. 'You bitch, you're sleeping behind my back. Who was there when you needed someone? I found the woman who raped you. I did it for you! I waited for two years to get you and two days in Delhi and you're fucking someone else!' shouts Shekhar. Avanti can almost see Shekhar's reddened face, the popping veins on his forehead and neck, and she throws the phone away. The phone hits the wall and the battery spills out.

She walks dazedly to her iPod, connects it to her father's speakers which starts to blast a medley of Devrat's songs. She slurps in the cold Maggi with a fork. Surprisingly, it doesn't taste all that bad.

FOUR

devrat

It's been two weeks since Devrat's last gig and his fan page
has seen a sudden spike of three hundred fans in this short
while. Videos of his performance are being shared in the small
community of English music lovers in Kolkata, and also beyond.
Three girls are seen crying in the pictures Thatplace Else
uploaded on their Facebook page. The people in the crowd
look drunk and euphoric and sad and amazed and the crying
girls look similar to the ones in any One Direction or Justin
Bieber concert. Only that these people are grown-ups and not
love-struck teenagers fixating on a cute smile and great hair.

Devrat knows nothing of it. He has been lost in a haze of
smoke and alcohol. Six of the ten thousand rupees he was
paid that day is already smoke and alcohol-processed-piss. His
phone has been switched off for a week and Sumit has made
five trips to his apartment to make sure he is alive. Sumit has
not tried counselling him though. He knows it's better to stay
away from young suicidal musicians. He loves Devrat and all,
but he doesn't want to have anything to do with him if he

decides to end it? Who knows what the police might come up with?

It is late afternoon when Devrat wakes up and is startled by how much his breath stinks—like a colony of rats procreated, multiplied and died. The room looks like a little grenade stuffed with clothes and newspapers instead of shrapnel exploded in it. He opens the window and stands by it and lights a cigarette. It's his last and he will have to go out to get another one. It looks like it will rain and he feels good about it. For a few hours, the entire city will be as glum and heckled as he is. He flicks the cigarette onto the pavement and checks if the geyser is still on and it is. It's out of compulsion that he takes a bath or he would have choked on his body odour.

As he bathes he remembers the sweet scent of Arundhati's body, the kind of smell that affluent girls reek off, the smell of flowers (Arundhati said it was a body mist by Victoria's Secret), and feels like smoking again.

He's running out of money, he remembers. Just as he's looking for his T-shirt, his phone rings. He had turned it on some time back. At first he ignores it, thinking it's Sumit. But the phone keeps ringing incessantly. It's his mom. Devrat takes the call.

'Hello!'

'Hello, Ma.'

His mother rattles off in Bengali about how worried she was when she found his phone switched off for the last couple of days. Devrat gives her a few half-assed explanations for his absence. His mother asks him if everything is okay and he says that it is. Every time his mother calls, Devrat puts up a brave front and tells his parents that everything is going great, and though he might be living in a cramped flat, which they should never visit, he's actually doing well for himself and there would be a day that they wouldn't regret their son dropping out of engineering college to pursue something that he really likes to do. Her mother disconnects the call after she's sure that Devrat's happy and doing well. His father, too, rattles off a few instructions from behind (*There are many road accidents happening in Kolkata, ask him to be safe. Ask him to not to keep the phone on charging all night. Ask him to keep the All Out on*).

He's the only son of doting parents, after all. They were a little miffed when they first heard that Devrat wanted to quit engineering and try singing for a bit but had relented over time. Devrat's constantly teary and puppy eyes (as his mother tells him) have always worked wonders for him.

They know nothing of Devrat's constant smoking, and of Arundhati. They are too nice for him to trouble them with his problems.

After his mother disconnects the call, he changes into the last clean T-shirt he has. He wears a jacket over it. The road is empty and except for a few kids scurrying about, jumping over puddles, rescuing their little paper boats, there is no one around. He buys two packets. He's smoking Four Square today. The cheaper, harder stuff. It starts to rain again.

The kids leave their boats in the puddles and soon water fills in and sinks them. The cycle of envisioning, building up, nurturing and then abandoning it is prevalent everywhere. His is the boat Arundhati nurtured and sank.

He steps into a sweetshop where other people have huddled up, waiting for the rain to stop. The sweetshop doubles up as a cyber café and he takes up a computer and logs into his various accounts. He doesn't think he can handle it but running away from his memories hasn't served him well either.

It took him a lot of alcohol, willpower and tears to stop accessing the Internet. He used to find himself on Arundhati's profile even though he knew how tough it would be to see Arundhati with someone else. It didn't make it any easier to see that his pictures with Arundhati had been deleted or hidden. Deleted, he was sure. Hidden, he wished. She had 'UnLiked' his Facebook page as well. He wondered if her fiancé made her do it. He thought of them talking about him in a coffee shop. The boy would pretend that he didn't remember Devrat's name and Arundhati would remind him, and the boy would go on to say that Devrat's music is pretty average and Arundhati would stay quiet and not defend Devrat.

For the first five minutes, he just deletes junk mails from Nigerian princes asking for money, companies selling penis enlargement pills and Viagra, Facebook and LinkedIn. This is all what we are about now, he thinks.

Then he checks the old mails in his account. There are a few people who keep mailing Devrat. Some twenty-odd people who have never stopped mailing him since he shared his first video. Every time he uploads a video, these twenty people mail him praising the song and they tell him they are waiting for more. Surprisingly enough, all these mailers are from Dehradun and one or the other from those twenty fans keep asking him to come over to Dehradun.

Then he types out Arundhati in the search bar, like someone types out the password to their most visited account: fast and without looking at the keyboard.

There she is. Sweet and pretty with her arms around 'him'. He tortures himself for a little more reading through her updates, looking at the pictures of the happy couple in clubs and restaurants, and in the Durga Puja pandals this year. It feels like his heart would sink to the bottom of his stomach. It's an actual physical pain. He feels he would vomit.

He goes to his own profile and is surprised by the number of friend requests. As a struggling musician he has to accept all the friend requests. He has to assume that they are fans, even though the profile pictures sometimes suggest that they are flowerpots and animals. Sometimes even Brad Pitt. By now, he thinks he has five girls in his list who look exactly like Angelina Jolie. Like. Exactly.

He accepts what feels like about a thousand friend requests, and checks the pictures he has been tagged in. They are about a hundred pictures from his last gig and numerous grainy videos. He sends the links of a few videos to his parents, so they can feel proud about their son, so that his father can put the video on a loop and his mother can watch him over and over again.

As he delves deeper into the messages, the wall posts and the comments on the pictures that people have posted, he is certainly happy. But the comments die down after the first week. Isn't that what always happens? People follow you, adore you, like you till you there, and the moment you're not, they forget you. If he is off the circuit for another six months, people are going to forget him and move on and he doesn't have any right to expect anything different. He has to be there, in front of people, to remind them of his presence. That's what he used to love, to sit amongst a group of school girls, and play his songs and bask in all the attention.

He types a status message and within two minutes, fifteen people like it. 'I am back. See you soon!J' He leaves the sweetshop-cum-cyber café and finds the children on the street playing with new paper boats now.

He enters his apartment and he finds his phone ringing.

Ugh, he thinks. There are three missed calls. Two of them are from unknown numbers and one of them is from Sumit. He calls back to find an exuberant Sumit on the other side.

'Finally! I am back!' he says and echoes Devrat's status message.

'You're such a stalker,' he says.

'Says the boy who only goes online to see what his ex-girlfriend is up to?'

'Let's not talk about it.'

'Yes, let's not. Let's talk about how many calls I am getting for you. And not just from managers, but from proper fans. One of your YouTube videos has seventy thousand hits, you know. I think you should shift to Mumbai. Who knows? You might even get an opportunity to do playback singing!'

'I can't do that,' he argues. It's not the first time he is in this argument and he knows it is not going to be the last time.

'Arre baba, why not? You have to be a little commercial. Devrat, you know me for a year now and you know I don't give this advice to the other rock bands or acts that I manage. But you're a versatile singer! You're like Sonu Nigam, like *badass-lost-in-love* Sonu Nigam. You should give it a try. Oh and by the way, Sonu Nigam makes upwards of 10 crores a year,' Sumit says fervently.

'Hmmm.'

Devrat knows Sumit's enthusiasm emanates from love and not greed but Devrat doesn't think of himself as that good and singing in Hindi isn't one of his strong points. To date, he messes his gender a few times. He knows he won't succeed and he can only handle so much rejection. Arundhati used to tell him that he's scared to step out of his comfort zone, that he's insecure, and damn right he is (though he never told her that) and why shouldn't he be? He's not as good as everyone around him makes him out to be. He doesn't want to have a dream in his eyes that will be abruptly snuffed out. It hurts and he knows this from experience.

'Get me another gig,' he says to Sumit.

'Fine. Keep your phone on. If only you would have contacted me earlier I would have got you something for fifteen thousand. I will still try,' Sumit says and disconnects the line.

He lights a cigarette and absent-mindedly hums a tune. It's his version of a Bengali song his father loves. It reminds him of the last conversation he had with his father when he had come down to Kolkata unannounced. Luckily, he was lost looking for Devrat's flat and had to call Devrat. Devrat threw him off for a good twenty minutes and cleared the flat of empty beer bottles, cigarette butts and the like.

'Is it going anywhere?' his father had asked Devrat.

Devrat told him that everything was under control and his career was going in the right direction. His father had nodded and told him, 'I talked to your dean at Durgapur Engineering College. They are keeping your admission on hold until next year. If you ever want to go back you can, you know.'

Devrat had nodded. His father had continued. 'It will be okay with us.'

'Let's wait for a year.'

And since then the time has started to tick.

It helps that he hasn't asked them for money in the past one year. They still call him and ask if he is okay or if he needs money and he assures them that he is fine and he will go back to the college if nothing becomes of him. Deep inside, he has already given up a little. He's miserable at times just thinking that he would have lost two years and a girl, and would have to go back to a college he left, doing something he loathes, having left something he loves.

The worst part is that he never even tried hard enough.

But for now, Devrat is wondering how those twenty people in Dehradun would react when they see his update. Would they mail him back? A part of him wants to go and check his mail box to see if they are still interested in his music.

A part of him says they must be.

FIVE

avanti

It was supposed to be a long weekend, the weekend she should have ideally spent in nervous jitters about her new job but instead she keeps reading Devrat's status over and over again. He has announced, 'I am back. See you soon! ☺', and that can only mean more videos, more gigs, and maybe in a city that she's in! She has just sent twenty mails to Devrat from her twenty fake accounts to boost his morale and to egg him to do more shows. She knows of Devrat's limited reach and she thinks she's doing her bit to encourage him. Who would disappoint twenty enthusiastic fans after all?

And Devrat did reply to some of her mails. She has maintained an account for quite some time now. She has often mailed him and asked him to come to Dehradun for a performance, at least once from each of those twenty accounts, but hasn't yet got an answer to that.

Her train of thought is broken when her phone beeps.

Have a good first day at work. Papa

She texts back saying thank you. As she dresses up in crisp

formals, looking the best she thinks she possibly can, she is suddenly thinking about her father.

The more time she spends in the house, the more she finds herself thinking about the sequence of events that must have happened fifteen years ago. Over a period of a few years, her father would have slowly started slipping down the slope of fixating with a mathematical problem he would never solve, her mother would have fought him and his preoccupation, there would be fights and silence and a crying child, and one day she would have just left. Their conversations are yet to move out from virtual space. She has given her father the benefit of the doubt. After all, he must still feel guilty about what happened to Avanti's mother, who died in a freak accident while returning from work. It was a year after she ran from his house with their three-year-old daughter in tow. All this wouldn't have happened if her father had a normal job. Like if he was an engineer. Or a bank manager. She wonders if her father had a stammer since childhood or if he developed it later.

She locks the door behind her as she leaves and makes sure the keys go under the mat and not in her handbag. She is not a big keys person and loses them at an astonishing rate. The road outside her apartment is like an F1 track with cars whizzing past her, leaving behind billowing smoke. There goes my make-up, she thinks. After much haggling she gets into an auto which will take her to the headquarters of the building of Indiago Airlines.

The auto ride is long and tiring. There are a million cars travelling in the same direction and none of them has more than a single passenger. 'People should be forced to car pool or this city will burst pretty soon!' she mutters.

'*Bas yahin*—here,' she says to the auto driver as she gets off at Nehru Place, where in the huge glass building adjacent to the sprawling five star hotel, Vasant Intercontinental, is the office of Indiago Airlines. The only airlines that flies to New York. Twice a day. Also Dubai. And Phuket. And Rio. 'This will be awesome!' she tells herself.

Then she takes a deep breath and a smile breaks out on her face. 'It's going to be good. You're pretty and you're smart. You don't have to be tense,' she tells herself. But just to spoil it all, it's Shekhar calling on her cell phone. She takes the battery out of the cell and keeps it in the bag. She closes her eyes and hums a song by Devrat, her drug, and pastes a smile on her face.

An hour later, she is sitting in a huge hall filling up an employment form with around a hundred other new flight attendants, all pretty and young. Everyone around her is decked up like they are in a club with a James Bond theme. No one has a hair out of place. Avanti, even though she was dead sure she looked gorgeous in the morning, is not so sure anymore. Even the guys have clear, flawless skin and bright pink lips. 'Kill them,' Avanti thinks. She's all for metrosexuality but this is just gay. She looks at a boy with a charming smile and slippery smooth skin. SO GAY. Not even legal now. Section 377 or something.

The hall was the target segment for fairness creams, body lotion, bleaching agents and every cosmetic aimed to help people become fairer and more Caucasian. From the brief conversations she has had with a few girls, she gets to know that the majority of them were aspiring models and soap opera actors but couldn't manage the struggle it entailed. Names of big television personas, fashion choreographers and photographers are dropped like they are old friends and soon, they are showing each other their portfolio pictures in shimmery dresses and dark lipsticks.

Flight attendants don't really need to be attractive but it helps if they are. When you're caged in a steel box thirty-five thousand feet above the ground with no escape routes, a pretty face can be the only calming factor.

Landing this job wasn't easy by any means. For the hundred-odd seats open for fresh applicants, there were a hundred thousand applications, making it tougher than getting into the IITs or the IIMs! Go figure.

'Hi, do you have an extra pen?' the guy sitting in the front row asks. She had noticed him stealing glances at her ever since they took their places. Or maybe he was just looking at everyone.

'Yes,' she says and hands over a ball pen. He turns around and faces her, throwing her a little off balance.

'It's a tough form to fill, isn't it?' he says and thrusts his hand forward. 'Ashutosh. Are you from Delhi?'

'Dehradun,' she answers and adds after a pause, 'Avanti' and shakes his hand. His grip is firm and strong as if trying to grind her bones to dust.

'Oh. So where do you stay here? Alone?'

That's a shady question to ask a girl. Alone? Why? She is already put off by his intrusive eye contact and how he leans into her while he speaks. The excessive gel in his hair, the perfect smile with gleaming teeth and pink lips, and the bulging muscles inside the white shirt are a put off. He's not real. He's a walking advertisement. He reminds her of Shekhar. *Sweet early on, but abusive later.*

'No, my father lives here. He's very protective about me. He's the worst. He doesn't even let me talk to guys. The last boyfriend I had, was punched in the face by my father,' she says as a means to ward off the gay boy.

'Oh. Are you liking Delhi then? Do you like to party?' he says as if he didn't just listen to what she said. 'Delhi has quite a few sick places. I can take you to some. My friends are party organizers here and I can get you in easily. Even your friends can come if they want to.'

That's it. That's so DELHI. Over-indulgent, curious, a shady approach. A boy you just met asks where you live, asks if you want to party, then casually drops a few names and plans out an evening even without asking you.

'No, thank you,' she says and gets back to filling her form. 'As I said, my father is real protective. He's the honour killing types.'

The guy returns to his form.

Soon after, their forms are collected and there are three-hour-long lectures on teamwork and its importance, the airline industry, expected HR practices and so on. As soon as the last session gets over, the room suddenly gets noisy and there are certain pockets busy with activity. She sees people exchanging numbers and BlackBerry PINs and making plans to come to the office together. A few guys ask her too, but she brushes them off.

She leaves the hall and the building and starts looking for an auto.

It takes her fifteen minutes to find an auto and soon Avanti drifts off. Despite the corpse-fair boys and the discomfort of being in a sea of beautiful women, she didn't mind the day at all and she knew the next six weeks would pass in a heartbeat too.

She can't wait to start flying and see the world. Midway through the auto ride she gets up to check if Devrat has replied to any of the twenty mails, but he hasn't, so she goes back to sleep.

SIX

devrat

Devrat is on a couch tired, spent and rich. The gig at The Music Factory, College Street, a new club that had opened just a week back went well and he was richer by ten thousand rupees. It's his third performance in three weeks and everyone knows that's a huge achievement for someone his age. Needless to say, there are other musicians in the circuit, more experienced and talented than him, who are disgusted by the music he plays and the following, no matter how little and limited, he commands.

They are in the back room of the club and Sumit tells Devrat that it was an awesome performance. Sumit uploads a picture of the event on his page. 'You look rather good in this,' he remarks. Devrat takes the laptop from him and checks his mail.

'Who are you replying to?' asks Sumit, curious.

'Some of my listeners,' answers Devrat.

'They write to you?' asks Sumit.

'Yeah. There are these twenty people who keep mailing me every time I upload something. Sometimes, it feels like they are the only people who really like what I do. Most of them are from Dehradun and they have asked me quite a few times to come over.'

'That's awesome. I'm glad you're replying to them. It helps build your base. Just a random question—are any of those girls?'

'Never checked,' he answers. A cursory glance on the names shows a skewed ratio towards girls, a demographic he has always been a little hit with. He's cute. And he's damaged. Girls love a lost puppy.

Most of his songs are half-baked self-composed songs about lost love and girls love it! Though writing them is a hard process. He has to sit in a corner and keep poking at his heart-wrenching break-up to write such lyrics.

Devrat knows his music is not pure rock, or pure pop or pure blues or pure jazz. His music is a mix inspired from whoever catches his fancy. Though he never sings songs written by others, he doesn't particularly mind singing a Justin Bieber in his rough, broken-down voice. Or Himesh Reshammiya. It's music after all. It's how you interpret it.

He is too young to figure out the music he makes and he doesn't want to rush or stick to rules and paths laid down by the ones before him. And it's working for him partially. He must be doing something right, he figures.

Tonight, too, he is involved in the same conversation. After his gig, he was invited to the table of a local, upcoming rock band (some fusion bullshit), which was yet to land their first gig and was looking to get Sumit's attention. Since they couldn't get hold of Sumit, they thought of chatting up Sumit's wonder kid, Devrat. And Devrat, as a rule, never turns down free alcohol and cigarettes. Five drinks down, the band forgot how much they hated Devrat and invited him over to one of the band members' houses where he lives alone. It was slightly better that Devrat's flat and a lot cleaner.

'What do you think you're trying to achieve with your music?' one of their senior band members asks Devrat. He doesn't look very drunk and is still a little hostile.

'I don't get you,' Devrat says and rolls his eyes as if he is drunk. He doesn't want to get into the same conversation again. He fixes himself another drink in a transparent plastic glass and hopes the question will die down by the time he is finished.

'You know what I mean. Your music is commercial and has no longevity. No one is going to listen to it after even five years. We don't get into music to make something that wouldn't even last our lifetime. We are into music so that we can contribute to it and add to its heritage, not spoil and distract people from real music. And it's not just music, it's books, it's movies, it's education, we are all looking for a shortcuts everywhere. Salman Khan! What's that about? Another shortcut! There are some things that are sacred and they should be. Books and music being two of them,' the old guy says and stops.

Devrat is pretty drunk by the time the monologue ends. He is just tired of the bullshit thrown his way for what he does and even though he has learned to be patient, sometimes the shit just hits the fan. And often, it's when he is drunk.

'I have a fully cogent argument in my head that I will present to you. . .' His head starts to spin. 'But I think I would need another drink for that.' He makes another drink and gulps it down. 'What I was saying was . . .' He looks at the man purposefully, points a finger at him and he . . . he pukes. It's not a normal puking-in-the-toilet-puke, it's a waterfall. With lumps. And out of his mouth. And onto the old guy. Devrat is smiling. Although he knows he's passing out and will probably be punched by the guy, he is smiling.

The punch doesn't come.

'Fuck you, man,' the old man says and walks to the washroom, smelling of rotten food and bile and processed alcohol.

'Fuck you, Devrat!' the others raise their glasses, pour it down their throats and start laughing. Devrat joins in the laughter.

Soon, they lose track of time and pass out. Musicians never drink responsibly. Also writers. It's goes against their nature. They drink to escape reality and they drink to pass out; they don't drink to dance or have a good time or to party.

When he wakes up the next morning, his head drums steadily and he is wrapped around another guy with long hair. He's still drunk.

He picks up his jacket and leaves the apartment. He enters the first coffee shop he can find and orders two strong filter coffees. His head is still bursting and his breath stinks like death. At least his pocket is full and he can buy a month's worth of cigarettes. That's good news. Life has taken a turn for the good in the last few weeks and he is finally thinking that he can get a hold on things. He has developed a new habit. Whenever he's a little down, he opens his mailbox and reads the mails by that group of fans who really like his music and keep mailing him. That gives him the strength to move on. Sometimes he thinks that they are all part of some group who collectively like his music. It always makes him happy.

Smiling, he blows on the coffee and pours it down his throat. He does the same with the next one. His tongue is sandpaper now.

He pays the bill, picks up a packet of wafers and leaves the shop.

Having just walked two blocks, he enters the cyber café and logs into his Facebook profile. A few more fans have liked the page, a few more of his pictures have been liked, videos have been recorded and shared, and his timeline has mentions of his stirring performances. Frankly, it feels slightly odd to be loved so much. Devrat's more comfortable when he's the underdog and he over-delivers, not the other way round.

There are sixty more people who have added him since yesterday. People really like these songs, he thinks and notes down the songs that people have most appreciated. He makes a mental note of writing more songs like that. But writing more songs about heartbreak and pain would mean thinking of Arundhati again, which he has been consciously avoiding. And just when he's about to log out of his profile, there's a notification that tells him that Arundhati has liked one of his pictures. He logs out. He's sitting there staring at the computer screen, his legs shaking nervously, wondering what must have gone through Arundhati's head before she decided to like his picture. It's not accidental. She must have searched for him and then liked his picture. It's a two-step process. He wonders if her fiancé knows that she still likes him. Maybe he should go and tell him about that because he's sure Arundhati tells his fiancé everything about him. He had spent sleepless nights thinking about Arundhati and her fiancé sharing a bed, exhausted, talking about how much better her fiancé is in bed than Devrat. Obviously they talk about him. Why wouldn't they? Devrat had talked and fussed about all the other boys Arundhati had kissed. Devrat's sure Arundhati is telling her fiancé all about Devrat's smoking habit, of how his mouth used to smell and how grubby and dirty his hands were. He's sure they talk about all that. And if they do, why is Arundhati going about seeking him and liking his pictures, torturing him. What is this? Pity?

He walks out and calls Arundhati. It isn't a well-thought decision and he doesn't really know where he is going with this. Maybe to confront her fiancé and tell him that he's better than him even though he doesn't really feel it. For all the pain he has gone through this is the least he can do. He can confront the boy and tell him that his fiancée reached out to him. That's going to be a big jolt for his ego, and should wear her fiancé down day by day for the rest of his life thinking about why his fiancée needed to talk to Devrat. That's enough damage. That should do it. That's just payback.

'Hey,' says Arundhati.

'Hi.'

'How are you, Devrat?' asks Arundhati.

'I'm fine. What are you doing?' asks Devrat casually though he really wants to ask her why she is still checking his profile online. It's JUST wrong.

'I was about to leave to buy a few things for myself.'

'Cool.' Devrat cuts the call.

He's pacing around the spot, running his hands over his head, now thinking that he should have never called her up. Everything comes rushing back to him. He thinks of Arundhati in her yellow summer dress waiting for the guy outside her apartment. He doesn't know whether it's the alcohol in his system or it's the anger but thirty minutes later he's outside her apartment building walking around in circles, waiting for her to come out. It isn't long after when he spots a white, well-washed Toyota Corolla screech to a halt before the apartment building. It's a face he has imagined with Arundhati a billion times before, a face he has imagined contorting while Arundhati and the boy . . .

The boy comes out, whips out his phone and calls a number. There's a big smile on the boy's face and the call ends with the boy saying that he is waiting outside. Devrat's losing it, bit by bit. He's not a big fighter, he never has been, but today he thinks he will get into one, and starts to imagine the boy's head smashed into the headlight of the car after he tells him that Arundhati still misses Devrat.

At a distance, he sees Arundhati walk out of her apartment's lobby. Instead of going to the boy, Devrat sneaks up behind her, trying to mask his anger.

'Hey,' says Devrat.

Arundhati jerks backwards, startled. 'GOD! What are you doing here?'

'I don't know what I'm doing here.'

'Devrat, you really need to go,' says Arundhati as she takes a turn, away from the apartment gate outside which her fiancé is waiting.

'Why?'

'Because Arnab is waiting.'

'Arnab? That's his name?' smirks Devrat. 'Is that how people are choosing men for their daughters these days? With the same alphabet.'

'Look, Devrat. I'm sorry whatever happened between us, but you need to move on!' says Arundhati irritably. Devrat still thinks she looks beautiful and hates to think that Arnab has kissed that face.

'I need to move on? I was doing fine until this morning when you decide to poke into my life. Why did you fucking like that picture?' snaps Devrat, stonewalling his tears.

'I was just happy that you had moved on. I was happy for you! Why can't you just see that?'

'I can't see that because you walked out on me and our relationship and decided to get engaged to a guy within days. And you want to know why can't I see that?' fumed Devrat.

'Our relationship? What was our relationship, Devrat? It was a constant stream of your negativity! All we did was to sit in your dingy flat and brood over your future! I was just a punching bag for your fears of what will happen to your career, your music, your engineering. That was our relationship! IT WAS ALL ABOUT YOU! IT WAS ALL ABOUT YOUR INSECURITIES AND YOUR FEAR OF FAILURE. Anyone, absolutely, anyone who tried to tell you that you were good and you could achieve things was bad in your eyes! Even SUMIT! As if we were all misleading you into something that's not good for you. It was all about you, Devrat. It was all about you!'

'And why shouldn't it have been? Didn't you do exactly what I had feared? The minute you saw that my career wasn't going anywhere and I was doomed to be a shitty engineer, you walked out. Didn't you do that? Didn't you always want a guy who stands outside your house all the time and drives a pretty, little white car!'

'Listen, Devrat!' raged Arundhati and dug her index finger into his chest. 'I was okay wherever you were. I never waited for you to be successful or anything. If I had it my way, we could have been stuck in your dingy flat, you could be a failed man and I would have still loved you! Devrat, the only thing that drew us apart was your insecurity that I would leave you and be with someone more successful. All your fears were unfounded.'

'Unfounded? Who are you with now? Who's that guy! I

don't think he lives in a one-room kitchen, does he? DOES HE?' thundered Devrat.

'It doesn't matter. You have to understand that it wasn't because of him. It was because of YOU,' argues Arundhati. 'If you, only you, would have looked at me and asked if I wanted what you think I wanted. If only you would have asked me this once, I would have told you that I didn't care. Your fears were unwarranted and I had been listening for so many months but then I had had enough.'

Devrat doesn't say anything. All he remembers is her disappointment in him, the constant niggling about which friend's friend is going to the IIM, which friend's boyfriend had found a job in the US and so forth. It was never for him, it was always for her.

'Take care,' says Arundhati.

Tears streak down his cheek and he can't bring himself to let go of Arundhati's hand. Arundhati jerks it out of his grip.

'Do you love him?' asks Devrat

'I will learn to love him.'

'That's just shit, Arundhati.'

'It's all I have,' says Arundhati.

'Don't you love me even a little bit now?'

'I will not answer that. And even if I did, it would never work out between us. You will always be a child, Devrat, stuck in your world of fears and insecurities, always wanting someone to hang on to. I loved you but I'm not that nice.'

Arundhati walks away. He watches her exit the gate, hug her fiancé, the man she will learn to love, and he drives away with her. Of course she was happier with me, she will seek me out again, she will realize I'm the one she needs to be with and that I'm the one she is in love with, Devrat tells himself and closes his eyes.

SEVEN

avanti

Avanti sits in the cab and thanks God it's over. The three weeks of training where they learned everything about safety, service and first aid, were very strenuous. Getting up at six-thirty in the morning, dressing up in the blue and red uniform of the airlines, tying her hair up, putting on make-up, strutting unsurely on her heels, and looking for an auto was tough. By the time she reached the office, she had to do her hair and the make-up again. The day wouldn't end by ten in the night.

It was only by eleven she would return at night. Her father would be awake but there was no conversation at the dinner table. One day she had walked in early from work and had seen her father cooking and she thought it was adorable but she didn't know what to say to him. He's still practically a stranger to her. The irony was Avanti spent days at aviation training learning to talk to people, a skill at which she was already great and only improving, but at home she had no idea how to broach a conversation with her father. Should she be angry? Should she tell him that it's okay? Should she tell him that, frankly, nothing matters? She's clueless about how to go about this. So she just shuts up every day when they are sitting at the table next to each other eating their breakfasts and dinners. There's one thing though that she loves. It's her father's tea. It's always perfect and she's kind of getting addicted to it. She never told her father that but it's kind of the only thing she looked forward to those days when chaos had taken over his life.

The instructors who took the lessons were ruthless and unforgiving. They were also wrinkled and old. Misses in the lipstick and the hair department were looked upon as cardinal sins, a creased uniform was like killing a puppy, and turning up late in the class was intolerable. But she's glad it's over.

It's her first flight and she's still stuck in traffic.

Even at seven in the morning, the circuitous roads of Gurgaon are choking with bumper to bumper traffic. The newer, wider roads have helped but every second seven more kids are born in India. One of them dies instantly, three of them never see a school in their lives and ply rickshaws, two of them end up in the lower rungs of the society and drive scooters, and the rest buy cars. Big cars. Sometimes SUVs. The traffic grows every day. Unless people find a way to teleport, this city is going to burst.

She's flipping through her roster for the month while in the car. It has a Kolkata flight later this month and she's most kicked about it. Devrat had replied to all the twenty mails a few days back. What she really liked about those replies was that they weren't standard. He wasn't copying and pasting the same answers. He was typing the answers out, and even though he was answering to people who didn't exist, it felt like he was talking to her, the way it has always been. That reminds her that she hasn't checked Devrat's profile in over two weeks; her training had been really strenuous.

The car stops at a red light. She has just logged into her account with her head on the glass window of the car when she hears a loud honking. She takes notice. And the other flight attendants who are in the car with her wake up with a start.

Avanti looks to her side and it's Shekhar in a two-door car shouting at the cab driver. The red light turns to green and Shekhar's car screeches to a halt in front of their cab. The driver of the cab walks out to confront Shekhar, but Shekhar pushes him to the ground. '*Neeche rahiyo, bhenchod* (Stay down, sisterfucker).'

Scared, Avanti walks out. 'What are you doing here?'

'Where the fuck were you? Why isn't your number working?' He's shouting at Avanti as he snatches her handbag. Avanti's trying to stop him, her eyes have welled up. It feels like she's still in a relationship with him. Back in those days, the minute Shekhar used to start shouting, she used to think she must have done something wrong. Even now, she's wondering what she might have done wrong.

She's looking at the flight attendants who were sitting in the car but are now out as well and ready to stand by Avanti. And then she's looking at Shekhar, who's rummaging through her handbag to find the phone. He finds it and dials his number. 'Oh! So now you have taken a new phone. Who gave you this number? WHO? YOUR NEW BOYFRIEND?'

'Shekhar! Stop it! I'm getting late.' She's hitting Shekhar on his arm but he's not budging. He's into the recent calls list and luckily, he finds nothing. 'Stop it!' She has almost broken down into tears but Shekhar doesn't even give her a second look.

'Who are you?' the two other flight attendants are shouting

at Shekhar. They are about to call for help, but Avanti waves them down.

Shekhar throws the bag and the phone on the ground. 'You better pick up my calls. And if I get to know that you're dating anyone, I swear I will kill you. I know you have deleted his number now, but I will catch you soon enough.'

He gets in his car and whizzes off.

'I'm sorry about that,' Avanti apologizes, a little ashamed, still shaking from the ordeal.

The two flight attendants behave like they didn't just see what happened. Avanti sits in the car, wipes her tears and does her make-up again. The flight attendant sitting next to her whispers in her ear, 'Never take shit from boyfriends.' Avanti nods. She doesn't know why she takes it from him. She never really even loved him. And right now, even though she's crying a little, she's furious and she can kill someone.

She puts the battery in the cell phone again and checks if it's working. She stuffs her earphones in and increases the volume on her favourite playlist. She opens her roster again. There are three layovers, at Kochi, Mumbai and Kolkata. A brief smile comes on her face when she reads 'Kolkata'. Layovers are when you fly to the destination city and come back after a day or two. All she wants is to see Devrat play and sing in front of her eyes, maybe shake his hand, and hug him endlessly. The very thought of it makes her so happy. She's finally going to meet her little puppy, her saviour. And just like that, what happened minutes ago is history. 'Thank you,' she mutters.

'Are you okay?' asks the flight attendant sitting next to her, seeing the sudden change of mood in Avanti, who's smiling widely now. 'Weren't you just crying a moment ago?'

'I'm okay, now.'

'Are you sure?'

'Yes. I'm sorry for that. That guy is slightly deranged.'

'Go the police, then,' says the girl.

'Some day,' says Avanti.

'Was he your boyfriend?' asks the girl.

'No, he was an ex-boyfriend. My boyfriend is in Kolkata,' chuckles Avanti. 'His name is Devrat.' Avanti realizes anyone would think that she, not Shekhar, is deranged, but that's okay. She rightly compares Devrat to a little puppy. No matter how angry or depressed or suicidal you are, you look at a picture of cute puppies and everything is fine and fuzzy. Devrat's Avanti's puppy.

Still stuck in the jam, she logs into her accounts. *What?* She immediately starts to curse herself over and over again. *Damn. Damn. Damn. This is not happening!* There are seven updates, tens of new pictures, and new videos on his page. There are people, girls, who claim to be the biggest fans of his music. There are over a hundred likes on some of his pictures, girls gushing over his music and how gorgeous he looks, and she can't help but feel envious.

There are a few sound clips uploaded on Soundcloud and she downloads them on her phone. She doesn't enjoy the music; she is too angry to think about anything else. Devrat was *her* discovery. She was the one who was amongst the first ten people to like his page, to like his music, to share his lyrics and the grainy videos of his performance on her Facebook profile. How can other girls claim him as theirs? She decides not to share or like anything. The two new songs, *Ridiculous Smoke* and *Perfect Futures*, play on a never-ending loop on her phone. She likes all his pictures. 'I hate this! Why is this guy getting popular! Not fair!'

The taxi parks close to the airport and she jumps out. Focus, Avanti tells herself, and tries not to think of Devrat's new-found popularity.

The other two amble out, still nonchalant, their faces expressionless, their chins held up high, sunglasses perched on their foreheads, as if they do this every day. As they walk in to the newly constructed Terminal 3 of the Delhi Indira Gandhi Airport, she notices uncountable pairs of eyes on them and she shrugs her shoulders and walks in.

'Papers.' She is broken out of her reverie by the moustachioed guard, who is standing upright with his right hand outstretched in front of him.

The other two show him their IDs and stride in, their chins still facing the ceiling. She fumbles, looks for her ID in pockets in her handbag, and finally finds it hanging around her neck. The guard smiles and lets her in. She smiles back.

'*Pehla din hai?* First day?' the guard asks.

'Yes,' she says, '*Aapka?* Yours?' And they both laugh. 'I will see a lot of your moustache from now on . . .' Avanti looks at the guard's badge and the guard answers, 'Kareem.'

'Okay, Kareem bhai. Wish me luck.' The guard smiles widely and wishes Avanti luck.

With the trolley wheeling behind her, she tries to catch up pace with the other two who are still walking with unmatched confidence and look like they know where they have to go. Their IDs are checked again and then their small suitcases. Her luggage has lipstick, a manual and a spare set of uniform just in case. She upholds the image of a quintessential flight attendant: a twenty-something girl in a well-fitted uniform, walking in high heels with a colour-coordinated trolley behind her.

They are ushered into the lounge where all the flight

attendants, flying all across the breadth and length of the country and beyond, are waiting for their call outs. The room is uncharacteristically silent and most of the girls are sleeping. Some of them are tapping on their BlackBerries and flicking on their iPads or doing their hair. She lies down on a couch, surprisingly soft and inviting, and listens to the songs again and they are awesome, notwithstanding her hatred for other girls who have started liking Devrat as well. So unfair!

Girls keep exiting the room and are replaced by more girls. There is no conversation.

'Is it your first time?' asks Avanti to a girl who's clearly a veteran.

The girl frowns for she, too, was trying to sleep. 'No.'

'It's my first time.'

'Hmmm.'

'Any tips?'

'Be disciplined.'

'Anything more? Oh, by the way I love your hair,' says Avanti and it's a genuine compliment.

'It's the same as everyone else's,' says the girl and closes her eyes. Avanti shuts up.

After an hour, names are called out for her flight and a big smile bursts out on her face. Four girls get up and head for the exit. Two of them use the mirror briefly to reign in their stray strands of hair into the buns and join the others.

'First flight?' the most senior-looking of the flight attendants asks Avanti as she nervously follows the lead of the other three flight attendants. They enter the flight and go through the preliminary checks they are supposed to carry out regardless of how stupid or superfluous they might seem. A little later, the first batch of passengers walks past them. The next half an hour passes by in greetings. 'Good morning.' 'Welcome.' 'Indiago Airlines welcomes you.' 'Thank you for flying with us.'

Avanti's in the alley waiting for passengers and although she's just supposed to smile at them and welcome them, she finds herself in long conversations with a lot of them. She's flitting between Hindi, English, Bengali and the bits of Punjabi she had learnt from her friends back at school.

Avanti's jaws hurt by the time the last few of the business class passengers pass her by, but she's so glad she finally has someone (actually three hundred people) to talk to. That one hour in the lounge staying shut was just annoying.

Avanti is in the economy class and she would eventually, if she sticks around, graduate to working in the business class, but she's not looking forward to dealing with business and first class passengers. They have the most calm and relaxed faces of them all as they walk past, smelling as if fresh out of a scented shower. Rich housewives, upper-rung business executives on company money, spoilt kids, and TV models. Good-looking people. The business class cabin reeks of money and she doesn't like the way they look at her. It's with the face of a customer, someone who's bought something. Or someone.

She moves on. The economy class is bustling with activity as passengers try to fit their hand baggage, clearly twice the size allowed, into the overhead bins. Had it been a train, expletives would have been exchanged and bags would have tumbled out and hands would have risen. Here, grumbles would have to do. She reaches out and helps a few people manage their hand baggage and find their seats. The bags are heavy, Avanti realizes. And why are big, burly men taking her help in stuffing bags in overhead bins? It's not as if flight attendants are diploma holders on 'How to Stuff Luggage in Overhead Bins.' But she helps them anyway and incorrigibly, finds herself in a conversation about which schools their children go to. 'Shut up, Avanti,' she tells herself.

The seat belt sign is on and the captain makes the announcement over the grainy PA system in his monotonous voice:

'This is flight 6EG 787 and we are flying from Delhi to Chennai today. In the cockpit are Captain Saurabh Mittal and Co-captain Tarun Dalal. The cabin crew comprises Bhavya Dabas, Guneet Kaur, Avanti Bannerjee and Taruna Seth. The flight will take two hours and thirty minutes to reach Chennai. We hope you will enjoy flying with us. Thank you.'

Soon after, the seniormost attendant asks the passengers to watch and listen to the instructions on the screens attached at the back of every seat. Avanti thanks God for the screens (this is one of the new aircraft) as she is not expected to stand in the galley and explain to people how to put on their seat belts and what to do during emergencies or lack of oxygen. It's not that it's embarrassing but often while practising it in the training college, Avanti felt like breaking out in a little dance while doing it. Or at least wiggle her waist a little and do a little belly dance. Then, she thinks, people will look. It should be actually a pre-flight dance. It's no joke, it could actually save lives.

Click. Click. Click. Seat belts snap all around her as walks up and down the aisle and makes sure people fasten their seat belts. The young boys blush while she tells them how to buckle it. The men leer. The women curse under their breath and they clutch on to their husbands tighter. 'God! We're not here to snatch your husbands! It's not as if they are any desirable,' she thinks.

The aircraft is lined on the tarmac and it's the second in line to take off. This is the part Avanti loves the most. She is sure she will be bored of it after a few flights but right now, she looks forward to it.

'What were you doing there?' one of the flight attendants remarked.

'Huh?'

'Why were you talking to everyone, Avanti?'

'Umm . . . because they were talking to me?'

The girl rolls her eyes. 'You don't do that. You just smile, help them and move on.'

'But why?'

'Why? Because it's draining! And you talk to one, and then suddenly everyone wants to talk to you!' complains the girl.

'So what's wrong in that?'

'You get drained.'

'I'm okay for now,' says Avanti and smiles at her.

'You are, but don't make them feel like they can talk to anyone. I'm not going to do that,' says the girl and makes a face as if the passengers are like cattle. Stay as far away from them as possible; just make sure they land alive.

Five minutes later, the metal cage is up in the sky and people have already started unsnapping their seat belts and getting out of their seats to visit the washroom.

'What do you do if a newly married couple tries to enter the washroom?' asks Avanti, rubbing her hands in obvious delight.

'We don't allow them,' comes the answer from one of them.

'That's boring,' says Avanti. 'I heard from somewhere that at Virgin Atlantic they used to give such couples champagne and cigarettes. That's pretty cool, right?'

'Where did you hear that?'

'I don't know. Somewhere?' says Avanti, trying to dig her

brain for that conversation where this might have come up. It's a useless pursuit. She has had ten billion conversations just today.

Lights are up on the main passenger panel, which means people have started pushing the buttons to call the flight attendants. The first half an hour passes in running around. The flight attendants are blamed for everything, and one of her colleagues is just short of telling them that she didn't make the aircraft by hand and she really doesn't know how to make the screen work! But not Avanti, who's gliding from one seat to another, sometimes talking to a Sardarji about his petulant teenage daughters to solving the love life of a pesky thirteen-year-old.

A couple of hours later, the flight lands and the scene inside the aircraft suddenly changes to a rickety Rajdhani where everyone is trying to get off the aircraft first. Avanti slumps into a seat, tired and a little thankful that the flight is over.

Just then the senior attendant walks up and says, 'Just halfway through, kid. Don't screw up. Your service was slow and you need to know who you are talking to and who deserves being talked to. You can't just go about talking to everyone. They are passengers, not your friends. Now, clean up the aisle. We have fifteen minutes to go.'

She feels she would die. Her feet are hurting and so is her back. She is exhausted from running up and down the aisle.

The passengers are again waiting at the step ladder the minute the four of them are done running checks again. Another three hours of exhaustion. Avanti braces herself, her forearms strain, and her calves make their pain known. She reminds herself that she doesn't necessarily need to talk to everyone on the flight but that invariably happens.

Four hours later, she collapses on her bed after putting Devrat's new songs on a loop on the speaker, hoping she would dream of him. She can't wait for the new song to release. Shekhar calls her phone twice, but the calls go answered. She looks at the missed calls on her phone, half-sleepy, and mutters, 'You're an asshole.'

EIGHT

devrat

Being successful doing music in India, especially Indian music, doesn't compare to being successful in other careers. The cash flow is irregular and uncertain, the public is fickle, and the tastes in music change like the direction of the wind. Most independent musicians know this and try to do as many live shows as possible while they are still on top. People talk of musicians over-exposing themselves and eventually dying out because of it, but they are not naïve and know that people will move on eventually.

Sumit has been trying to make Devrat understand this for a long time but hadn't been able to crack through Devrat's strong and stubborn skull. As a rule, poorer musicians are more uptight about ideals than the ones making money. So, do riches corrupt ideals? Or you have to be corrupt inherently to be rich?

Devrat smokes a cigarette and watches while his friend Karishma cleans up his flat. Three months have passed since the last time he saw Karishma and Devrat is not sure whether he is happy to see her. Karishma was the root of all evil, his wingman for the night he met Arundhati.

'When was the last time you talked to her?' Devrat asks and Karishma doesn't answer the question. She starts to separate the clothes she thinks are dirty from the clean ones and ends up with just one pile of dirty clothes.

'Didn't you just say that you're over her? That you were in a Zen state and you really don't care about her? And do you have a maid? Or a washing machine? What do you do for clothes?' she asks.

'Dry-clean,' he says.

'Perfect,' she says sarcastically and gathers the clothes in a bedsheet, tying up the edges when they are all in. She leaves the room and comes back after fifteen minutes. 'The washerwoman will come with your clothes tomorrow. I have talked to her and she will pick your clothes every Sunday from now on. Don't miss her!'

Devrat nods. 'I hope you know I change my flats every three weeks.'

Fuck you, says Karishma's face. 'I have no idea how you live in a mess like this? It's horrible,' she says and washes her hands.

'You should have seen how clean the flat was when I was dating her,' snaps back Devrat.

'Oh shut up. I think you like being depressed,' argues Karishma. 'Adds to the whole mysterious musician shit. But let me tell you it gets boring pretty fast.'

The flat looks quite bare now. The used utensils are in the racks, the clothes are missing, and the shoes are stacked in a clean line near the door.

'Hey. I have a performance tonight at Green Frog, do you want to come?' he asks.

'Sure, I will come! But, Green Frog, that's awesome. Going places, eh?' she mocks. 'Do you want to order something? I am hungry as hell. And oh! Karan says hi.'

'Ask him to fuck off,' says Devrat.

'Why do you hate him so much?'

'He snatched my best friend away from me. You would be here every second day earlier and look at you now. That fancy guy with an MBA degree and a tie around his neck wrested you away from me!'

'Oh please,' snaps back Karishma. 'You were too busy with your depression to give a shit about me.'

'Did you know you kind of look cute when you're angry?' asks Devrat.

'It's been ten years that we've known each other and your lines haven't ever worked on me,' says Karishma.

'They were never meant to. If I wanted those lines to work, they would have probably worked.'

'Blah.'

And that was right. Devrat had literally seen Karishma shave her hairy legs. Like hairy legs. Like when the hair on your legs becomes long and they curl. Once you see that you can't go back. You can't fall in love with the girl ever again. Though Karishma was kind of cute. Small. Petite. Full lips. Big eyes. And a really cute face made of cupcakes, candy and smiles of little puppies.

'The pizza place's number is in my phone. Call them,' Devrat says and throws his phone at her. She orders a pizza with minimal cheese and a lot of toppings, most of them vegetarian and none of which excites Devrat.

'So how much are they paying you? Green Frog?' she asks.

'Not much. I am not doing a whole show, just a couple

of songs. The owner's girlfriend heard me play somewhere and asked for me. So, I am not really wanted there. It's just a demanding girlfriend. Otherwise there is a techno-house band, Fried Jalebies, that's playing there,' Devrat smirks.

'I see. You still don't like dance music,' she laughs.

'I don't have a problem with it,' he says and lights up the first joint. 'Just that . . .'

'You can't dance.'

'Yeah. Whatever.'

'Are your parents happy now with what you're doing?'

'My mom is okay with it. A little concerned, but my father still thinks I will give it all up and go back to college.'

'And will you?' asks Karishma.

'I will try not to, but if nothing works out, I will have to,' says Devrat.

'It will work out.'

'From where I stand, it doesn't look like it will,' sighs Devrat.

'Stop being so negative all the time!' snaps Karishma. 'You're performing at Green Frog. That means something, right?'

'But not alone.'

'Forget it,' retorts Karishma.

Devrat lights a cigarette.

'Can you smoke after I'm gone?' she begs. He complies and extinguishes the cigarette against a wall. 'Now tell me. When are you going to start dating again? I have many single friends. And I think some of them already like you.'

'Do they know I smoke?'

'Maybe.'

'Do they know my house looks like refugee camp?'

'I don't think they care.'

'Do they know that I would look for Arundhati in them?

Do they know that she's going to come back one day? Do they know that once she does I'm going to tell her that I don't need her? Do they know I talk like this?'

'Not yet.' Karishma rolls her eyes and throws a pillow at him. 'You need to be over her. Aren't people like you always buried in women?'

'Not if you don't want to.'

'And why do you not want to?' Karishma's tone is almost begging. Like it's her responsibility that Devrat is alone and depressed and is not getting any action.

'You need to stop trying to get me with someone. Last time wasn't that good. Oh! Is this why you're trying so hard? You're guilty?'

Karishma looks at her feet. 'Maybe.'

'You don't need to do that!' exclaims Devrat.

'Seriously,' he continues, 'It's not that bad. Like today, I almost didn't check Arundhati's profile. And that's new! I'm getting better. But I doubt that someone's going to take Arundhati's place in the near future.'

'I'm happy for you then.'

The doorbell rings. It's the pizza guy. Karishma reaches out for her handbag but Devrat gets the door. He says, 'I can pay. For now at least.' A little later, Devrat has to leave for his recording, his first ever legitimate recording for a YouTube channel.

'You're not as big a failure as you make yourself out to be,' says Karishma while leaving.

'Maybe you're right. I do have about twenty fans in Dehradun!' quips Devrat.

'Eh?'

'You won't get it,' says Devrat.

~

'Are you are telling us that NOW? And who's this Karthika? Ask her to wrap up quickly. Devrat can't wait that long,' shouts Sumit on the phone. He's uncharacteristically aggressive. The recording studio Devrat is supposed to record in has pushed his recording an hour for the previous singer, Karthika, who is taking a little bit long.

Devrat gestures at him to calm down and Sumit smiles at him. Once he's done with the call, he tells Devrat, 'You have to throw your weight around. Artiste tantrums are also the reason why artistes become stars. Once everyone talks about the fit you threw they will think you deserved to throw a tantrum.'

'That weirdly makes sense to me. You're corrupting me, Sumit,' says Devrat and lights a cigarette. 'Sometimes I think I was better off studying mechanics of solids and worrying about end semesters.'

'You will be the most famous twenty-one-year-old musician in the country. That sure beats mechanics of solids,' says Sumit. 'And keep the smoke out of my clothes!'

Devrat checks his phone. He's moved on from his archaic Nokia and has a new phone in his hands. He was told by Karishma that it has a lot of applications and is fun to play around with it, but he doesn't know what to do with it. He sure wishes Arundhati likes another picture, or mails him, anything that gives him a sign that she's not happy and she would be back with him soon enough. And that's when he doesn't even want her anymore. It's just revenge now. He wants her just to show that she wants him.

He swipes across left, then right, and then locks the screen; he admits to himself that Candy Crush is pretty addictive and Temple Run is kind of good.

He checks his Facebook profile. There are people from his

college congratulating him for whatever he's doing, people he didn't really talk to when he was with them, and Devrat is thinking that maybe they are little jealous of him, maybe there are wishing that his music thing is short-lived. Devrat, too, is scared about that. The student Devrat always keeps reminding the musician Devrat of that. The opportunity cost of trying to be a musician is high. He has already lost a couple of years, a girlfriend, and a little bit of his sanity.

He updates his profile, *'Going to the studio to record a new song. Excited!'*

Within seconds it's liked by a few people, the first of whom is a girl called Avanti. Usually, he wouldn't check anyone's profile but the phone's new and expensive and it's uselessness is making him feel guilty about buying it. He swipes to her profile and sees the thumbnail picture of the girl who looks kind of pretty and out of Devrat's league.

'Hey!' shrieks Sumit.

Devrat is startled and he closes the application, as if he was caught watching porn. 'What!'

'You just updated your status. That's the way to go! Social media and all that, connecting and engaging with fans! Who's profile were you on? She looked pretty!' exclaims Sumit.

'I don't know what you're talking about.'

They reach the recording studio after a brief stopover at a roadside stall for a quick meal. Sumit tells Devrat he would soon have to stop doing this, because after he records this song, and he shoots the video, and the video goes viral on YouTube, he would be mobbed.

'Who's the last person with whom this happened?' asks Devrat nonchalantly.

After thinking for about fifteen minutes during which

Devrat played the same level of Candy Crush over and over again, Sumit answers, 'Justin Bieber!'

'Exactly my point,' says Devrat, fully knowing that video and the song would sink without a trace. Who cares about pop/rock songs anywhere? Most independent singers spend their lives singing hit Bollywood songs on garbha nights, or worse, record devotional songs on their tunes.

They are in the waiting room when the owner of the studio walks in and apologizes for the delay. He tells Devrat and Sumit that they can wait in the recording room if they want to. Devrat says a 'why not' and they walk into the heavily insulated recording room. There are two sound technicians working and they look back and acknowledge Sumit. Handshakes are exchanged.

'Should we give it another try?' the sound in the recording room booms.

The technicians look in the direction of the glass window that separates the singer from them. It's a girl, more like a woman. She's looking at the lyrics sheet in front of her and mouthing the lyrics. She has wild, frizzy hair and is slightly on the plump side. She looks like a younger and a better-looking version of Usha Uthup with tattoos on her forearms.

He knows her from earlier, having seen her on quite a few posters of cultural fests of colleges across India, and was at one point quite jealous of her, not only of her multiple gigs but also of her voice.

'She charges a lakh and a half for a performance,' whispers Sumit in Devrat's ear. 'Though you're much better than her. She's old now. She was awesome when she was young. People say a lot of things about her these days. That you know . . .'

'Not interested.'

'I was just saying that she sleeps around.'

'Did I not say I wasn't interested in knowing about her?'

'Okay! Fine. Hey, listen. I need to go somewhere and wrap up some work. You're sure you will manage?' asks Sumit. Devrat nods and Sumit leaves the recording studio. Devrat sits on a small chair and listens to her sing. He mindlessly opens the application again on his phone. He swipes through the pictures as he listens to Karthika sing. The girl's beautiful, the one on his phone. She's from Dehradun as well. He wonders if the girl is one of those twenty people who mail him every few days. He tries remembering the name, Avanti, though he knows he will forget it again for he has always been bad with names and he still doesn't know half of his cousins' real names. He closes the application and finds himself daydreaming about a situation when Arundhati sees him with a girl, this girl from Facebook, who's clearly hotter than she is. That would surely have her begging Devrat to take her back but Devrat would just smirk, move on, and write a song about it. He's jerked out of his reverie by a high note that Karthika just hit.

Karthika is a stickler for perfection and does some lines a dozen times over, and each time it's better than the last time, quite different from what Devrat does—he sings it once and lets it go with the imperfections.

The song is finally over. Karthika leaves the recording room, still grumbling over the few notes that she hit wrong. It's Devrat's turn next.

The technicians get up, their backs aching, their ears sore. 'Do you mind if we smoke and come back?'

'Do you mind if I join you?' asks Devrat and they walk to the balcony of the studio and light up. There is silence, a silence that only fellow smokers can enjoy, something that makes no sense to people who don't smoke. And that silence is broken when Karthika walks in, with her creeper-like hair and her unabashed enthusiasm. 'And that was a fuck-all song and a fuck-all recording session! There's no way that's going viral. People are going to shit all over the song and forget it. I will have to pull a Poonam Pandey to get views on that song,' growls Karthika as she wrests a cigarette from one of the recording guys and takes a long drag. With the amount of cleavage that's on display right now, she's already pulling a half Poonam Pandey.

'It can't be that bad,' says the guy. 'At least better than the last time when you threw a chair through that window after singing a "fuck-all" song that got a hundred thousand views.'

'Still doesn't change the fact that today was just horrible. Horrible,' says Karthika and takes a long drag. 'And hi! You're Devrat, I suppose. I have heard a little about you. The mysterious, non-available singer. Nice marketing technique to get the demand up. I don't agree with it, but still, good effort.'

Truth be told, Devrat's a little intimidated now. He had never done well with women who are older, more accomplished. Not that he's an MCP but all the women he has been around with are docile women, so when someone like Karthika comes around, he feels a little overpowered, less of man, and he's not particularly proud of that.

'How old are you? Seventeen?' asks Karthika.

'I'm twenty-one,' corrects Devrat, and immediately thinks that 'I'm eight' would have sounded equally childish.

'I'm thirty-two,' says Karthika.

Shit. Thirty-two!

'How long have you been in this . . . industry?'

'Feels like forever,' says Karthika. 'Best of luck for your recording. Who are you recording it for?'

'A small YouTube channel. They wanted me to sing for them. Sumit arranged for it,' answers Devrat.

'Shall we record the song now?' one the technicians asks.

'Sure,' says Devrat. Karthika follows them inside. She asks Devrat if he minds her staying in the recording room and he says he doesn't.

Devrat goes to the room meant for singers, places his lyrics sheet in front of him, and puts on the headphones. As usual, he will be trying to knock the song out of the park in one go and not give it multiple shots like Karthika did. The music is on and he starts to sing. He stumbles on a few lines in the lyrics department, and has to repeat them, but other than that, it's perfect. In and out in half an hour. During the entire duration of the recording, he tries steadfastly to not look at Karthika. He would have dealt with Karthika with ease had this performance been in a club, had he been a little drunk, had he been a little baked out of his head, but when sane, he doesn't do well when being judged.

He comes to the recording room and asks the guys. 'How was it?'

'Awesome, bro!' says one.

'You killed it,' says another.

'It wasn't good at all, but they will obviously not say that. It makes their lives easier. You book them for two hours and then finish in forty minutes!' says Karthika. 'Work shirkers, all of them. Fuck you.'

'Oho, Karthika—'

They start to protest but Karthika asks them to shut up and asks Devrat where he lives, and Devrat tells her, and she asks if he needs to be dropped home. Devrat nods. Karthika doesn't slip into conversations, she bulldozes into them.

Minutes later, they are in her car, a decent Honda City, the older model, bought secondhand from a fan. A fan who later became a boyfriend, who wasn't even good in bed and Karthika tells him that it was a little creepy because they would only fuck when she sang. 'Could be harder than you think it is,' says Karthika and laughs throatily. Her mouth's open wide enough to fit a few children in. Karthika's a little disgusting and emasculating but there's something strangely sexy about her. She's a like a sexy, pointy-nosed witch.

'Don't you feel bad about the song you just sang inside?' asks Karthika.

'Why would I feel bad about it?' asks Devrat.

'You know . . . it . . . just wasn't as good. You could have sung a few lines differently than you did. And it would be a much better song,' says Karthika.

'It doesn't work for me like that,' says Devrat.

'You're cheating your listeners. You should give it the best you can,' snaps Karthika. 'Like I do.'

Devrat is not sure whether he's attracted to this opinionated older woman, or he's repulsed. 'I don't think it works like that for me. It's not like any other product that the best notes work the best,' says Devrat. 'If I try to sing every note the best I can, I end up losing the emotion behind the word and I start to concentrate on the singing more.'

'Surprise, surprise! You're a singer, and you're supposed to concentrate on that,' mocks Karthika.

'Maybe. Here, right,' says Devrat. 'Here's where I stay.'

'Oh that's nice,' says Karthika. 'Hey! Do you want to go out right now? I can sure have a beer.'

Devrat shrugs his shoulders and says yes. Karthika is a little annoying but she has this quality about her, which makes him want to stick on, or maybe it's just the fact that she's an attractive singer. And you don't meet a lot of people who are into this full time.

Karthika drives away from Devrat's apartment onto the main road and within fifteen minutes they are sitting in an 'okay-ish' pub in Salt Lake. It's just starting to fill up. They order pints and discuss the posters of the music bands that line the walls around them.

'You have a girlfriend?' asks Karthika.

Devrat shakes his head. The question has always made Devrat nervous and hopeful. Why do people ask this question? Does she fancy herself with him, which doesn't seem like a possibility since she's kind of old, but she's also asked him out, so that's in no-man's land. Or it could be that she wants in on some gossip about him.

'So you're a player, aren't you?' probes Karthika.

'Not really,' says Devrat, and just to deflect the questions off him, he asks Karthika the same question.

'I'm divorced,' she says. 'Got married at twenty-three, divorced at twenty-five and swore that I will never get married again, and I'm sticking to it for now.'

Devrat drinks from his bottle. He has no intention to dig into something that he has no experience or interest in but she continues, 'He cheated on me. And well, I cheated on him as well. But then it wasn't why we broke up. We just didn't love each other enough to stay together. Oh, and he was an asshole as well.'

Devrat nods.

'Also, he liked the wrong music.' Karthika laughs throatily again.

Devrat is still confused whether he's attracted to her, because quite clearly, she's not just an arrogant, perfectionist singer, but also someone who probably thought that love is the centre of the universe, and now doesn't. She's also damaged, cheated on, and dumped.

'It happens,' says Devrat. 'I just got dumped recently. She's engaged now. Imagine.'

'Marriage is a sham.'

'I'm too young to know about that,' says Devrat.

'It's just a lot of lacklustre sex, responsibilities, fixed deposits, and house loans and questions about when's the child coming.'

'Maybe.'

And just like that Devrat drifts off thinking about Arundhati and the boy she's engaged to. He finds himself wondering if the two of them have slept together, and whether the sex is good, and mostly because he hasn't slept with anyone since Arundhati walked out and is thinking whether sleeping with Karthika, if the chance arises, would make it any better.

They both finish their beers and order for another one, and finish that as well, and order for another one as Devrat and Karthika make their trips to the washroom. They are too drunk to stop now. Then Devrat finds his phone ringing. It's Mom. He's sane enough to walk out of the pub and talk to his mom. His mother asks him if everything is alright, if he's eating on time, and if they can come and visit. Devrat tells her that things are swell (and they are this time), and that she shouldn't worry and maybe they can come next year when he shifts to a bigger, better flat. Her mother tells him that she misses him, and Devrat says the same. His finds his parents to be mighty cute and he hopes he can tell them that some day rather than just being a cause of worry for them.

He staggers inside and finds the pub a lot darker than before. In the corner, where Karthika and he were sitting, is Karthika, now dancing to the slow beat of the song, her waist moving in perfect harmony, her lips mouthing the song, and he notices that she's a lot more desirable than he earlier thought of her to be. Or maybe he's just drunk.

'You took long,' says Karthika and puts her hands around Devrat's neck, who's almost immediately comfortable. He orders another pint of beer while he's slow dancing with her. He would be lying if he says he hasn't, in the past half hour, thought of how it would be like to kiss someone like Karthika, a woman far older, wiser and talented than he is. He has thought about it, but every time he has, he isn't lost in how the act would be like, but in the words he would say later, over drinks, to his friends and acquaintances about his fling with a woman, divorced, no less, when he was just twenty-one years old. The story gives him more pleasure than the arms of Karthika that are firmly wrapped around his neck. And if he had not been thinking about what would give him more pleasure, he would have already tried kissing her, but he hasn't. Because he knows it makes no sense to do so. He will not miss out on anything if he doesn't make out with Karthika. Maybe except a little bit of thrill, a little sense of victory, a story to tell his friends, but that's it. He wonders what Arundhati would think of it.

He keeps dancing, matching his steps with her, while she keeps making her hair dance, lashing his face with her surprisingly soft and fragrant hair. Her lips hover dangerously close to his and he can smell the beer. Karthika jerks him forward and whispers in his ears, 'Do you want to get out of here?'

'Sure.'

They ask for the bill, Karthika stuffs his hand with a few five-hundred rupee bills and excuses herself. Devrat pays the bill and is waiting at the door when Karthika comes back. Her hair is tastefully tied now, her red and blue earrings are showing, her lipstick is redone and she looks . . .

They sit in her car. And this time Karthika drives slowly. There's no conversation. One part of Devrat clearly wants this, the next part that's going to happen here, but the other part is terribly against it. The part that wants this is twenty-one years old and it says he deserves it. The other is questioning the motive. After all, she's a decade older, and there's nothing new that he can offer to her, and this will be just another story which wouldn't make any sense later. Will he be any different from Arundhati if he sleeps with her? But then, does he need to?

The car screeches to a halt. Devrat instinctively jumps out of the car.

'Aren't you going to invite me?' asks Karthika.

'My mom's upstairs. She's waiting,' answers Devrat.

Karthika nods. Devrat searches for any change of expression on her face and there are none. Karthika drives off.

Devrat walks up the stairs of his apartment, feeling liberated, feeling different. There's no victory in giving in.

NINE

avanti

Avanti's feet are killing her now. It's been three hours since they started off and the flight has been hovering around the Mumbai airport for an hour due to the heavy incoming traffic.

The passengers are getting anxious and the frequent announcements from the captains aren't helping. The passengers look at Avanti like it's her fault that Mumbai is the busiest airport in the country. She doesn't mind tending to the old, frail people who are scared, but the men, who think they have bought the entire airlines with their cheap, discounted air tickets, have no business shooting her looks like she's the one not doing her job well.

'Can you please confirm when we are going to land? Our grandson must be waiting outside,' an old man asks. See! That's not hard now, is it? Asking someone something politely. Avanti calls the cockpit and a firm voice tells her that it's going to be a while. The voice is authoritative and little bit sexy, but she doesn't read much into it. Most pilots, she now knows, are raging alcoholics with potbellies snuck in tightly behind their crisp white uniforms.

As she passes the last few seats of the economy class, she hears a few men talk.

'That's the problem with all these Indian airlines. They can't even land their planes on time. How do you think they will compete with the foreign airlines when they come in? I once travelled with Air France. Impeccable service!'

Avanti turns back, wanting to ask him what the fuck his problem is, but then she looks at the man—he's in his mid-forties with a belly the size of a whale and his teeth are bright red and half-eaten.

Avanti leans over and asks, 'We, at Indiago Airlines, are always at your service. Can I help you with an extension to your seat belt to accommodate your paunch? No? The smaller one is doing just fine? Okay. Thanks!'

The man shifts nervously in his seat and says he's fine. The men around him stare at his bulging belly and the seat belt that's straining around it and they muffle their laughs.

Avanti walks off. They are still in the air and Avanti's bored. 'The guy has been to the washroom at least thrice in the past one hour,' notes Avanti, pointing out to young guy who's constantly watching something on his phone. 'God knows what he's doing in there.'

The senior laughs and says, 'I have walked into old men with magazines in there.'

'Disgusting!' says Avanti. 'Hey? Can I go into the cockpit?'

'Sure!' says the senior flight attendant.

Today, the cockpit is being manned by Vikram Singh and Arun Gawli. Arun is a middle-aged guy whom Avanti has no interest in. He can quietly get sucked out of the cockpit window for all she cares. Vikram, on the other hand, is painfully handsome, and not only that, Vikram has conveniently ignored her and that makes him slightly desirable. He looks a little old though, like twenty-eight or something, which makes him a decade older, but ogling is okay, she reasons. She already feels she's cheating on Devrat.

'How much time will it take?' Avanti asks Vikram, pretending to look in the direction in which Vikram's looking. She doesn't get shit. And staring at the blinking, glowing light panels only makes her more nervous. So instead, she stares at Vikram's jawline. Oh God! That twenty-eight-year-old jawline!

'We should be there in fifteen,' says Vikram in an irritatingly dispassionate voice.

'That is if we don't crash, right?' says Avanti and giggles.

Arun and Vikram stare back at Avanti. They shrug their shoulders as if to say, 'What the . . .?'

Avanti smiles nervously and slithers out of the cockpit. Just as she's leaving, Vikram leans back and asks Avanti, 'Are you guys going out somewhere tonight?'

And so much for the beautiful jawline. Vikram's over-eagerness and his leering eyes just killed it for Avanti. She realizes she only likes men till the time they are not interested in her. 'My boyfriend is in Mumbai. Devrat. So I will be a little busy with him,' says Avanti and leaves the cockpit.

A little later, the flight lands and the passengers deplane, muttering the choicest obscenities, swearing to themselves that they will never take this flight again. Avanti still forces a smile and wishes them a good day ahead. She wishes they would fall off the stairs and break their necks or get run over by the airline bus.

The flight attendants retrieve their bags and wait for their car. Despite the long, tiring flight, the unsavoury passengers, and the slip of the tongue in the cockpit, Avanti's still looking forward to the evening. Today can be her first night out, unsupervised by anyone. Even though she's tried, she's excited as hell.

'So what's the plan?' asks Avanti, but her fellow flight attendants are already dozing off in the cab to the hotel. Soon, she drifts off, too. She wakes up with a jolt and finds the cab driver shaking her. Her mouth is open and she has drooled all over her uniform. So much for the weeks of training when you are taught how to act lady-like and professional at all times.

By the time she reaches the reception, after wrestling with her luggage and her heels and her wayward hair, the other girls are already on their way to the lifts. The entire airlines staff has checked in with the precision and timing of a Ninja.

She flops on the bed in her room while the bellboy arranges her suitcase. She can't positively stay in the room or she will go bat-shit crazy. She's not in her city. She's unsupervised. It's an eighteen-year-old's dream! She can't *NOT* abuse this freedom, for if she does that today, God knows what she will do tomorrow. Maybe she will turn down a free shopping trip. Maybe she would want to get married. Maybe she will want to have five kids and a fat husband. 'This is where it all starts,' she thinks.

Maybe that's the life of a flight attendant. To fly for a few hours, sleep in the cab/bus, and sleep like a log after popping a few pills for the backache, the bad skin and the eating disorder. Maybe her dreams of travelling to different cities, partying out with pretty girlfriends and hot captains was all a mirage constructed to fool willing, naïve girls into joining the aviation industry. Maybe there will be no Shahrukh Khan jumping ropes and getting past security lines to get to you, you, a beautiful flight attendant like in 1994's *Anjaam*.

She has to get out of the room!

She calls her three colleagues who flew with her. Two of them are old and they refuse to go out anywhere, straight out. They don't even have the courtesy to tell her that they are chumming and hence in great pain, or that they have a ginormous loan they have to pay off and hence can't afford to spend on anything other than water, air and food. They just say NO.

The third one, though, jumps and squeals, even lets out a few expletives, when she hears Avanti's voice. It was a surprise because this girl, Namita, was snapping at everyone throughout the flight. She almost even slapped a drunken passenger. Avanti had immediately judged her to be a veteran, someone who has been in this industry long enough to hate every bit of it.

Avanti is trying to pick what she wants to wear. Namita isn't a bad-looker at all and she doesn't want to look average.

She finally chooses a black dress that is tantalizingly little and uncomfortable, but she looks dazzling and that's what matters. She doesn't necessarily believe the feminist bullshit of what's inside is what matters. If it worked that way all feminists should make sure they get married to ugly, haggard men with facial hair concentrated on their earlobes.

She calls Namita and tells her that she's coming over. Namita doesn't believe in the feminist shit, too, and is rocking a leather skirt that ends inches above her knees and a halter top. She looks rather cute. Like an innocent girl who will have whips and handcuffs at the back of her cupboard.

They take the hotel cab because they think they will roll like that today, like rich girls. And it turns out that Namita is actually rich.

'Then why are you doing this?' asks Avanti, who now knows that Namita's father has factories that make cardboard boxes.

'I'm twenty-nine,' says Namita.

'Twenty-nine? No! You can't be! You look as old as I am!' says Avanti.

'And how old are you?'

'Eighteen.'

'That's the nicest thing anyone has ever said to me. But yes, I'm twenty-nine and I've been divorced for the last six years.'

'Oh.'

'Don't worry. It was a long time back and surprisingly, I don't feel any different. I still feel like I'm eighteen, twenty-one max!' chirps Namita.

'Okay.' Words are melting to mush in Avanti's mouth. 'Why did you . . . umm . . . get divorced?'

'It was just a wrong decision. We were in love. It had been a year and I thought this is it. We were too young. Our parents, especially mine had objected but we were too stubborn for our own good. Took us two years to realize we'd made a mistake and then we walked our different paths. He's married now,' says Namita.

'So now you're okay?' asks Avanti.

'It's been years that I have been okay! Time heals everything and this was just a divorce,' says Namita.

'But you still haven't answered why you're in this?' asks Avanti.

'I'm getting married in a year and this time it will be someone my parents choose for me.'

'So you're not looking for love?'

'I'm not sure I know what love is. I'm not sure anyone knows. I just wanted to do something before my time runs out.

My parents wanted to send me off on a holiday but that would have been boring. So I suggested working for an international airline. I have never worked in my life and this was the only industry that would accept me.'

'And your rich father was okay with it?'

'They threw a major fit! A MAJOR FIT! But then I cried, and it was okay.'

They enter WTF, a small Karaoke bar in Versova, and quite a few heads turn, only for a split second though because this isn't Delhi, and unlike Delhi, people have better things to do than mentally undress girls walking on the road. They take a table with high stools. Namita says she feels like a Long Island Iced Tea today and so they order two of those.

'I'm not sure I can drink,' says Avanti.

'Don't do that, now! You have to drink! Don't kill the vibe,' protests Namita. 'I don't want to be the only one drinking and talking shit.'

'Okay, fine. But only one!'

'Yeah. We will see.'

By the time the clock hits ten, the place is full. There are groups of good-looking men, good-looking women, good-looking men and women, talking animatedly. Three boys have come and asked if they can join them, and although they had asked nicely and they seemed like nice boys, Avanti couldn't let them join them.

'I have no idea why we asked them to go,' says Namita. 'They looked cute.'

'It's because I'm already dating someone in my head.'

'That's the strangest thing I have ever heard. What does that mean?' asks Namita.

'It means I have been sort of dating him in my daydreams

and he obviously has no idea of it. He's kind of like a hurt puppy and he's gorgeous. Also I have never met him. I have just heard him sing and seen his pictures. And I do know I sound a little bit psycho here so I will just stop talking and never mention this again,' says Avanti, embarrassed.

'That was interesting. But that doesn't mean we can't talk to anyone else,' argues Namita and winks.

'Okay, fine. There are three boys in that group,' Avanti says and points the straw in the direction of a big group in which two boys are constantly shooting looks at Avanti and Namita. 'If they come, we will let them treat us.'

'Done. And if they are not interesting enough, we will just leave and let them pay the bill!'

'Wait. Aren't you like insanely rich or something?' asks Avanti.

'It's not about the money, Avanti. It's about the little thrills in life!'

'Poor guys! They will curse us and every other girl for the rest of their lives,' says Avanti.

'Guys kind of deserve that, don't you think?'

'Yes,' says Avanti and thinks of Shekhar who, frankly, has gone mad after the entire Avanti Changing Her Number incident. He calls twenty times a day and Avanti picks none of them. 'Cool! We will wait then.'

Well, the boys come and they are cute, but not great to talk to. Namita and Avanti pose as investment bankers and fib about how tough their lives are. They tell the boys that they are rich, married and lonely. They can see drool collect on the tongues of the two boys. Namita and Avanti are drunk, but not as drunk as they are acting. Namita is now throwing her hands over a boy who's enjoying every bit of it. She complains that her husband is fat and is really bad in bed. She looks at the boys and asks, 'Do fat people have smaller penises?'

The boys, who by this time are ripe red tomatoes, stutter and stammer something only they can understand. Namita and Avanti are clutching their hands under the table, thrilled at how dumb these boys are.

'How do you, like, give a blowjob if it's too small? It's ridiculous!' says Avanti.

'I know, right? I know of this one time when I was really horny and I had to do with the guy who delivers courier packages to my place,' narrates Namita with overdone sluttiness. The boys look at the two girls in horror, and a little bit of hope.

'Oh! Yes, don't I remember him! You sent him over to my place as well, remember? And then you walked in . . . and . . .'

Namita stops her. 'We just met them, we shouldn't tell them everything!'

Avanti tells Namita that she's right and some things are better left unsaid.

'Please tell us! Please tell us!' the boys insist, by now thinking that this is the best night ever of their lives and they will find themselves in a steamy foursome after these two drunken women finish their stories. Namita and Avanti finish the story, a story that would make *Fifty Shades of Grey* read like a nursery rhyme, and by the time they are finished, the boys look . . . well, there's no other word really . . . they look horny. Like a story out of the Indian pornography comic, *Savita Bhabhi*, is just about to come true.

'Excuse me,' says Namita. 'I think both of us need to go to the washroom now.' Namita hovers near Avanti's neck and looks up naughtily.

Avanti looks at the boys and says, 'I hope you guys live alone.'

The boys nod, too dumbfounded to be smooth anymore. It's the best day of their lives.

'Give us ten,' says Avanti and they leave, smiling and winking at the boys.

The boys talk between themselves, slap each other's backs, congratulate each other, wondering if this is really happening, and start checking their pockets for protection. Avanti and Namita, who are watching all of this, walk out of the restaurant and burst out laughing.

They take five minutes to get a grip on the situation and then they burst out laughing again. It takes them about an hour of strolling around idly to get over it. It's almost after one and they are sitting on the pavement. The hotel cab is waiting.

'Have you had boyfriends after that? After your divorce?' asks Avanti out of the blue.

'Not really. My parents kept a pretty strict tab on me after it happened. And I kept feeling it was my fault for a really long time for having put the family through a divorce and all. Everything changes once a young daughter of the family is a divorcee. It becomes what your family is known by. So everyone is like, "Oh, yes, Mehras. Nice family but their daughter is a divorcee."'

They stagger into a cab, still drunk, and still giggling over what they did to the boys when Avanti's face suddenly droops. She's frowning now. She was checking Devrat's profile because a few days back he had updated, '*Going to the recording studio to record a new song.*' And she liked it immediately and was waiting for the song to come out. But instead . . .

'What happened?' asks Namita. Avanti shows Namita her cell phone. It's a picture of Devrat with an old woman, probably in her thirties, named Karthika. More stalking reveals she's a singer, too.

'Who's she? And who's he? Is he the guy you were dating in your head?'

'Yes,' nods Avanti.

Avanti briefly explains what Devrat means to her, and even though he isn't her boyfriend, he means much more. Namita consoles her and tells her, 'You're way prettier than she is. She must be his older sister or something.'

'But then why are they so close in the picture?' grumbles a drunk Avanti. Just then her phone rings. And it's Shekhar and she lets the phone ring.

'Now who's that?' asks Namita.

'My ex-boyfriend who still thinks he owns me. He's a bit of an asshole. He's constantly after my life,' answers Avanti.

'Why don't you tell him that?'

'I'm scared,' Avanti tell her, and Namita taps her on the head. The phone rings again and this time Namita answers the phone. She puts it on loudspeaker and before Shekhar can say anything, Namita starts to shout, 'LEAVE AVANTI ALONE, YOU ASSHOLE! SHE'S IN LOVE WITH SOMEONE ELSE! SO FUCK OFF!' Avanti and Namita are giggling and Shekhar starts to abuse from the other side of the phone.

'AVANTI? Where are you? And who's this girl? And what guy? ARE YOU DRUNK? TELL ME WHERE YOU ARE! I WILL COME. Tell me where the FUCK are you?' Shekhar shouts, but Namita cuts the call and Avanti switches it off.

An hour passes by, and Avanti's is in her hotel room now, wondering who the hell Karthika is? She wonders where Devrat must have met her ... she sends Devrat a few mails from those twenty accounts, telling him that he deserves someone much better and goes off to sleep hoping they would break up by the time she wakes up.

The following day, she wakes up with a massive headache and promises herself that she's never going to drink again. Groggily, she switches on her cellphone and it has fifty missed call alerts, from Shekhar and from her father. She calls up her father.

'Hello?'

'Hello, A . . . vanti.'

'Umm?'

'You're in Mumbai.'

'Umm . . . yes?'

'A friend of yours, Shekhar, came to our house today. He was shouting at the top of his lungs. He was asking for you. He was abusing you. I felt really bad.'

Crap! 'And?' asks a fuming Avanti. Avanti can kill a puppy right now.

'Nothing. I . . . I . . . chased him away with a bat. There were other members from the resident's welfare, too. So we chased him outside the apartments and told him to never come back again. He is y . . . our friend so I didn't allow the society *wala*s to call the police. I'm sorry, but he was abusing you and creating a ruckus. Can you give me his parents' number? I will talk to them and tell them what their son is up to?'

And just like that Avanti feels calm; she stops pacing around the room and flops on the couch. For a moment she goes 'awww' in her head and smiles. Her father, a powerless middle-aged man, trying to stand up for her, wanting to complain to Shekhar's parents as if they are all students in the fifth standard, is cute. She thinks how her father must look like with a bat in his hand, chasing after that huge, muscular guy.

'It's okay. You don't have to call them.'

'Okay.'

'And I'm fine.'

'O . . . kay.'

Avanti realizes that the conversation, if it carries on, will only get more awkward and decides to tell her father that she's getting late, and she disconnects the call. It was cute, nonetheless.

She has to leave for the airport in a bit. She checks her phone again. The picture of that woman, 'Karthika' is still there, and the question is still haunting her.

'Who the hell is this Karthika and where did he meet her?'

TEN

devrat

Devrat is waiting for Karthika to stop singing. This is Karthika's fourth gig in four consecutive days and Devrat has been to every one of them. All of them have ended with guys lining up to talk to Karthika, Karthika signing her albums' CDs for them, Karthika and Devrat ending up getting drunk, that either led to one of them puking their guts out, or the two of them indulging in nasty, angry sex. Today, it's going to be the latter.

Devrat had thought he would not meet Karthika, and that giving in was easy, but then when he heard about Arundhati's wedding date, he couldn't quite take it. What made it worse was that Arundhati uploaded pictures of them snuck in a blanket in what seemed like a hotel room. All this while there was a slight hope in Devrat's head that probably they haven't had sex yet. But now they have and that's something Devrat refuses to take lying down. No matter how progressive, a guy can't take his ex-girlfriend sleeping around with another man.

Now Devrat doesn't know what kind of revenge this is, but but he is set on his plan—he would have sex with Karthika everywhere that he had with Arundhati, and when Arundhati eventually breaks up and comes crawling back to Devrat, he can tell her, in explicit detail, that all of Arundhati's memories are now tainted with memories of Karthika and him having sex. So it's important for Devrat that he doesn't pass out today even as he downs his fifth pint of beer.

A few days back, he uploaded a picture of him and Karthika, his arm around her, her face stuck to his cheek just so Arundhati can see it. Quite a few people liked that picture, calling them a beautiful couple and they can't wait for Karthika and Devrat to perform together. But surprisingly, his fans in Dehradun weren't impressed. They mailed Devrat telling him that he deserves much better and they weren't too happy knowing that he's dating Karthika. They were angry to say the least. He's trying not to think about it that much.

On the other hand, much to the happiness of Sumit, the video they recorded for the song went viral and notched up two million views in the first two weeks itself. Gigs were now easy to get, and for the first time, they were in the position to negotiate their terms.

'That girl, Arundhati, was bad luck for you,' said Sumit. 'See! Ever since she has gone, you're doing so well for yourself.'

'That's what. Ever since she's gone I have been a better singer. For every time I go on that stage, I'm thinking about her,' argues Devrat.

No wonder most singers and actors and artistes have such screwed up love lives. They are all looking for that heartbreak, that failure, that death, that will change them as a person. And the pursuit of that leads to strange people and strange places. So what after Devrat gets over Arundhati? Will his music lose its soul again?

It's obvious that he will not fall in love with Karthika and when Karthika decides that she has had enough with the little boy, he will not be heartbroken, maybe a little bored for a while but definitely not heartbroken.

But he does have to admit that the sex with Karthika is great. In fact it's much better than what he had with Arundhati. He's forced to compare because now he has legitimate reasons to; Arundhati, too, must be making the same comparison.

With Arundhati it was never sex, it was always kissing, prolonged kissing. It was like they kissed, and bumped into sex, like it was an object and they used to think, well, not bad, we can try this too. But it always never about sex. Sex was the thing they never talked about.

Devrat isn't sure if he really enjoyed having *sex* with Arundhati. Sex for Devrat was more about pressure than pleasure. Arundhati was the first girl Devrat had done it with while Arundhati had been with other men. So it was always a competition going on in Devrat's head. He had to be better than all the guys Arundhati had been with before him. So more often than not, sex wasn't enjoyable at all. It was an assignment Devrat wanted to ace. He didn't want to put a single foot wrong.

Even when she was naked and wrapped around him, he was thinking of how her ex-boyfriends must have performed. He wanted to last longer than her ex-boyfriends so he used to start thinking about failures in his life to distract himself from the act. He wanted to be perceived as passionate so he kissed her a lot. He had read somewhere that love alone can make sex better and hence he would slip in an 'I love you' somewhere during and after the process. He would always snuggle and try hard not to fall asleep after they used to come. It's like if the dessert is nice, you're fooled into believing that the dinner was, too. Having sex with Arundhati was science. It was calculated and measured to make Arundhati believe he was the best in bed she had ever had.

'That was the best sex. EVER. Nothing even comes close,' Arundhati had said once. More than seeing her naked, those words used to turn him on more, even now. He feels victorious whenever he replays these words in his head. Like he beat all her previous boyfriends!

But with Karthika, it's easy. It's just sex.

He doesn't give a shit about whether he's big enough for her or not, whether he is man enough for her or not, whether she's happy with all his moves (not many!), whether he's satisfying her, whether she comes, too, or not. For when he's with Karthika, it's all clear and on the table. It's like Russian Roulette. Some days you win, some days you lose. And they talk about it. 'You sucked last night,' Karthika would often remark. 'As if you were any better,' Devrat would retort. It is easy. There is no pressure.

Devrat wonders if Arundhati's fiancé undergoes the same pressure, in fact, he wishes it on him. But he's with her for life and that's enough time to prove himself. But what if Arundhati already thinks her fiancé is better than Devrat?

He has found himself thinking on this same loop almost every few hours, and it makes him sad and furious. Thinking about it and getting sad has also become his superstition now. He does it just before his show starts. He likes going up on the stage, a little angry, a little disappointed, but as his listeners say—mostly awesome.

He sees Karthika walk up to his table, her male admirers fall back when they see Devrat stand up and claim Karthika as his own. They sit down and Karthika looks at Devrat. The question is in her eyes and Devrat is supposed to answer it before she says it.

'You were great today!'

'Oh. Was I? You're just saying,' says Karthika as she looks at the waiter and orders her pint.

'No, I'm not,' says Devrat. He was just saying. He has heard the same song so many times now, he even knows the parts Karthika doesn't like or screws up slightly.

'Thank you,' says Karthika and she says it while her lips hover close to Devrat's ears. It's sexual. Everything Karthika does is sexual and Devrat now believes that every older woman who's single has major sexual needs.

'Is your friend coming? What's her name? Karishma?' asks Karthika.

'Yes, she is coming. She's a little late though.' He has not seen Karishma in a while now. Karishma LOVED the video and the song that went viral and has wanted to see Devrat for quite some time now, but Devrat has been avoiding her. Meeting her meant telling her about Karthika and he wasn't sure how comfortable he was with that.

'Who's this girl you have uploaded a picture with?' Karishma had asked a few days back. 'I hope you're not dating her! Are you? Are you? Please tell me you're not. She's way older than you, Devrat.'

Karishma was clearly not fond of this new woman in Devrat's life. Devrat had given a noncommittal answer back then but now he has tackle the problem head on. Not only meet her and tell her, but also make her meet Karthika and tell her what's going on between the two of them.

'Here she is,' says Devrat as he sees Karishma walking through the door. Devrat and Karishma hug and Karishma hits Devrat for being so elusive all this while.

'Big celebrity you're now, huh?' mocks Karishma.

'Yes, obviously. Don't you see all these girls flocking around to see me?' Devrat says mockingly looking around him. 'A video going viral doesn't make anyone a celebrity or anything.'

'But it did make you into an asshole,' quips Karishma.

'Oh, by the way, this is Karthika.'

Karthika embraces Karishma. It's not a hug, it's an embrace. It's a very elderly thing. Her arms wrap around Karishma in the most comprehensive manner, like she's consoling Karishma, like someone close to Karishma has died. When they are in that embrace Devrat realizes how ridiculous he and Karthika must look together. Karthika is . . . old.

'You must be Karishma,' says Karthika.

Karishma is still looking at Devrat, searching his face for explanations. 'Yes, supposedly, I'm his best friend but I don't know about you.'

'Oh, there's nothing to know really. We just met on the music circuit and we talk music. That's it,' says Karthika. Devrat is confused here.

'Oh okay! I thought of something entirely different! I thought both of you were dating! I got scared for a moment!' says Karishma and starts to launch into a How Stupid Of Me laugh.

'Naah! He's a kid,' says Karthika and ruffles Devrat's hair. It's all very confusing to Devrat. Never before did Devrat feel so young in front of her, but suddenly Karthika, is in his head, like a school teacher he's sleeping with. Karthika adds, 'I need to go. Both of you can carry on. I need to get some work done.'

Devrat protests but Karthika insists and leaves. Devrat's

phone rings and it's Karthika and she's telling him that she will see him at his place later when he's done.

He's still thinking of what to make of all this when Karishma asks him, 'I hope there's nothing going on between the two of you.'

'What? No! Obviously not!'

'Okay, okay. Don't be offended now. She's hot though, for her age,' says Karishma. 'Oh! There's something important I need to tell you. There's this girl in my apartment who I knew from earlier. And only yesterday I saw her listen to your song for hours on end! She's rather cute. If you want I can . . . you know.'

'No, I don't. And fun fact, by the way, do you know that Arundhati and her fiancé are putting after-sex pictures on their profiles?' asks Devrat. He swipes and taps his phone and shows Karishma the picture.

'You don't know if it's an after-sex picture. And even if it is, you should delete it,' says Karishma.

'He isn't even that good-looking.'

'And that should be none of your concern. You should delete it and move on.'

'He even writes statuses in wrong English, Karishma,' grumbles Devrat. He orders another pint.

'I have no doubt that you were and are a better guy than whoever this fucker is,' says Karishma. 'But you have to move on. There's no other option left.'

'Whatever.' Devrat takes a large gulp of his beer. And burps. He tells Karishma that he really needs to visit the washroom. By the time he reaches the washroom, all he had eaten and drunk in the past two hours was gurgling at the back of his throat and within a few nanoseconds he was flushing it down the toilet. Then he sits on the toilet seat and drifts off. It's only when he hears faint knocking he wakes up. Karishma is banging on the outside door and Devrat can hear her talk to a few waiters about the need to knock the door down. He stands up with a start, tries opening his eyes wide, tells himself that he's in control, walks out of the cubicle, splashes water all over his face and walks out with smile.

Karishma sees through him though.

'You need to take better care of yourself. Do you feel better now?' she asks.

'What do you mean better? I just pottied.'

'First of all, pottied isn't a word. And second, I know you puked and passed out. It's not that we have met today. Oh! Also since I was getting bored, I checked your phone,' says Karishma nonchalantly. Devrat snatches it from her. 'And I deleted her pictures. But that's not the point. The point is that I saw pictures that made me want to join you in the washroom and puke with you.'

'What the . . . but. . .' Devrat checks his phone and tries to remember what was on it. Other than a few pictures from the little shows he has done, the gallery is empty. All the pictures of Karthika are gone. The teasing selfies of Karthika in minimal or no clothing, the pictures she used to send him clicked early morning naked in bed, the pictures they took before, after or during sex, they are ALL GONE. It's a sexless phone now and it hits Devrat.

'Why would you do that?'

'Devrat? Are you OUT OF YOUR MIND? I don't know where to start? First, you're sleeping with her! She's more than a decade older than you. She will screw with your head. You can't afford that right now! One mistake and you will end up in the engineering college again. I hope you know that. And as if that's not enough, you have naked pictures of her in your phone! Do you have any idea how much trouble you can find yourself in?'

'Quit it.'

'Shut up and listen, Devrat. What if someone came across this cell phone instead of me? You would be dead then. You wouldn't be in engineering college, you would be in jail!'

'You're over-reacting!' says Devrat.

'I'm not. If you want to check, why don't you upload a few of those "sexy" pictures of yours online and see if you can wriggle out of that,' says Karishma, referring to Devrat's and Karthika's chats where Karthika used to call her half-naked pictures as 'sexy' pictures. Sounds rather odd, thinks Devrat.

Karishma suddenly turns soft and holds Devrat's hand and tells him that she's always there for him, and if he needs anything he can just call her. They can talk, and that they can solve this and get through this. Devrat protests that he's fine, and Karishma points to the cell phone and tells him that he's not.

'I just want you to get it together. If you ever need me, I'm here.'

'What if I need "sexy" pictures?' chuckles Devrat and Karishma hits him on his head.

Karishma's phone starts to ring. The name Karan flashes on it. Karishma takes the call. Apparently, Karan is waiting outside. Karishma asks Devrat if he wants to hang out with them and Devrat waves her off. He has never met Karan and doesn't intend to so when Karishma asks him to come out and say hi, he ignores it. Karishma leaves.

Devrat knows where he stands but sometimes he just loses

sight of it. He knows he's on the perfect path of losing it all and ending up penniless. He's practically illiterate, he's unambitious, careless about money, and he spends an ungodly amount of time trying to be depressed because he thinks it helps his music. But now that he's sitting in the bar and getting depressed, he thinks it's not because it helps his music but because it helps him being lazy. Most depressed people are like that, isn't it? Someone who doesn't have the time to be depressed might not be happy but he's too busy to think about how sad he is.

Given his new-found fame, he should be doing a whirlwind of shows but he doesn't. He has categorically told Sumit that he would not do more than one show a week. It hadn't gone down well with Sumit but sometimes there's no arguing with Devrat. He stubs his cigarette and calls up Sumit.

'Get me as many shows as you can get,' says Devrat.

'What? Oh! Are you sure?' asks Sumit.

'Yes, I am.'

'I have one lined up in five days. They wanted you but since you didn't want to do it, I was pushing for someone else.'

Devrat weighs the scale on this. Lying in bed with Karthika the entire day or doing a small gig for fifty people who may or may not know him.

'I'm sure. Push me for it.'

'It's at Insomnia Café. Update your pages and your profile,' says Sumit.

Devrat does just that. He deletes the picture of Karthika and him from his page. When he's deleting it, he remembers the mails he got from his fans in Dehradun telling him that they weren't too happy seeing him with her. As soon as he deletes the picture, a host of his recent pictures are liked by a girl. He remembers the name somewhere. Avanti(?). Where has he heard the name? He visits the profile of the girl. He gets a sense of déjà vu when he visits the girl's profile. It's like all this is familiar and that he's done it before, in exactly the same way.

He thinks of liking her pictures but refrains from it. After all, he's the singer and she's the fan and he should let the equation remain that way.

ELEVEN

avanti

Avanti is ecstatic. She's over the moon really. This can't be happening! No, it's not because Shekhar hasn't called for two weeks now and his contact has dwindled to a few text messages and the like where he calls her an ungrateful slut, a fucking whore and other synonyms. It's because she's flying to Kolkata tomorrow and Devrat's gig is scheduled on the exact same night. And the cherry on the cake is that he has deleted the picture of him with that God-awful-looking singer, Karthika. She has already sent a mail thanking him for that.

She checks her roster and she checks Devrat's updates again. This is divine intervention. But just as the news sinks in it's more distressing than it's gladdening. Firstly there's this entire thing about what she's going to wear, and God willing she does find something to wear which she knows she wouldn't, she has to go up and talk to him, and she doesn't know how she's going to gather the courage for that.

She's sitting in room making plans to shop when her father knocks at her door. She gets up, opens the door, and walks back to bed and sits there. Her father keeps standing on the door. He's in his work clothes, which means an ill-fitting shirt, a pair of brown trousers and a chunky set of sports shoes.

'I'm sorry I c . . . hecked your roster,' he stammers. 'I saw you're flying to Kolkata.'

'And?' asks Avanti. Conversation is still scant between Avanti and her father. She doesn't know what to talk to him about. And he only has one question to ask her, if Shekhar is still troubling her. Beyond that they really don't talk.

'I'm flying on the same day to Nagpur. From what I can see we will need to reach the airport roughly about the same time. I was wondering if you were thinking of sharing the cab?' asks the father.

'Sure,' says Avanti.

Her father nods. He's still standing there. Avanti tells him that she has stuff to do and her father slinks away. Avanti's not angry with her father, just awkward, and she will always be awkward.

She shuts these thoughts off and thinks of what she's going to wear and she's clearly at a loss. She doesn't want to look like a groupie, or a one-night stand, but she does want to stand out as well.

Her anxiousness gets worse as the time of the flight approaches and she starts to feel sick in the stomach. Like really sick. She wants to call in sick and not go to Kolkata, not now, not ever. She has gone over and over the words she would say to him but every time it sounds more stupid and she doesn't know a way around it. The little black dress she bought a couple of days back, a dress that she thought made her look like a total style diva, now seems to have become tight and loose simultaneously from all the wrong places. Frankly, she looks like a skinny elephant in it now. She has spent the entire night talking to Namita who asked Avanti to take it easy but it's easier said than done.

Her alarm rings and she has hardly slept—she looks like an old troll, absolutely hideous. She wants to bury herself inside her blanket, if possible, below the top soil, the lithosphere, the asthenosphere, right down to the core. She's surprised she remembers the break-up of the earth's crust or whatever, right down to its very centre. She's still wallowing in self-pity and anger when her door is knocked. It's her father and she shouts that she will be ready in just a minute.

Avanti jumps out of her bed, changes into her clothes, checks if she has packed everything, wonders if she's looking like a housemaid and is convinced that she is, and runs out of her bedroom. Her father is waiting at the breakfast table and there are two bowls of cereal, he's eating out of one of them. Avanti quietly goes and sits there. She pours milk into the muesli, a kind she hasn't tasted before, and starts to eat. 'Not bad,' she thinks. Better than the cornflakes. Her father's phone rings and it's the cab driver. They both get up. Her father locks the door behind her. He's just carrying a small hand baggage while today, Avanti is travelling heavy.

The cab driver zips through the Ring Road and there are no words exchanged between them. Avanti is busy checking and rechecking her Twitter account. There's nothing new on her Timeline but it's better than just staring at the road and being more aware of the silence that hangs in the air.

'Which hotel are you going to stay in?' her father asks.

'I haven't checked yet,' says Avanti and keeps the phone on her lap.

'Do you like flying?'

The question is innocent but Avanti still feels offended. 'Yes, I do. It's fun.'

'I'm sure it is. So do you also go into the cockpit? What's that like?' her father asks, rather excitedly, and for a moment, Avanti looks at him strangely. He's fifty, no less, but his face is one of an excited poodle, eyes wide open, like he's talking about Narnia behind the cupboard.

'It's quite confusing if you ask me. There are little lights everywhere and beeping stuff and it's a little claustrophobic.'

'Have you been inside it when the plane is taking off?'

'Not really but shortly afterwards, yes,' says Avanti.

'Have you t . . . ouched the lever that makes it go up?'

'No. I think I will be in jail if I do that,' answers Avanti.

'Oh.'

Her father almost looks disappointed as if being told Santa isn't real. The cab reaches the airport and both of them get off. Her father helps her to load up her suitcases on a trolley and they make for the entrances of the airport. She walks towards a different gate, meant for airline employees only. She looks back once to see her father gingerly move towards his gate with his eyes still on her. She looks away and walks inside, trying hard not to look back again.

Once inside the airport she starts to panic again. She tells herself to calm down. At the counter where she enters her attendance, she checks the flight timing again. She's on time. And just like that, she checks the flights to Nagpur from Delhi, to see which flight her father is on. There are thirteen flights to Nagpur today from Delhi but none of them are until late afternoon. She walks to the gate again, she peers out and her father is still standing where she last saw him. He's still scanning the crowds. She wants to wave at him but she doesn't. She watches him walk away, get into a cab, and leave the airport. Avanti smiles. She thinks of dialling her father's number and calling his bluff. She wants to tell him that she knows that he's trying to reconnect with her but she doesn't. Her flight is announced and she walks towards the security check.

The flight is uneventful, though she's slowly losing her mind. She didn't want to work at all today, so she faked a painful break-up and her empathetic colleagues didn't let her lift a finger. There's nothing stronger than a break-up for two women to bond over.

In the cab back to the hotel, Avanti feels rather nervous and pukish. Avanti checks Devrat's update and is disappointed that his gig at Insomnia hasn't been cancelled yet. If only it were cancelled she would have the pretext to not meet him. But now, she will have to go. She will have to talk to him. And she will have to come back, disappointed, with the information that Devrat, though only twenty-one, is hitched and is never going to be hers.

Three very nervous hours later, she finds herself in Insomnia, an hour before time. There are still people there, milling about, sitting without a care in the world, and she's shivering. She clearly remembers the first time she heard Devrat sing. It was from a time Devrat's fan page had less than ten followers and she had stumbled on it by pure mistake. There was just one video on it, a grainy video of a skinny guy with a guitar, whose voice had more static than the video itself. She was listening to the song, crouched in the corner of her room, crying. Seven hours later, she was still listening to the song on a loop, smiling. The puppy-faced boy had won over her heart.

She nursed the obsession she had on him, an obsession she

could truly calls hers since no one shared it with her. But now she feels nervous seeing the posters with Devrat's picture on it. He has grown rather handsome in the past few years, irritatingly so, and girls have started fawning over him for that. Avanti wants to slap them and claim her right. He was hers before he became this edible, sexy-looking hot singer.

Slowly and steadily, the bar starts to fill up, and much to her dismay, a few people are talking about Devrat as well. They know he's playing and they know he's good, and Avanti wants to bang her head against the wall and die. Why did he get known or popular or 10 per cent of popular, whatever it is!

He's already fifteen minutes late. Avanti had ordered a beer to calm her nerves and is already a little tipsy; but it's only made her more anxious.

'WHAT'S UP!' a voice booms from behind Avanti. Avanti jerks back to see Namita standing with her arms wide open.

'What!' Avanti shrieks and they hug, and as they hug Avanti feels like someone's lifted a boulder off her chest. 'What are you doing here?'

'What am I doing here? I just wanted to see what's the big deal with this Devrat,' says Namita. She pulls up a chair and sits next to Avanti.

'You came all the way to see how I embarrass myself in front of Devrat?' asks Avanti.

'That's what friends do, right?' says Namita.

Avanti really likes how they have seamlessly taken up the role of being best friends for each other. There was no awkwardness, no pulled back words, and no pretences.

'I'm so nervous. Just look at him. So cute!' says Avanti. 'And I didn't mean to say cute. I meant to say something more meaningful, deep and profound. But he's so cute, too.'

'I will have to agree to that,' concurs Namita. 'So have you thought what you would say to him?'

'I have waited five years to see him. So I think I'm going to pass out in front of him. That sounds like a perfectly plausible plan right now.'

'Oh shut up, that's not going to happen.'

'You have no idea.'

'Just get it together, Avanti.'

'This is the best I can do.'

'Then drink more.'

'I'm already a couple of drinks down, Namita, and you know I don't handle it well.'

'Two more wouldn't hurt,' says Namita and waves to the waiter to repeat their drink and he does. She makes Avanti gulp them down.

By the time Devrat welcomes everyone to Insomnia, Avanti has a silly smile pasted on her face. Devrat's voice envelops her like a hammock and she feels she can just sleep off wrapped around in his words.

'I'm glad you guys came here,' says Devrat. 'I don't know how to indulge you in small talk and make you laugh before I sing my first set of songs, so I will just dive in. The song is . . .'

Devrat strums his guitar and is yet to start singing, but Avanti is already digging her nails deep into Namita's forearm.

'Chill.'

'He's about to sing! He's about to sing!' murmurs Avanti excitedly.

'That's what he's here for, isn't he?'

And then Avanti loses it. Devrat's voice fills her up, sexually and spiritually, in ways she didn't know she could be filled up. Devrat sings one song after another, and slowly, people who were at the pub just to have nice evening have their eyes stuck on him. So are Avanti's. She can stay here, stuck in this moment, forever . . . listening to him . . . watching him sing while the neon lights make him sweat a bit . . .

After about twenty minutes, he takes a break, thanks the crowd and tells them that he will be back after ten minutes. The crowd cheers. Avanti frowns. 'He's mine,' she thinks, 'I found him!'

'He's damn good,' says Namita.

'I wish he was not. I wish he sucked. I wish he was the worst singer ever.'

'Excuse me?'

'Look at the girls, Namita. They were staring at him! Why were they staring at him? How dare they stare at him?'

'Because he's cute, Avanti, that's why!'

'But I noticed him first. I found him,' says Avanti and mock-cries.

'Aw, that's sweet.'

'It's a lost cause, Namita. He will get famous some day, cut his own music album, sing for movies, sleep with movie stars, get married, cheat on his wife, and get divorced. Please take me to a mental asylum. I think I belong there and not here. If I stay here for a minute longer, I will pack him up in my handbag like a little Chihuahua, throw in a few puppy treats, and take him home. Damn it, Namita, I will never be able to get married now,' sighs Avanti.

'And why is that?' asks Namita.

'After he's successful and divorced, alcoholic and abusive, I will marry him. I will be the only one around and we will grow old together and shit,' answers Avanti and bangs her head against the table.

'You're over-reacting. Here, take this,' says Namita and pushes the drink in front of her. Avanti gulps it. The taste is immaterial now, her tongue is flapping around, drunk, and her tastebuds are either dead or have passed out.

'Where is he?'

'Let the guy rest, Avanti. He just sang non-stop!'

'Why am I not happy listening to the songs I have listened to a million times now? No, I'm happy, but I'm not. Why is that?' asks Avanti. *Oh God! I'm drunk again. Why am I so stupid?*

'Chill. We will go talk to him when this ends. I will make a cordon and make sure no girl gets to him,' announces Namita.

'Fuck me.' Avanti bangs her head on the table. 'I'm going back to the hotel.' Avanti tries to get up but Namita holds her down.

'You need to get it together. It's not a big deal.'

And just then Devrat comes back. The crowd cheers and he belts out a few songs which are even better than the ones he sang earlier.

'I'm in love for life and beyond,' whispers Avanti in Namita's ears.

TWELVE

devrat

The break always screws it up for him. Everything goes right till the time his phone vibrates and it's time for him to let his throat rest. It's not because he needs it. It's because the pub needs to sell. And breaks are the time (if the singer is good enough) when people while waiting for the gig to restart order the most. He's behind the door, watching the crowd order their next round of drinks and french fries and pastas. In the crowd, there's one girl who caught his fancy. Far well dressed than anyone who would come to listen to his music, she was the only one in the crowd who was mouthing each word of every song.

The girl looks strangely familiar. He tries to think where he has seen her but he draws a blank. He remembers having seen her not once but quite a few times but can't place her.

And now that he's back on the stage and singing again, he's trying hard not to look at her, he's trying not to stare at her hair that's in a bun a moment and is falling all over her face the next, he's trying not to want to touch her skin, which seems more

106

airbrushed than a *Vogue* cover, he's trying to get his fingers stuck in the strings, and bleed. And he has to bleed to sing better. *Where have I seen this girl? God! She's beautiful!*

He's getting frivolous in his head as he's singing as he's happy. He's in a pre-crush stage, and it's apparent in his singing. So to make sure he's depressed, he forces himself to think that he's already dating the girl in the crowd he has been looking at, but has just got to know about her affair with another guy, a guy richer and more accomplished, possibly more endowed in the groin area as well. Now he's suitably depressed and he's singing well. In his head, he's in love with the girl and the girl has already broken his heart.

Damn it! She's so gorgeous!

The fact that the girl is still swaying her head from side to side singing every lyric in the song only makes Devrat try harder. It's the last song and he fears that the girl will leave the pub after he's done so he sings another song, a song he doesn't sing often, but the girl knows the lyrics of that song too.

The song ends. Devrat takes longer than usual to wrap up his stuff. Usually after any performance, Sumit and Devrat take to a corner table and sit there for a while. Sumit always insists on it. It gives the people the chance to walk up to and talk to whoever was singing, and gives the singer the chance to tell them about their next performance.

Today, there's no Sumit and he's nervous. He packs his guitar and the help takes it inside. He makes his way to the crowd, some ignore his presence, and some of them say, 'Great job man!' and a few talk in loud voices as how it wasn't that great.

He sits at a corner table and orders a beer. He doesn't feel like drinking though. He feels like talking to the girl who's now talking animatedly to her friend. She looks positively drunk but yet insanely cute. He tries not to stare in her direction.

He's sipping his beer, which is warm and bitter now, when he sees the girl shuffle in her chair. She's walking towards him. Definitely a fan, nothing to panic about, Devrat thinks, although his palms are already sweaty and he can feel his pulse throb.

'Hi,' the girl says, 'Avanti.' She thrusts her hand out and Devrat shakes it. He smiles back at her. 'Big fan,' she says. Devrat thanks her and smiles. He doesn't want her to just leave after saying this—he's searching for words to say to her, words that will make her stay, continue the conversation.

'I'm not that good. I'm pretty average. It's not a surprise that out of the fifty people here, you're the only one to walk up to me and tell me that I'm any good,' he says. It's the best he can come up with.

'Never say that. I take offence to that. You're not just good. You're God,' Avanti snaps back, the smile on her face, gone.

'Excuse me?'

'I mean you're good. You're very good!' Avanti gushes. She's still standing near the chair facing Devrat, awkwardly, and Devrat doesn't know how this conversation will go on. Should he ask her to join him and tell him more? Should he just tell her that it nice meeting her and send her off on her way? Since he doesn't know he just sits there looking at her, and she looks at him, and they are smiling and shifting in their places. Devrat heaves a sigh of relief when Avanti starts to talk. She says, 'I was just telling my friend back there that I have been listening to your songs for so long now.'

Devrat looks in the direction to Avanti was pointing. 'There's no one there.'

Avanti looks back and rolls her eyes. Namita has left. 'I swear I came with a friend and she has left without telling me. Please don't think I'm a freak with imaginary friends. You're thinking that, aren't you?' says a panicked Avanti.

'I saw the two of you when I was performing, so I believe you. And you can sit, that is, if you don't have any other plans,' says Devrat, and mentally taps his own back for being uncharacteristically cool. *And you can sit, that is, if you don't have any other plans?* From where did he learn that?

Avanti thanks him and takes the chair. Silence engulfs them.

'Who are the songs for?' asks Avanti, the words shoot out almost like a surprise, like a bullet from a gun she was holding beneath the table, her fingers place lightly on the trigger, something that she meant to do eventually. Eventually but not now, but she couldn't control it, She panicked and just fired. 'I'm sorry. You can choose not to answer that. I don't know why I asked that. I think I was just jealous of whoever you were thinking of while you wrote them,' says Avanti and touches Devrat's hand instinctively.

'You don't have to be sorry,' says Devrat, trying not to look at her fingers that are still on his knuckles, a sensation he is acutely aware of. 'I wrote those songs for whoever I have dated or liked.'

'Oh.' A tinge of disappointment comes on her face to think Devrat has dated before. It's unreasonable, she knows, but that doesn't help. Her eyebrows furrow and she quickly retracts her hand. The radiance of her face dies down a little, and with that Devrat's heart shrinks, too.

'The songs are exaggerated. I used to imagine that I loved them far more than I actually did, and that I was far more sad when they left me. It helps me write the songs better. And it helps me stay depressed.'

Avanti giggles, which comes as a surprise to even herself because she never really giggles. 'So you're saying you stay sad and stay happy intentionally so that you can write better?'

'Does that make me a freak?' asks Devrat.

'No matter what you do you will never be a freak. I can find a head in your` freezer and think that there might be a logical explanation to that.'

Devrat laughs, much to his surprise as well. It's probably a defence mechanism against the warmth that is taking over.

'So? What do you do?' asks Devrat. He has to remind himself that he's the singer, and she's the fan, that she has to be shy and he has to be rude and arrogant like a rock-star.

'I'm a flight attendant,' answers Avanti.

'Are your parents okay with that?' Devrat regrets the sentence as soon as the words leave his mouth for it's kind of hypocritical of a guy who left his studies to be a moderately successful singer to ask what the parents of a flight attendant think.

'My mother died when I was young and my father doesn't really care, I think,' says Avanti.

'I'm sorry.'

'It's okay. It doesn't bother me much now. And whenever it does, your songs make it alright.'

'You're too kind.'

'So how's it being a flight attendant?' asks Devrat, trying desperately to keep the conversation going, not wanting Avanti to say 'nice meeting you' and then walk off.

'Shouldn't we be talking about what you do, Devrat? What I do is boring and uninteresting compared to what you do.'

And while Devrat tries to find an answer to that, he wants her to say his name again. It sounded so good. And he doesn't want her to leave.

'I think what you do is awesome,' says Devrat.

'If you insist I will not try to contest that.'

'Do you want to have coffee somewhere?' asks Devrat, in an uncharacteristic burst of confidence. But mostly it was panic that she would soon leave.

'You haven't finished your beer yet,' points out Avanti.

'I don't need to. I ordered it to look cool and singer-like. I would rather have a strong coffee right now.'

'Has no one told you that you don't have to look cool and singer-like because you already rock that look pretty well?' says Avanti and Devrat blushes profusely. She continues, 'And there, you're not only a cool-looking singer, but you can also blush. What more can a girl want?' She's looking so adorably at Devrat that he feels like a little two-year-old wrapped in a blanket. She adds, 'And of course, I would love to go for a coffee although it's slightly unbelievable that you just asked me to have coffee with you? You did, right?'

'Yes.' Devrat nods shyly. Devrat disappears in the back room of the club and picks up his guitar and his payment for the night.

'*Aapki girlfriend hai* (Is she your girlfriend)?' asks the club's help, pointing at Avanti who's visible through the little glass window of the back room. Devrat doesn't answer. He stares out of that little window, his nose pressed against the glass, his breath fogging it, like a little kid outside a candy shop, and he sees Avanti pump her fist and she's doing a little victory dance. There are people looking at her but she looks happy, almost a little deranged, but so happy that it's infectious.

Devrat leaves the back room and as soon as she spots him, she stands straight, smiling, lady-like and extremely beautiful.

'Let's go?' says Devrat and they walk out from the pub. They walk next to each other, not talking much, just there, with each other. 'Here?' Avanti points to a roadside chai joint. 'I love chai. My father makes the best tea ever.' Avanti's so excited with something so inconsequential as tea that Devrat's just amused and he says, why not.

'Aren't you a bit over-dressed for this place?' asks Devrat just as they take a seat at one of the wooden benches.

'I'm from Delhi. I'm a flight attendant. I am always over-dressed. That's my superpower. Don't take that away from me.'

'That sounds legit. I should put that on Twitter,' says Devrat, laughing and that's kind of new and Devrat's liking it. If ever there would be a competition of developing a crush in the smallest timeframe possible, Devrat's developing crush on Avanti would be right in the top rungs.

'Twitter is hard. Facebook is better,' says Avanti. 'Upload pictures and wait for people to like it. Twitter is where people judge, Facebook is where people get jealous. Being intelligent all the time is hard and time-consuming.'

'See. You can put that on Twitter.'

Avanti giggles. 'Stop giggling!' Avanti tells herself.

They order two masala teas and Devrat is smitten by how deft Avanti is with the little steel cup and the tumbler, pouring the tea between the two to cool it a little, while he struggles with it. Avanti helps Devrat out with it. Devrat is quite fascinated by it all, by the tea pouring, by the quick wit, and by her superpower.

'Does it make it taste better?' asks Devrat.

'Does being sadder make your songs better?' counters Avanti.

Devrat smiles. They both sip from their tumblers.

'I still can't believe that I'm sitting right in front of you. RIGHT. IN. FRONT. OF. YOU. I have to tell you this. I have imagined this in my head so many times. I always thought what

I would say, what I would do, how it would all turn out to be. And every time I used to think of it I would remove some detail and add some other detail in,' says Avanti and after a pause adds 'Sorry.'

'Why are you sorry?'

'You look like I have freaked you out.'

'No, you haven't. I'm just surprised. Because nothing of this sort ever happens with me. It's the first time. And . . .'

'Oh shut up!' exclaims Avanti. 'I'm sure it happens with you all the time. Look at your YouTube video. There are girls screaming in the comments section.'

Devrat almost senses a tinge of anger in Avanti's voice as she says that.

'That's now. But it's been years since I first uploaded videos and sound clips and I always used to wonder who listens to them. It turns out that you used to listen to them!' says Devrat.

'What's so surprising? You're good. You always have been. I made so many girls listen to your songs when I was in the hostel. I'm sure a few of them believe in love because your songs made them believe that everyone had a guy out there waiting for them, who would be just like you, who would be everything that you are.'

'I'm nothing.' Devrat's cheeks are flushed and warm and he's blushing.

'You need to stop with that, Devrat,' says Avanti. 'When I say I take offence to that, I really mean that. No one says a word against my favourite singer.'

'Not even if he's undeniably flawed.'

'Not even then. It's not that I have followed you, the person, I have followed an idea of you, an idea I had perfected over years, and you're insulting that. Please let me hang on to that.'

Devrat sips from his tumbler, thinking how naturally and effortlessly he has slipped into a conversation with a girl who was a stranger twenty minutes ago but now seems like a safe repository for all his secrets. It's true that she's pretty beyond words, but now it doesn't matter what she looks like. Even if she were a baby gorilla with buck teeth, scratching her belly, Devrat's crush would have remained as is.

'That's kind of deep,' says Devrat, not finding anything suitable to say. But if he's a star in her mind, everything that he says has to be gold, right? It's like lines from famous novelists are always quoted and re-quoted no matter how ordinary, while the lines from others languish in unsold books.

'Is it? I think that's because I'm a little drunk.'

'Why would you think that?' asks Devrat.

'I'm usually very vain. I'm all about make-up and pretty clothes. That's what defines me,' says Avanti.

The bill arrives and Devrat pays. Avanti tries to pay but Devrat protests and tells her that she shouldn't insult the idea of him.

'Knowing that you're all about make-up and clothes makes you deep. At least self-aware,' argues Devrat.

'And what defines you?'

They both get up. The roadside chai shop is about to shut down. The roads are almost deserted, with a sprinkling of a few yellow taxies, a few couples are walking on the pavement, out for a walk after the *machher jhol* and *bhaat,* in their sports shoes and sarees.

'I don't know what defines me,' says Devrat. They pass a shop that sells rubber chappals and rip offs of expensive sneakers. Just before the owner pulls the shutter down, Avanti quickly buys a pair after a brief but effective negotiation where she tells the seller that she's not a tourist and he better not try to rip her off, puts her heels in the poly bag and starts walking in those chappals. This is nice, thinks Devrat.

'Okay. Fine.'

Avanti doesn't talk for a while and they walk randomly taking unknown turns, often reaching dead ends, at which they smile and turn back.

'So you dropped out of engineering?' asks Avanti after a while. Devrat nods.

She doesn't ask him why but he still tells her, 'Because I was scared.'

'Scared of?'

'I didn't like it. I feared what if I didn't make a good engineer? What if at the end of four years I have like ten back papers? If that makes any sense.'

'But didn't you want to sing? Rather than being an engineer?'

'Yes, but I could have done both. I chose this. There are less chances of me failing here. At least I will fail doing something I like more,' says Devrat softly, wondering if he should open up more.

Avanti nods. Devrat wonders what he has to say to keep this conversation going. He's almost a little scared by the idea of 'him' in Avanti's head and whether he's even close to matching up to that.

He walks on hoping she wouldn't be disappointed by who he really is.

THIRTEEN

The first time she would meet him, that first look, that first conversation, that eye-lock, that laugh, things that Avanti had planned in explicit detail have all gone out of the window. Her first rendezvous with Devrat is nothing like she had imagined it to be. Nothing like what she had constructed him to be in her head.

She'd thought he would be the definition of a bad boy with a broken heart, someone who would be inaccessible, hard to talk to, someone who would be easy to be labelled as arrogant, someone who you could look at in the future and say that you had a crush on him till the time you actually met him. But this is different. Devrat is different. He's human, more like a puppy, but yeah, human. She can talk to him, like actually talk, and he answers like he's not the Devrat she had obsessed over since forever. The question in her head is not whether to like the Devrat who's in front of her, it's how not to fall for him, how not to cling to him, how not to let this walk end. Because he is not the bad boy she had imagined him to be, he's way better than that.

'When do you leave?' asks Devrat.

'Tomorrow morning.'

'Oh.'

Avanti likes the sound of that 'Oh'. It's filled with disappointment.

'So a layover is just one day?'

'Yes, a day and a night. I'm staying at the Taj,' answers Avanti and wonders if Devrat would take it as an invitation. She panics suddenly, what if he does, what if he comes over, what if he kisses me like he probably kisses girls he picks up from his performances, what if something more happens? Avanti hasn't been as promiscuous (with the exception of Shekhar who was just a mistake) as a lot of her classmates have been and she's proud of it. But now she's thinking she should have been. A little experience would have helped a long way. Right now, she's just a nervous wreck. Devrat doesn't take the invitation.

'I live two blocks away,' says Devrat. 'It's the poorer pocket of this area. We have been walking for long.'

'I hope it's not an invitation,' says Avanti and drops the ball in his court.

'It never is. Usually, I just tell people where I live and show them my dilapidated apartment from the outside so that they can pity me,' answers Devrat. Avanti looks for hints of sarcasm in his tone but there's none.

'I'm sure it's not that bad.'

'You have no idea, Avanti.'

'But you're . . . Devrat? Aren't you almost like a celebrity?'

'Yes, for you, I am. Maybe for someone on the Internet, for someone who's sitting two thousand kilometres away. But for my landlord I'm still someone who's ruining his flat and pays rent three days late.'

'You're a boy.'

'What's that supposed to mean? I'm supposed to be a boy, am I not?' asks Devrat, confused.

'No, but I like you and I don't like boys. I like tall successful men with cars and big houses and not boys.'

'My bad.'

'But I like you.'

'I don't know how to react to that because that statement can mean a lot of things,' says Devrat.

'Don't react because let me figure out first what that really meant,' says Avanti. She mutters 'I like you' again in her head.

They sit down on a bench. It's two in the night now. Avanti is sure that Devrat thinks of her as a clingy, confused, psychopath of a girl who just told him that she likes him and where she's putting up for the night. *God! I'm such a loser!*

Avanti, just to sound modest and to ensure it's not the last time she's meeting Devrat, gets up from the bench. 'I think I should leave. I have an early morning flight tomorrow. It was nice meeting you.' She thrusts out her hand, totally formally, hoping this would be enough to leave Devrat with an impression that she's not clingy. (Though she tries to remember what Devrat has done till now to suggest that she has been the only participant in the night's proceedings.)

Devrat shakes her hand. 'Let's get you a cab.'

Avanti's devastated but she, too, joins him at the edge of the pavement trying to wave down a cab. Five cabs pass by and none of them stops. Avanti suppresses a smile. She hopes they don't find a cab at all.

'They are probably thinking I bought you from somewhere.'

'What does that mean?' asks Avanti, feigning anger, fully knowing what it means.

'I would have no business doing anything with you at this time of the night. You could be some model moonlighting as an escort.'

'Strangest. Compliment. Ever.'

'I don't think it's strange at all. Look at you and look at me. You're way too pretty to be standing next to me.'

Avanti blushes and wonders if he can see her red cheeks in the dark.

They wave down a cab. Avanti curses under her breath. *Why did the cab drive have to stop?*

Avanti and Devrat have an awkward moment where they neither hug nor they shake hands. They just end up waving at each other. Avanti puts on a smile that's as fake as it gets because inside, she feels like she's dying, and the cab is not a cab but a Dementor, a monster sucking out all of her happy thoughts.

'Bye,' she says, her heart sinking to the bottom of her stomach. She doesn't want to leave.

'Bye,' Devrat says and it only makes Avanti sadder.

She's is in the cab, the cab begins to move and it looks a little bit like a movie scene as the cab picks up speed and Devrat's walking, and then jogging.

'Hey! Hey!' Devrat shouts.

Devrat knocks on the window just as the taxi guy is about to put the car into the third gear. The car stops. Devrat knocks on the window. Avanti first smiles, then realizes she has to open the door, a little confused as to what's happening.

'Open the door,' says Devrat. Avanti complies only too happily.

Devrat shuffles inside the cab and sits right beside her. Avanti wants to beam at him, maybe throw her arms around him, but she tones it down to a weak smile.

'I just thought it was a little dangerous for you to travel alone late in the night. So . . .'

The driver who understands, frowns.

'That's so sweet of you,' says Avanti. 'Also, the food back at my hotel is great. That is, if you don't mind. You know, Devrat, it will be a lot less painful if you can at least act like the celebrity you are.'

'But I'm not a celebrity.'

'It would have been easier if you still did. You would have been a lot less adorable,' says Avanti.

The car humbly rolls on, and the cab driver struggles with the gear box that juts out from the steering column every time the car comes to a halt.

'Thirty-five rupees,' says Avanti.

'What?'

'Our tentative cab fare to the hotel.'

Devrat looks on surprised. 'Umm?'

'Oh. I'm sorry. It's just a little game I play with myself every time I sit in a cab.'

'What game?' asks Devrat.

'I kind of try to guess what the cab fare will be like. It's a function of the speed, the rate per kilometre and the expected traffic.'

'Are you still drunk?'

'I'm sorry?'

'No, I was kidding. It's fascinating!' says Devrat. 'So you don't guess, you calculate?'

'Kind of.'

'Don't you think it's a little too intelligent for a flight attendant to do that?' asks Devrat.

Avanti blushes. 'Maybe.'

'But why do you do that?'

Avanti tells Devrat that her father taught her this. It's one of the only few incidents she remembers of her father—sitting in an auto trying to calculate what the cab fare would be at the end of it.

'Your father is?' asks Devrat, unsure whether he should venture into that territory.

'He's a mathematician. Usually, all these mathematical geniuses go crazy after they have stumbled on something great, or solved something, but my father started the other way around. He started crazy.'

'Umm.'

'It's okay. I don't feel bad about it. Maybe a little bit about my mother, that I couldn't see much of her, but not so much about my father.'

'But you live with him?'

'Yes. But it feels like a paying guest accommodation. We don't talk. If anything I feel a little guilty that I don't feel anything for him. Except a little pity,' says Avanti, remembering how her father had come to the airport, lying to her that he, too, had a flight, shared a seat with her on the cab, and then went back. She clearly remembers the searching eyes of her father.

'What about your parents?' asks Avanti.

'I'm their weakness I think. They obsess over me. I'm an only child after all. So they do try to shackle me at times, lay down rules, but they eventually bow down to whatever I say.'

'I don't blame them. You can be a weakness for anyone.'

The cab stops near the lobby of the hotel. The fare is thirty-six rupees. Avanti shoots an 'I told you so' smile at Devrat who acknowledges her brilliance.

And then, just like that, they are in her room.

FOURTEEN

'I think I will just come out and say it,' says Avanti. 'I'm not going to sleep with you tonight.'

Devrat chuckles. 'Should I go back then?'

Avanti's face drops. Devrat laughs and says, 'I wasn't looking for that.'

For the first time in forever Devrat isn't concerned about the little sexual vibe between the two of them. He has taken it in his stride and he's enjoying the journey. The prospect of her not sleeping with him doesn't bother him, but the prospect of him having to leave the room disturbs him.

Avanti makes the coffee in the hotel room's machine and it isn't half-bad.

'I love hotel rooms,' says Devrat.

'I do, too,' beams Avanti. 'I just love how I can mess up the room and come back and the room is all cleaned up.'

Devrat looks around. There's a pile of clothes, neatly folded, lying in a corner. 'So this is what you left for the cleaning guy?'

'Yes, kind of. I'm a nightmare to the bellboys.'

Devrat wants to go and sit on the fluffy bed in front of him, where Avanti's sitting, but not because of her, but the bed. Maybe a bit because of Avanti as well.

Devrat drinks from the complimentary bottle of water. 'I love room service.'

'Here.' Avanti throws the receiver towards him.

Devrat orders a pizza, a one with a lot of toppings, an expensive one, thinking it must be paid for by the airline. It's only later that he comes to know that it comes out of Avanti's allowance.

The pizza arrives and the bellboy keeps it next to the bed. Devrat finally takes this as an opportunity to shift to the bed.

Avanti excuses herself.

'I just need to change,' she says and comes back a little later in loose, faded pink pjyamas and an oversized Kolkata Knight Riders T-shirt. She's carrying a room freshener in her hand.

'What's that for?'

'Umm. If we eat on the bed, it's going to smell like that all night and tomorrow morning.'

'You mean you don't eat on the bed? Then what do you eat on?' asks Devrat, shocked, for all his life has been spent eating on beds with newspapers covering them. Lately, the only reason why the bedsheets of his apartment were being washed was because they had one too many stains on them.

Avanti squeamishly looks at the table. 'Fine,' Devrat says and shifts the pizza back to the table.

'It smells amazing!' they both say together and then laugh.

'You look nice,' Devrat says as he cuts a slice that is floppy and dripping with cheese and toppings.

'Aren't you late with the comment? I just changed.'

'No, you look better now. I like your hair, ruffled and

unkempt, also the loose T-shirt and the pyjamas. It makes me feel like I'm on a holiday. And an expensive holiday at that,' says Devrat and looks around the room.

Soon they find themselves on the bed, three feet of distance between them, yet sharing the same blanket, the remote lying midway between them. Devrat's feet were on the blanket for a little over half an hour, and he was shivering yet not acting on it. Avanti made him get inside the blanket and since then he has been a little awkward about the proximity of Avanti's legs with his.

The movie isn't all that funny, but at the slightest joke Devrat laughs and looks at Avanti who looks back and they laugh together. Devrat is frightfully aware of the distance between them. He doesn't want to get any closer. It's like doing that would spoil everything that had happened and everything that could happen. Yet the knowledge of her bare feet a few feet away from his toes tickles him and his heart beats harder. Even a little tug at the blanket makes his heart go aflutter. She looks beautiful. Her lips without the lipstick now are a faint pink, always a little parted, a hint of tiredness. Her skin now without the compact is marred with little marks, making it real and soft and human. She looks prettier tired and haggard than made-up and proper.

'You're beautiful,' says Devrat.

'Hmm?'

And then there is a knock at the door.

'Must be the bellboy to get the empty plates,' says Avanti.

Devrat tells her that he will get it. He jumps down and heads towards the door. The door is knocked on again. This time more firmly. He fiddles with the lock, opens the door, and a fist comes rushing to meet his face. It crashes right into his nose, he can hear the slow crunching sound it makes, and then he's on the ground.

'BASTARD. YOU FUCKING BASTARD.' Devrat can hear someone shouting.

Before he can get his hand up to his face, which is now bloodied and battered, he feels his jaw shatter against a knuckle. It's hard. 'This is what Admantium feels like,' Devrat's thinking as he's passing out . . . I just got hit by the Wolverine, that's a cool way to die, he thinks.

'I will kill you! I will fucking kill you!' He hears a boy shout. And just before his eyes close Devrat sees the heavy boots of the boy hover over his face.

He can hear faint noises of Avanti screaming in the background.

'What the hell are you doing here?' she's screaming.

Devrat turns and lies prostrate on his stomach now, too dazed to get up and start walking towards him. His nose is dripping with blood and the carpet is crusted now. Devrat shakes his head and tries to make sense of what the two of them are talking about. This is his heroic moment, he thinks. He will find the dying shreds of life in him, stagger to his feet, and just when the boy would be about to hit her, he would smash his face with something . . . umm . . . with the iron that's lying face-down on the ironing board. Yes, perfect, he thinks. He tries getting up but falls back on the ground, his head spinning. So this is what a concussion feels like, he thinks.

'Who is he? You have been fucking other men behind my back, aren't you? I knew it! All air hostesses do that. All of you are sluts! Goddamn sluts!'

'We are flight attendants. We call ourselves flight attendants, not air hostesses,' mutters Avanti.

'WHAT! WHAT DID YOU JUST SAY?'

'Nothing.'

'Why did you do this to me?' thunders the boy. 'I had everything. I gave you every damn thing! I will kill him. I will just kill him!'

Devrat hears the boy's feet thump on the carpet and inch towards him but they stop when Avanti rams into him.

'Leave him! It's not him. It's me. I'm so sorry. It's my fault!' says Avanti.

The boy still walks towards Devrat, grabs him by the collar and rams him against the wall.

'Did you fuck her?'

Devrat tries to tell him that he only just met her but the boy thunders again, 'DID YOU FUCK HER?'

Devrat's face is all bloodied but he still says with a smile. 'I wish I had because you have beaten me up any way.'

Avanti chuckles at that but stops. 'Stop it, Shekhar.' She's wrestling with Shekhar's arm but it's a big arm and Avanti is frightfully weak against it.

'DID YOU FUCK HER?'

Shekhar's hand is wrapped firmly around Devrat's neck and even though Devrat is trying to talk he can't. He still mutters illegibly. 'You are asking the same questions twice.'

'TELL ME! You fucking, rotting piece of Bengali shit.'

'I'm a Bengali, too, asshole!' mutters Avanti, not knowing from where she got the strength to call Shekhar that. She's not even crying right now and that's a first.

Shekhar's grip loosens a little on Devrat and he says, 'And we gave you the national anthem and the national song. Also, the *roshogolla* and communism.'

Shekhar tightens his grip around Devrat's neck. Devrat flaps around a like a dying fish. Quite ironical because Shekhar shouts, 'You fucking *machher jhol!*'

Devrat wonders why that is an insult. It's like him calling Shekhar butter chicken, which is quite delicious. And if Devrat dies today, he will never get to eat it again.

'TELL ME! DID YOU FUCK HER!?'

'YES. HE HAS,' shouts Avanti. 'Now let him go.'

And just like that, he lets Devrat go, who slumps to the ground and mutters to himself, 'I have?'

'I'm sorry, Shekhar. But I think you need to go now. Whatever happened between is now over and you need to understand that,' says Avanti.

Shekhar is walking around in circles, holding his head, cursing, sometimes half-charging at Avanti as if he's going to hit her but then he doesn't. Avanti is looking straight at him, unfazed, unaffected. She's looking at Devrat who's slumped on the ground, crawling towards the ironing board. 'All my friends were right about you. You're just a fucking slut!'

Avanti wants to ask which friends is he referring to here, but that's not a discussion for now. Bitches, she thinks.

'I'm sorry, Shekhar,' says Avanti. 'But thank you for what you did to me.' She's looking at Devrat who has the iron in his hand, but he's still on the ground, flapping, battered and bruised.

'Thanks? You slept with him! YOU. SLEPT. WITH. HIM. LOOK AT HIM! He can't even bench press.'

'That he can't. But I didn't sleep with him.'

'You didn't? But you just said you did?'

'I'm just seeing him. If I had to sleep with anyone, I would have slept with you,' says Avanti. 'Look at your biceps. It's the only thing every girl wants. Your bench press is 210 pounds and you can squat a baby elephant. You're every girl's dream.'

Oh. Now she has tears. Devrat meets her eyes and she meets his. She's not smiling, but her eyes are. And while Shekhar paces around a little more, clenching his fists, Avanti winks at Devrat. Avanti is surprisingly herself right now. She mentally pats her back and says, you go, girl!

'Fuck, yes! I'm alright. It's you who's wrong,' grumbles Shekhar. He's in a war-like pose. He punches the wall. 'I should have never started to date you. I was so happy with my girlfriend. I should have stayed with her. You're just a fucking slut. . .'

Avanti frowns. She fires her opening salvo. 'You never told me you had a girlfriend!' Suddenly, every instance of Shekhar shouting on her, abusing her, picking a fight with her whenever he used to doubt her loyalty comes rushing to her head.

'Oh yes, I did. I HAD A GIRLFRIEND. And I'm still dating her. And thank God I'm still dating her because you're a piece of shit!' shouts Shekhar.

Avanti's face clenches and she looks straight at Shekhar. 'Get out.'

'What?' asks Shekhar. Even a dimwit like Shekhar knows now that he has overstepped limits.

'Get out, Shekhar! I don't want to hear a word now.'

'You will kick me out? I will go out myself, you slut.'

'You call me that once more, and I will call the police,' grumbles Avanti. She takes a few steps towards Shekhar and she's not kidding. She's positively furious and is looking straight into Shekhar's eyes. He's quivering like a little puppy (on steroids).

'Avanti.'

'Get out, Shekhar,' says Avanti, who turns away from him and sits on the bed. She's holding her head in her hands now. Shekhar takes a few steps ahead and keeps a hand on her shoulder. And almost instinctively, she brushes away the hand and slaps Shekhar and bellows, 'Go away, right now!' And then as if possessed by a foreign force she gets up and pushes a squealing, begging Shekhar out of the room. She slams the door on his face. 'FUCK YOU, SHEKHAR. FUCK YOU! I HOPE YOU DIE, YOU ASSHOLE!'

She comes back to help Devrat to the bed. He's still clutching the iron he meant to hit Shekhar with. 'You didn't tell me you were dating Hulk Hogan's cousin.'

'It's the ex-boyfriend I have been trying to get rid of,' says Avanti and whips out the first aid kit from the drawer of the washroom. 'I'm sorry.'

'It's okay. I just like how it all feels like a movie. Though I feel like I might never be able to walk again without a wobble.'

Avanti chuckles. 'It's not that bad.'

'Is it not? He was built like a Transformer. Though I think I would have been able to smash his face with the iron had I been able to get on my feet. I wish I could have helped you a little though.'

'You already did help me a lot. You just didn't notice,' she says and looks at him. 'Okay. It is a little bad.' Avanti wipes the blood off of Devrat's face. 'At least your nose isn't broken.'

'That's sort of the high point of my day. I'm so glad your Hulk boyfriend didn't break my nose for sleeping with you. Oh wait! I didn't sleep with you!'

'Stop making me feel guilty!' protests Avanti.

'Fine. Fine. I was just taking your case. But really, it hurts like a bitch,' grumbles Devrat.

Avanti asks him to hold the cotton to his nose so it stops bleeding. She bandages his head up.

'So it clearly showed you were never in love with him, but

why did you turn so scary at the end? You have heard the term, "*Maata ghus gayi usmein*"? You were a bit like that. Possessed,' asks Devrat.

'I never really had the courage to do it before. I'm not sure how I got the courage today,' says Avanti. 'I think I'm a bit of a freak magnet.'

'I concur,' Devrat tells her.

'Oh shut up, Devrat. You are, too. I saw the picture of you and Karthika and she looks every bit a freak like Shekhar.'

'Umm . . . I never dated her.'

'Liar,' says Avanti, a bit jealous.

'No, seriously. It was just something.'

'I don't want to know, but yet I want to know. Tell me the short version of the story,' says Avanti.

'But I did get dumped recently and that led to Karthika.'

'Not that short,' says Avanti.

'The girl I loved went off with the rich guy. leaving me poking at my memories of her so that I could feel . . . I don't know . . . alive? She was all I was holding on to. He was everything I wasn't. To avenge that I started sleeping with Karthika.' Avanti frowns. Devrat continues, 'I had no idea why she was sleeping with me and did not ask. I had no inclination to know about her. I don't know why that happened. That in short, is my story.'

'You're damaged, Devrat.'

'So are you,' says Devrat. 'It's all hiding behind those layers of make-up and the pretty clothes you wear.'

'I'm not wearing any make-up.'

'That's why I can see the scars.'

FIFTEEN

It's four in the morning. They're sleeping now. Or at least lying down, trying not to sleep, hoping that their time together could stretch out infinitely. Devrat's head is bandaged, one of his eyes is snapped shut and he's three feet away from her. The lights are out except for the little red light of the television, but it's enough for Avanti to see Devrat's face and it's beautiful. He's like a little child, a lost one.

'You can sleep,' says Avanti.

'I can't stop thinking of your ex-boyfriend.'

'Is it?'

'What else would I think about lying three feet from you?' asks Devrat and Avanti blushes.

The more she sees Devrat in pain, the more Avanti falls in love with him; there's something deeply romantic about a hurt singer, or writer, or painter. Not so much a hurt engineer or a hurt investment banker. Every few seconds she panics thinking Devrat's asleep but settles down when she realizes that he's still all ears and looking at her.

'You have your flight in four hours,' says Devrat.

'You didn't have to remind me of that.'

Avanti wants to hold his hand, wrap her fingers around his, and stay in bed and watch him sleep.

'You're beautiful.'

Avanti blushes. 'You're just saying that.' Avanti doesn't know why she just said that. She has always known that she's beautiful and every time someone repeated that, it was just a validation, not a discovery, but this time it was. She feels beautiful.

'I'm sure you get that a lot.'

'But somehow it never meant so much,' says Avanti.

And just like that, they fall asleep. It's one hour from her call-time when she wakes up and finds Devrat sleeping. He's curled up in a ball and his face is smiling. Avanti has always hated mornings, and her job as a flight attendant has only made her hate mornings more, but this morning she loves. Only she knows how hard she has to restrain herself from not running her fingers over his face.

She's late. She jumps off the bed, quickly puts some water to boil in the kettle, stuffs all her clothes in her suitcase and forces it shut. She needs a bath but for that she will have to leave Devrat's side. She spends a few minutes looking at him, not wanting to go, but then decides to take a quick shower. In the shower, she burns herself. She wipes herself and rushes out, already missing him, knowing that she would regret the few minutes she didn't spend with him.

She's in a towel and she wets the wooden flooring. Devrat is awake and he's looking for something in his printed boxers. Avanti laughs seeing those boxers and Devrat is startled. He turns and looks at her.

'I was looking for my jeans,' he says. He's trying hard not

to look at Avanti, who's wrapped in a towel, somehow feeling sexy now. He's still looking at her, blushing, trying to tear his eyes away but failing. And it only makes Avanti feel better about herself.

'Oh,' says Avanti and then points to where his jeans are lying on the floor. She keeps standing there, hoping Devrat would look at her again, and he does, sort of a stolen glance, and Avanti feels strangely turned on knowing that Devrat's looking at her. It makes her feel beautiful, wanted. She doesn't want to go, instead she wants Devrat to look at her, fantasize about her. *How can you be so dirty in your head?!* Avantika is asking herself. Embarrassed and blushing at her own thoughts, she walks back to the washroom with her clothes, replaying the moment in her head when Devrat looked at her.

She changes into her uniform and puts on her make-up, trying to perfect it, yet not look like part of a homogenous group of flight attendants.

She finds Devrat on the table, drinking coffee, reading a newspaper and for a moment is thrown two decades in the future when the hotel room would be a house and Devrat would be a grumpy forty-year-old man with failed dreams of being a musician, and she will be an old, yet slim, irritating wife. 'Perfect,' she thinks.

Devrat turns to her. His eyes are on her for a few seconds too long before he says anything. Avanti wonders if he's still imagining her in a towel and she feels a little more alive.

'You look great,' says Devrat.

'I look like every other flight attendant. An exact copy.' Avanti frowns.

'We are all meant to be exact copies of each other,' he says.

'What does that mean?'

'I'm not sure. I just thought I would say something deep and profound and I came up with this but it isn't deep and you look amazing.'

'You should fly with me some day,' says Avanti. 'You will find five exact copies of me.'

'I refuse to believe that.'

Avanti believes in every word Devrat says. Although she tries to refute them and contest them, inside she hangs on to every word he's saying. And today, now that he has said it, she feels different, beautiful and amazing.

'Do you want to eat something?' asks Avanti.

'Sure. Let's order?'

'There's a free breakfast buffet downstairs.'

'I LOVE free food,' says Devrat and jumps from his chair.

'That's some enthusiasm.'

'Why shouldn't there be?' asks Devrat. 'When there is free food in buffets I feel like I'm ripping off somebody even though I'm not. So today we will try to feel good about ourselves while we try make the hotel go bankrupt due to our demonic early morning hunger.'

'As you say, sir.'

'I like that.'

'What?'

'Sir.'

They smile. Avanti lines up her suitcases near the door, does last minute checks on the room, takes out the hotel key card from the slot and they leave for the breakfast buffet.

It's lavish and there's food for the entire world, from the entire world, and more.

'I don't want to sound greedy, but this might be the best day of my life!' says Devrat who piles his plate up with sushi, something he had only had once in his life and never again because it's too expensive.

'I'm glad I can help,' says Avanti. She doesn't eat much. The Towel and the Stolen Glance incident is still weighing heavily in her mind. The next time it happens, if there's a next time, she has to be at her fittest. She's already Googling Hotel-Gym-Routines. Her plate only has small pieces of pineapple and watermelon, both of which she's sure has more water than anything else.

'I think I'm full,' says Devrat. His plate is still full and he has hardly eaten. 'I'm not used to food.'

'As in?'

'I'm used to cigarettes.'

'You haven't smoked one since you met me.'

'I figured you wouldn't like it,' says Devrat.

'You can have one if you want to.'

'I don't want to.' Devrat's looking at Avanti and, frankly, it's too much for her too take. In the past twelve hours, Avanti has realized that Devrat isn't too fond of eye contact and she's happy about that because every time he looks straight at her, she's a molten mess of nerves.

They eat in silence for Avanti doesn't want to break it to him that she needs to go and it's slowly killing her inside.

'You need to go?' asks Devrat.

Avanti nods.

'Right now?'

Avanti nods. 'I have five more minutes to check out.'

Devrat and Avanti look in the direction of the check-in counter where a few flight attendants, in the same uniform as Avanti's are checking out of their own rooms.

'When will you be back?' asks Devrat, playing with food, not eating.

'Not this month for sure. I don't have any day free. Pretty busy month, flying wise. Probably next month.'

'Cool.'

'Cool.'

The conversation is depressing. Avanti feels like a mom leaving on a business trip, and Devrat's acting like a little child who's sad but he's mature enough to understand and can't throw a fit and cry and lunge at Avanti's feet.

'I think you should leave,' says Devrat. 'You will be late.'

They both get up from their chairs, and drag their feet towards the check-in counter. They look away from each other and shift in their places uncomfortably.

'I will see you next month then,' says Avanti, more to herself than to Devrat.

'Cool.'

They exchange numbers, the colour of their faces gone.

'You can join them. I will leave,' says Devrat. Avanti nods and they don't hug. They awkwardly shake hands and Devrat heads towards the door.

Avanti looks at him disappear down the stairs, into a cab, and onto the streets of Kolkata. She can't help but cry.

SIXTEEN

Devrat is in the cab looking at the number he's just saved. He opens Whatsapp and searches for Avanti's picture in her contact information. There's a wait before the picture uploads. Avanti is in her uniform, smiling, and the picture seems to have been taken inside the aircraft. He's staring intently at the picture, as if hoping it would magically get him inside the picture. The phone starts to ring though but it's not Avanti. It's Karishma and her daily call to check whether Devrat is still alive and depressed, rather than drunk and dead.

'Hey! Open the door! I'm standing outside. All your shitty neighbours are staring at me as if I'm a prostitute!' barks Karishma.

'I'm not home. I will be there in . . .' he checks his watch. 'Thirty minutes.'

'Shit. Thirty minutes! Where the hell are you? And how many times have I asked you to keep a key on the window sill? Why can't you remember that?'

'I forget it intentionally. Because what if you enter with your own key some day and find me naked?'

'Ugh! Disgusting.'

'Exactly!'

'You seem happy today,' remarks Karishma.

'I'm not happy. I'm sad. I'm almost depressed. It's a good kind of sad. The kind of sad I was when I saw Free Willy escape into the wilderness.'

'I don't get what's that kind of sad. Wait. What happened last night? Did you get some action?' she asks.

'Not really.'

'Where were you last night?'

'In a hotel room.'

Karishma wants to sound concerned but her enthusiasm is too overwhelming. 'What! With who?'

'Someone who really likes my music.'

'Don't tell me it's Karthika or I will puke. I have seen her naked pictures and I don't want that image in my head again,' grumbles Karishma.

'No, no! It's someone else.'

'Who? Did you sleep with her?'

'Yes, I did sleep with her, but nothing happened. We just slept. Though I did see her in a towel even though I tried not to and she looked beautiful. Like if you kind of grind Scarlet Johansson, Sonakshi Sinha, Katrina Kaif and Jennifer Lawrence into a fine paste, put it in a cauldron, boil it, distil all the good parts and put the concoction in a girl, you will get her.'

'I'm quite sceptical if that process is scientific.'

'I see no other way she could have been made otherwise,' argues Devrat.

'Wait. So you slept together, and she was in a towel and you saw her and she saw you seeing her and nothing happened. Why? How?'

'I think I was overwhelmed by her awesomeness.'

'Overwhelmed by her awesomeness?'

'It felt like I had created her out of my will. She was beautiful. Like beautiful, beautiful. Not like you enter a store, someone gives you a makeover, dresses you up, sprays at your hair and you're beautiful. She's beautiful in her sleep, in her faded pink pyjamas, in her ruffled hair and the puffy eyes. No one else could have carried off that face.'

'Umm . . . and still you couldn't get yourself to score?'

'I wasn't thinking about it,' he responds honestly.

'You weren't thinking about it? Are you, like, gay?'

'I just realized that I did sound like that.'

'Now come soon! I will be waiting downstairs, warding off other customers,' complains Karishma before disconnecting the call.

Devrat's smiling, still wondering if what happened the night before actually did, and is struggling to piece together the sequence of events before it ends up in one jumbled mess.

Just as he's doing that, remembering that his head is still pretty bashed up and there could be internal bleeding and he could die, his phone rings.

> **AVANTI**
> *Umm. Hi.*

> **DEVRAT**
> *Umm. Hi.*

> **AVANTI**
> *How's your head?*

DEVRAT
I was just thinking about that. There could be some internal bleeding and I was wondering if I could die because of that.

AVANTI
It makes me feel worse. If there's anything worse.

DEVRAT
?

DEVRAT
?

AVANTI
Would you think of me as a clingy, overbearing fan if I said I think I already miss you?

AVANTI
God. I sound desperate.

AVANTI
See. I think you just blocked me.

AVANTI
Damn.

AVANTI
Well. Bye.

DEVRAT
Haha.

> **AVANTI**
> What?

> **DEVRAT**
> *I wasn't replying because I was reading each of your messages thrice.*

> **AVANTI**
> *At the cost of making me feel like shit.*

> **DEVRAT**
> *But I needed to read them again.*

Time passes by. There are no messages exchanged but both Devrat and Avanti are looking at their phones.

> **AVANTI**
> *I want to write something to keep the conversation alive but don't know what.*

> **DEVRAT**
> *I was thinking of sending a smiley too but those are conversation killers.*

> **AVANTI**
> *True that. About to reach the airport. I don't think I have ever been sadder to see an airport. *feels like such a pile on* *Kills herself**

> **DEVRAT**
> *runs* *saves her*

> **AVANTI**
> *dream comes true* *blushes*

DEVRAT
Reached?

AVANTI
Almost. Can we not talk about how I'm leaving?

DEVRAT
How can we not talk about that? You're my only legitimate fan and you're going. If you were a true fan, you would have stayed.

AVANTI
Don't make me feel bad now.

DEVRAT
I was kidding.

AVANTI
That's a conversation killer.

DEVRAT
Would it help if I said that I kind of . . . miss you too?

DEVRAT
?

DEVRAT
Was it too soon?

DEVRAT
Damn. I should have acted like a celebrity.

AVANTI
reads it thrice *giggles* *colleagues look on strangely* *ask a million questions*

DEVRAT
Did you tell them?

AVANTI
I wouldn't know where to start. Did you tell anyone?

DEVRAT
Karishma. My best friend.

AVANTI
What did you tell her?
P.S.—I still can't believe I'm texting YOU. You were supposed to be unavailable. You were supposed to be on Facebook. You were supposed to be not someone I would know and text.

DEVRAT
blushes

AVANTI
That's a little girlish.

DEVRAT
lifts dumb-bells with hair stubble *Bashes people around* *drinks protein-shake* *Farts and burps*

AVANTI
That's more like it. But what did you tell your friend?

DEVRAT
Everything.

AVANTI
What did she say?

DEVRAT
She was disappointed I didn't get laid.

AVANTI
:O

DEVRAT
SHE was disappointed. Not ME. SHE.

AVANTI
Not YOU? Not even a little bit?

DEVRAT
You're making me think about it now. I don't want to think about it.

AVANTI
Why not?

AVANTI
Oh. Shit. Today is a bad day. I didn't want to come out that strongly.

DEVRAT
Why not?

> **AVANTI**
> I'm a bit of a hypocrite in these matters.

> **DEVRAT**
> Elaborate.

> **AVANTI**
> I talk and behave . . . like someone on a hormone overdrive.
> I send out all the wrong signals, and when people catch
> them, I run the opposite way.

> **DEVRAT**
> That's kind of cruel.

> **AVANTI**
> I'm a bit of coward that way.

> **DEVRAT**
> Hmmm . . .

> **AVANTI**
> Do you think I can call?

> **AVANTI**
> Are you still there?

> **AVANTI**
> Shit.

> **DEVRAT**
> Of course. Hehe.

> ## AVANTI
> I will kill you.

Devrat checks his hair on the rear-view mirror before he receives the call.

'Hi, again!' says Devrat. 'If we talk this much, I'm afraid I will run out of my charm, if there's any, and you will realize that your fascination with the boy whose music you like is starting to wear off.'

'That wore off the minute I first talked to you,' says Avanti. 'I found someone better.'

'I'm sure someone pays you to be nice to me,' says Devrat and pays the cab driver.

'I think it's the other way round. Wait. Gotta go inside.'

Devrat holds. He likes this and he has never liked this. He was never the person who talks on the phone. He was a 'texter' once, then he was an 'emailer', but never someone who would want to talk at length. It was boring, but this is refreshing, he likes this.

'Yes, sorry. Are you sure you're not busy?' asks Avanti.

'You're forgetting that I'm an engineering dropout who's struggling at being a struggling musician.'

'Stop saying that. I'm serious.'

Devrat can almost feel the anger in her voice. He can see her face contort, her eyes narrow and her fist slightly clench. 'Fine.'

'What are you going to do today?' asks Avanti. 'I'm sorry, am I boring you now? I am, right? I should probably disconnect, find a hole and hide my head in it.'

'If you become a bore, I will disconnect and switch my phone off. So till the time I don't do that, you're in the safe zone.'

'That just scares me. Now every time I find your phone switched off I will think it's because of me.' Then she adds after a pause. 'Not that I would call you a lot of times. Ummm . . . but can I call you?'

'Of course.'

'I'm making such a mess of myself here. Usually, I'm a lot smoother.'

'You're still smooth.'

'I think I'm just panicking a little,' says Avanti.

Devrat can hear heavy breathing noises from the other side.

'I think it's cute,' says Devrat.

'You're way cuter,' says Avanti

'If there were any of my guy friends around and they were to hear this, they would laugh at me. It's exactly the kind of conversation that guys are mocked at for having.'

'But it's also the kind of conversation that you always remember,' argues Avanti.

'. . .'

'. . .'

'Security check,' says Avanti.

'I will hold.'

SEVENTEEN

Avanti doesn't care if she loses her job today. She's in the washroom of the aircraft and she's still on the phone.

'I don't think this phone call is worth your job,' remarks Devrat.

'You have no idea what it's worth,' whispers Avanti.

'I have never flown.'

'Never?'

'Never.'

'Are you scared of it?' asks Avanti.

'Air travel is for people in a hurry to get somewhere. I'm never short on time as you would have noticed by now.'

'You should fly with me now.'

'I could be highly claustrophobic.'

'That's what I would be there for,' offers Avanti. There's a knock on the door and the senior flight attendant wants her to come out. Avanti grumbles audibly. 'Terrible stomach-ache. I think it's food poisoning,' says Avanti.

'Oh I'm sorry, take your time,' comes the reply from outside.

'So food poisoning, eh?' asks Devrat.

'See, what all you are making me do?'

'It's your own free will.'

'You sure do know how to make someone feel like a pile-on, don't you?' growls Avanti.

There's an announcement on-board that tells the captain and the other flight attendants that boarding has been completed.

'Damn. We are about to take off,' wails Avanti. 'I will call you later. If that's okay with you?'

'Sure.'

'Bye.'

'Bye.'

Avanti's fingers linger around the 'CANCEL' button for a little while before she taps on it.

'I miss you,' she says after the phone's disconnected.

Soon she will be thousands of miles away, pining for him, and he will be back to his old life, maybe remembering last night as an adventure to be talked about at dinners with strangers. It makes Avanti feel a little dizzy. She can't get Devrat's gorgeous face and puppy-like eyes out of her head.

'Are you okay?' asks the senior flight attendant when Avanti comes out of the lavatory.

'I don't think so.'

'You can rest if you want to for a little while.'

'I would rather work to distract myself.'

Her trick clearly doesn't work. The magazines all lie— burying yourself in work doesn't help when trying to forget a pretty, lost boy with a broken yet brilliant voice. She looks at her phone and wonders if Devrat's leaving her texts and Whatsapps and Facebook messages and Twitter favourites while she's flying. She frowns at her desperation to be around him. But she reasons that he has been her longest standing obsession.

'Hey.'

'Yes, Avanti?' asks the flight attendant.

'Suppose? Just imagine you meet someone on a layover and the boy really likes you. Would he wait for you to be in his city next month? Or would he do something more?'

The flight attendant thinks for a while. 'He wouldn't wait for a month.'

Avanti frowns. She feels like a bit of a failure now that she knows Devrat may not wait for a month to see her again. Maybe she didn't make the cut. Maybe Devrat didn't like her as much. *But why?* She was always the prettiest in class, she was never really dumb (she was good at geography and history), and she could tell the last five Presidents and Prime Ministers along with the length of their terms. Maybe she should have told him that. Maybe that would have impressed him. After all, Bengalis from Kolkata are raging fans of politics and afternoon naps.

'What do you know about Varahgiri Venkata Giri?' asks Avanti, a little angry at herself.

The flight attendant frowns. 'Who's that?'

'He was the fourth President of India, 1969–74.'

'So? You're dating his grandson or what?' winks the flight attendant. 'Didn't know you were into south Indian men. I mean they are hot but I'm not a big fan of moustaches.'

Avanti ignores that and gets back to work reimagining situations from last night, thinking what she could have done different to make Devrat fall in love with her. Would dropping the towel have helped? Would not calling him have helped? Would not texting him so much have helped?

The aircraft is now cruising at 35,000 ft. To Avanti it seems like a crushingly slow speed. 'Get me to Delhi quickly!' Avanti wants to shout out. She's wishing the aircraft blows an engine and they have to turn back to Kolkata! And she wishes there's a terrorist threat and they close the Kolkata airport forever.

She's reading the texts they had exchanged and she is cursing herself for she could have written different, wittier things. Annoyed with herself, she almost deletes the string of texts but somehow keeps herself from doing so.

She Googles 'how to be interesting when texting boyfriends' but realizes that she's in a flight and there's no network.

The call bells start to ring. The last thing Avanti needs now is to tend to someone's kids' ear popping, or someone needing a newspaper. The other attendants do the needful when Avanti frowns and they assume it's still her stomach.

'There's a petulant kid at 21A who's pressing the bell as if he has bought the aircraft and every one of us! He's already pressed it twenty times!' complains a flight attendant to the senior one.

'Jerk.'

The bell rings. 'Here he goes again. Can we not go?'

The senior flight attendant tells them that they have to.

Avanti's colleague attends to the irritating passenger, comes back and slumps next to her, fuming. 'I'm not going again. He wanted a pencil. Now is it my job to get him a pencil? My job is to fucking get him to land safely. Asshole.'

'I'm sorry,' says Avanti. 'Let me go the next time.'

'Is your stomach okay?'

'What if it's not? As unlady-like as it may sound, I might end up farting there.'

'Ew!' the other flight attendant says. Avanti manages a little smile even though her heart's sinking imagining Devrat hundreds of miles away.

The bell rings again. Avanti and her colleague look up. It's 21A again.

'Pervert,' the flight attendant mutters.

'Your wish is answered,' growls Avanti's colleague.

Avanti gets up, suitably irritated. As she walks through the aisle she's trying to frame her words into well-veiled insults. She's hoping to get into an argument which would distract her from Devrat.

18 . . . 19 . . . 20 . . .

'Excuse me, you may have bought. . .' Avanti's words trail off.

'I'm sorry to bother you again,' the boy says in his raspy voice, 'I just started to feel a little claustrophobic and I thought only a pretty flight attendant could help me out.'

Avanti struggles to find words. 'Umm . . . You could have just called me.' Looking at the pretty boy in front of her, she feels all her anger melt away slowly and it's replaced by a little, silly smile.

'I tried.'

'I'm glad you did,' says Avanti. Only she knows how hard she's trying not to burst into tears and hurl herself at Devrat who's smiling as if him being on the aircraft is nothing more than a little prank.

'Excuse me,' says Avanti to the two men sitting next to Devrat. 'Will you allow us to shift you to the business class seats at the front of the aircraft? I know you're being inconvenienced by this strange, but gorgeous passenger sitting at 21A. Please allow us to help you.'

The two men are more than happy to do so and they huddle to the front of the aircraft, smiling, thanking Avanti.

'What are you doing here?' asks Avanti in a loud whisper, trying not to draw too much attention. *Oh my God! He's here!*

'You asked me to fly with you and it was an offer I couldn't refuse.'

'I don't know what to do now.'

'Huh?'

'You're seriously here, right?' asks Avanti. She touches him. 'Shit. You're here.'

'Yes, I think so, too,' answers Devrat with an impish smile on his face.

'This is so screwed up. Oh. God. I'm panicking. Oh. My. God. But why? How?'

'Sit. Sit.'

'I can't! This is my aircraft! I'm supposed to be attending to people and not sitting next to you! YOU!'

The people sitting in rows around Avanti look at her palpitating and slowly losing it.

'Shhh,' says Devrat.

Avanti sits next to Devrat and holds her head.

'The fact that you're over-reacting is cute.'

'I spent the last twenty minutes freaking out wondering if you have already forgotten me. I was trying to come to terms with that and here you are! Why? You're purposely screwing with my head, aren't you? Are you sure you're still here?'

'Yes, I am. And couldn't it be that I, too, was freaking out that you would fly to Delhi and not come back until next month?'

'Why couldn't you just come with me? I wouldn't have wallowed in self-pity for the last hour.'

'I wanted it to be a surprise. And had I told you I would have missed out on this reaction!'

'I hate surprises,' grumbles Avanti. There's an awkward

silence and she's debating mentally if this is the beginning of something, whether him spontaneously jumping on a flight to Delhi means something more than an interesting story to be told over dinner.

'Is everything okay here?' asks the senior flight attendant looking at Avanti and Devrat.

'Yes, it is,' answers Avanti. 'He's a friend.'

The flight attendant smiles knowingly and walks from there.

'Does this mean something, Devrat? Because I'm kind of freaking out here.'

'I would like to think so. And I think I'm a little freaked out as well. In a good way though,' answers Devrat. His words make her feel warm and fuzzy.

'You're really here, aren't you?'

'Yes.'

'Dr Rajendra Prasad was the only President to serve two terms in India.'

'Huh?' Devrat looks on, confused.

'Just in case.'

EIGHTEEN

Devrat boards the bus meant for the passengers and Avanti gets on the car that takes the flight attendants to the terminal.

'Will see you inside!' shouts Avanti from the car, beaming, waving like a madwoman. To think that he's the reason behind Avanti's happiness is strangely comforting and uplifting. Devrat's phone is ringing continuously while he waits for Avanti outside the airport, still trying to wrap his head around his spontaneous trip.

'Hi, Sumit.'

'Where on earth are you?' bellows Sumit. 'I have been calling you for the past two hours, Devrat. A college in Durgapur has asked for you and I'm quoting fifteen thousand for a two-hour performance. It's day after tomorrow and you better be there.'

'Confirm the event. I will need the tickets to be booked from New Delhi.'

'Delhi? What Delhi? What are you doing there? Don't tell me you picked another manager. I will kill you—'

'Stop over-reacting! I'm here to meet a friend. Send me the ticket and any special requirements that the college has,' says Devrat.

'You don't have to teach me that. Tell me something? Who's the friend? It's a girl, right? Who's it? Don't tell me it's Karthika! No, man. She's hideous.'

'She's not THAT bad-looking. And it's not her anyway.'

'Whatever. Just tell me who the girl is and I want details,' probes Sumit.

'Shut up, Sumit. I will call you later,' says Devrat and disconnects the line.

Avanti's walking towards him and she has a shy, goofy smile on her face. 'I still can't believe you're here. Are you? You are, right? I am not crazy and talking to thin air, right?' asks Avanti.

'Well, I am here. And you should stop saying that.'

Avanti shuts up, embarrassed.

'It's okay,' whispers Devrat. 'Even I don't believe I'm here. So that makes two of us.'

They get into a cab. Devrat's thinking of how to break it to Avanti that he has about two thousand rupees and two days to spend in Delhi before he flies off to Durgapur and gets paid again. For all he knows Avanti will take him to an expensive hotel and get him to check in there. Though he loves hotels and he loves to see Avanti in hotel towels more.

'Where are we going?' asks Devrat.

'Home?'

'Home? What home?'

'My home. You need a place to stay, right? So stay at my place. I talked to my grandmother and she said you can stay over.'

'You spoke to your grandmother about me? What did you

say? How did she allow you? She stays with you? Didn't you say you live with your father?'

'Too many questions,' snickers Avanti. 'She lives in Dehradun and I told her that you need a place to stay. She's pretty chilled out. She will talk to Dad and tell him.'

'She didn't say a thing?'

'I would be lying if I said she didn't. She threw a big tantrum but then calmed down after I threw a bigger tantrum and blamed her for sending me to Delhi and not loving me enough! So she allowed me. She loves me a lot and it always works in my favour,' Avanti chuckles.

'Can't I stay somewhere else?'

'Why would you do that?'

'Because I've known you only for a day and it will be mighty awkward to face your dad?'

'Join the club. Even I feel awkward in front of my dad.'

'But still! I'm very awkward around older people. I have nothing to say. Every conversation with my own relatives feels like a terrorist investigation.'

Avanti laughs at that. 'It will be okay. My dad doesn't talk a lot. He spends hours inside his room working on some mathematics theorems and stuff. He won't ask you anything.'

'It still is very awkward.' Avanti starts to laugh and Devrat asks her what happened. 'You're cute, Devrat. Like a pug or beagle! I could just keep you in my handbag and keep playing with you.'

'Okay, now you're emasculating me. Stop comparing me with puppies. Should I start doing deadlifts and pull-ups?'

Avanti smiles.

'Now what!' snaps Devrat.

'I just imagined a puppy doing pull-ups!'

'Uffo!'

They both smile. The cab is stuck in traffic and Devrat's quite happy about it. Meeting anyone's parents hasn't been his strongest point. Both Karishma's and Arundhati's parents had looked at him like he was a parasite, a rat, a pest control problem their daughters should get rid of.

Devrat's now thinking of the last time he met his parents. It's been a couple of months already and he misses them. He thinks of how different life would have been without all the pressure he has put on himself to succeed in something it's very hard to succeed in. He could have been an engineering student, slogging every day, got himself a job, given his parents the pleasure of looking for a girl for him. And every time he thinks of them, he thinks he has been selfish to not give them that pleasure.

'I'm a pile of nerves. I can die right now,' says Devrat when they reach her apartment building.

'You will be gone before my father even manages to string a single sentence. He's conversationally challenged,' assures Avanti.

They trudge up the stairs, and Avanti jimmies a key into the lock and opens the door. Devrat's thinking of whether he should greet Avanti's father with a 'Hello' or go with a more acceptable 'Namaste'. He's quite nervous because strangely enough he cares what Avanti's father thinks of him.

'Where's he?' whispers Devrat.

'I don't know. He's like a jack-in-the-box. You think he's not there but then he pops out from his room with ink-spot stains on his shirt and face.'

'Why do you say it like it's a bad thing? That's quite a cute definition for any dad.'

Avanti doesn't respond and is surprised to realize that it's actually true. She shrugs it off. 'Let me get you to your room.'

'Aren't we rushing into this too soon? My own room? Have you strewn flower petals all over the bed as well?' Devrat winks.

'Very funny.'

The guest room is spanking clean but it smells of abandonment. It's sparsely furnished but it's much better than what Devrat would have got in the money he has. And that Avanti would be in the adjoining room was a big bonus.

'You can change,' says Avanti. 'I will be back in ten?'

'Sure,' says Devrat and tries not to imagine Avanti, too, changing.

Devrat lies on the bed for a few minutes, closes his eyes. For a moment he's thinking of what to wear and that's when it hits him that he doesn't have clothes and he has been in the same T-shirt for over forty-eight hours now. He sniffs his armpits and a part of him dies. He smells rotten.

The washroom has a new shaving kit, packed toothbrush, a tiny tube of toothpaste, shower gel and a clean towel. He bathes thoroughly to beat the ungodly smell of his T-shirt. He's drying himself when he hears music and running water from the other side of the wall. A little later, he hears Avanti humming the songs as well. *God! She can sing!* Devrat foams his two-day-old stubble, slowly and deliberately, trying hard not to imagine Avanti in a bathtub, or shower, naked. She does look like a bathtub person, like a movie star, pretty even without make-up and with wet, clumpy hair. Devrat stands there, betting against himself, whether she's in a bathtub or a shower, and the Devrat who's betting on the bathtub is winning. And then just like that, he says out aloud, 'I can hear you from here.'

There's silence from the other side. The music stops.

'Umm . . . hi!'

'Hi,' says Devrat. And just to make sure the conversation is not about whether she's in a bathtub or a shower, he adds, 'I don't have a clean T-shirt to wear. Think we should go shopping after this?'

'Sure,' says Avanti.'Or I will get your one of my father's T-shirts if he has one in his cupboard. Though I'm not promising you anything. I have only seen him in dull oversized shirts.'

All of this is not weird at all, Devrat tells himself. It's a natural progression in a story where a girl meets a boy in a bar in Kolkata, they spend the night in a hotel room, and find themselves in the girl's house in a different city where the boy is wearing the girl's father's T-shirt.

'Sure,' mumbles Devrat as if wearing her father's T-shirts is perfectly ordinary.

Devrat can't help but think of her in the bathtub, lined with lit candles, her body submerged in foamy water, her legs propped up on the edges. In the image, he's there, sitting on the toilet seat with the lid down, talking to her. Just to push that image out of his head, he says, 'I'm done. I will see you outside.'

There's no answer from the other side of the wall for a few seconds. Devrat wonders if he should barge in through her door with the excuse that he thought she might be drowning.

'Sure. You could have come over and we could have talked but as with most things, I'm sure this will sound flirtatious and you will come and expect something and be disappointed when nothing happens,' rues Avanti.

'Why do you think I would come over thinking that something would happen? I'm a perfectly decent boy. And I didn't imagine you in a bathtub at all,' says Devrat.

'I'm sure you didn't,' chuckles Avanti. There's silence again, after which, Avanti says, in a voice softer than usual. 'Come over.'

'Okay,' says Devrat. 'But only if you promise not to flash or try to do anything dirty with me.'

'Whatever.'

'Give me a minute.'

He leaves the washroom, already sweating and nervous. What if she's looking absolutely devastatingly hot? What if he's staring at all the wrong places? What if it affects him physiologically? What if she notices?

Devrat psyches himself up, tells himself that she will be covered in foam from head to toe, and that's equivalent to a girl in a burqa or something. And also it's totally harmless; people do this all the time!

Devrat tells himself that and enters Avanti's room, which seems to have undergone a little explosion of clothes and make-up stuff. Devrat's palms are sweaty and the bathroom door is slightly ajar. A part of him, a huge chunk, doesn't want to enter, rather wants to stay out, run to his own room and later tell Avanti he got caught up. She's going to be naked. Like naked. Not even a towel. But naked! *Stop saying that word!*

Devrat walks in and tries not to look directly at her, instead looks around the bathroom and into his phone.

'You can sit there,' says Avanti and points to a small stool that's a little too pretty to be in a washroom. The washroom, itself, is too pretty to be a washroom.

Avanti's covered in foam alright, just like he had imagined. He can see two little bumps that are her knees. But he's imagining much more. Maybe he shouldn't have taken up on the offer. This is torture.

'You look pretty,' says Devrat. 'Fresh.'

Avanti blushes. The mirror in the bathroom has fogged up and the room is perfectly warm.

'I have this thing of bathing in very hot water. I heard somewhere it's good for the skin,' says Avanti.

'If that's true, you must have been born in a hot water spring,' says Devrat, his tongue failing him a little. 'Sorry for that cheesy line. I couldn't come up with anything better.'

He can't help but notice the wet strands of hair that are stuck to her skin, and every time she moves her legs inside the water, something flutters inside him. He stares at his phone, locks and unlocks it.

'When does your father come in? I mean I don't want him to walk in on us and see us like this. That wouldn't be so great, I am thinking?' asks Devrat.

'He won't. And why are you so concerned about my father. He barely talks, Devrat.'

'I think I'm just little nervous. I just want him to like me.'

NINETEEN

Avanti's glad that she's not visible from inside the water. Devrat's last words are simple and yet they open up a plethora of possibilities, many of which she doesn't want to think about.

I want him to like me.

Avanti has been trying to act perfectly calm in Devrat's presence and it's been hard to keep up that pretence because the bottom line is that she's naked and he's here, the only thing that separates both of them are the rapidly disappearing bubbles and air.

But still, it's not shame that's eating her up. Well, it's shame but it's a different type of shame. It's like watching and enjoying a movie that you shouldn't enjoy. It's like a hardcore Harry Potter fan choosing to re-read *Fifty Shades of Grey* over *The Goblet of Fire*.

This, by far, is The Boldest Thing she's ever done. This is dirty. Like hot, dirty, like not pornographic dirty, but still dirty, dirty in a good sense, a kind of dirty she can't explain.

Quite frankly, she feels a bit like a pervert right now to be enjoying this. She likes how Devrat is stealing glances at her, she likes how he's all shy about it, she likes how he's red in the face, just like she is, she likes how he must be thinking in his head, and she likes how he thinks that she's pretty.

'I think I'm done,' says Avanti when she realizes that most of her bubbles are gone and her refracted nakedness might be visible from outside.

'I'm not sure if I'm happy about it,' says Devrat.

'Stop being a pervert. You don't play it well. You have been looking at your phone all this while!'

'I'm a shy pervert.'

'See you outside,' says Avanti. Devrat leaves. She dries herself, wipes the condensation on the mirror and watches herself intently. While dressing up, she also searches for the term 'exhibitionism' just to check if she's slowly turning into some kind of a desperate weirdo.

When she comes out she finds Devrat on the floor, in front of the television, flipping through the comic books she remembers having seen in her father's cabinets.

'I see you have busied yourself,' says Avanti.

Devrat looks back at her and it takes him an extra second to react. Avanti has come to like these little amazing pauses he takes, the double takes, how he stops looks at her, smiles coyly, looks away and then answers.

'This is awesome! I have never seen a collection like this before,' remarks Devrat. 'Come! Sit. Look at this! I never thought people owned these in India. This is pretty awesome.'

'I didn't know you were a comic book fan,' says Avanti, a little disappointed because she thought they would talk about how big a fan he is of Seeing Avanti Bathe thing. *You're a pervert, Avanti, stop it!*

'A big fan! But comics weren't really widely available. So I had to stick with Nagraj and Doga and Super Commando Dhruva and Shakti. And they weren't that good.'

'I haven't heard any of those names,' says Avanti. 'But tell me about them.' She likes how Devrat's eyes have suddenly lit up. She picks up a comic and immediately hates Wonderwoman for her huge bust, and keeps the comic out of Devrat's reach.

'Oh! There's so much about them. I remember renting them for ten bucks for a week. I liked Nagraj the most though. His backstory itself used to be so intense. And hey! Look there's the Dog Welder.'

'Dog Welder?' asks Avanti, immensely amused by this supposedly half-famous singer getting excited like a kid.

'Oh. He's one of the worst superheroes! He used to weld dogs to bad people's mouths so they died of starvation. I had only heard of him and his pack of eight superheroes. Never saw a comic that actually had him!'

'What used to happen to the puppies that he welded? Just asking because ever since I have started comparing puppies with you, I'm deeply concerned about them.'

'Why don't we find out?' asks Devrat and picks the three comics that feature the Dog Welder and his pack of superheroes. Avanti hides the one with the huge-breasted Wonderwoman by sitting on it. And just like that they are sitting on the couch, reading the first of the three comics.

'Spoiler alert,' says Devrat. 'The dogs are all dead.'

'That's a relief.'

They start reading the comic and Avanti, surprisingly, is into it. It's more because Devrat narrates the backstories of the characters like it's his own.

'So this guy dressed in a black jacket and shades, quite burly, a little bit like your ex-boyfriend, is called The Defenestrator. He throws criminals out of the window that he carries,' explains Devrat.

'So I'm guessing it was the lowest point of comic writers, was it?'

'There are only so many superpowers that you can give people. You're bound to run out of them! Okay, what superpower would you give yourself if you had the choice?' asks Devrat, smiling, because he's thinking his superpower will be what every boy wants, to be invisible. For *obvious* reasons.

'I would be Wonderwoman!' says Avanti without thinking.

'Why?'

'Umm . . . because she's hot?'

'You're hotter, Avanti. If you and Wonderwoman were in a to-death match in hotness, she would cover up and shy away.'

Avanti feels rather shy at this and they get back to the comic, which is getting hilarious as they read on. A guy named Flemgem is now producing ungodly amounts of phlegm to blind the enemy.

'They could have got any middle-aged north Indian man to do that,' remarks Avanti and they laugh.

Then there is Bueno Excelente who defeats people by acts of perversion. He's not shown killing anyone but there's a newspaper byline in one of the comics that screams that one of the villains was fatally sodomized. So he was a pervert with good intentions.

They finish the three comics, which made little or no sense, but Avanti still felt she had spent the best two hours of her life.

'That was interesting, very interesting . . .' says Avanti, a bit sarcastically.

'You think it's crazy, right? You have to suspend all belief to like them. Comics are like Salman Khan movies on steroids.'

'Don't get offended. I liked it. I just have to get used to Bueno Excelente killing people by having sex with them,' says Avanti and chuckles.

'Yeah. Whatever.'

And they are still arguing who would win between a three-way match between Phlegm, Bueno Excelente and the Dog Welder, Avanti is placing her bet on the sex-guy and Devrat on the animal rights welfare nightmare when they hear the study's door unlock. Avanti's father walks in; dressed in oddly fitting faded blue trousers and a shirt that hangs over the belt.

Avanti knows Nani would have talked to Dad but still she's wringing her fingers thinking what he would say seeing a boy in his house.

'Namaste, Uncle,' says Devrat.

'Namaste,' says her father. 'Your parents know that you're here?'

Devrat nods.

Dad looks in Avanti's direction. She is quite amused by her father's measured behaviour. 'Your Nani called,' says Dad. 'If y . . . ou need anything, do let me know.'

'I will,' says Avanti. She's strangely proud of her father for being so well behaved and chilled out.

'I have ordered pizzas for you,' says Avanti's father and looks at both of them. 'I hope you like pizzas?'

Devrat nods and Avanti has half a mind to throw a tantrum because as a teenager she's supposed to do that but she refrains. Avanti's father disappears in his study.

'Sweet,' mutters Devrat.

'He's not like this,' says Avanti. 'Usually.'

'What's he like?'

'I don't know. He's always lost, always a little nutsy. He just says a few words and locks himself in the study. As long as he lets you stay, I'm okay with him. Though he did chase Shekhar away once with a bat . . . ,' she trails off and she is thrown back to the time she was leaving for Kolkata and her father lied about his trip to Nagpur so that he could spend some time with her. 'He's trying to reconnect with me,' Avanti thinks, smilingly, and says this aloud.

'Then what's stopping you?' asks Devrat.

'I hardly know the man.'

'You hardly know me as well and I saw you bathe today.'

Avanti is about to find the words to argue with that when the bell rings and Dad comes running out of the room to pay. He struggles with the boxes and Devrat reaches out and takes them from him. He's then about to go back to his study when Devrat invites him to share the pizza with them.

'I'm okay. I will eat what the maid has cooked,' says Avanti's father.

'But Uncle, eat with us. It's too much for two people.'

Avanti wants Devrat to let her father go, but Devrat insists and her father joins them. There's awkward silence at the table and Avanti wishes the Defenestrator would throw her out of his window and put her out of her misery.

'Six-pack never realized what his true power was,' mutters Dad.

'Huh?' Avanti mutters.

She finds Dad looking in the direction of the three comics. The Wonderwoman remains hidden, but it doesn't matter anymore since Devrat said Avanti's hotter.

'But wasn't his superpower the strength he got when he was drunk?' asks Devrat.

'No, it wasn't. It's an awful comic but the main guy is said to be a commentary on alcoholics. Six-pack was so busy being drunk and imagining his successes that he never found out what his real powers were.'

For the first time, Avanti's father, doesn't seem like a man whose hopes are lost; who's leading a slow life that eventually ends in old age home or death or both. Her dad's excited when he shows the last few panels of Hitman #18 to Devrat and they are reading it like eight-grade students would.

For the next half hour, Devrat and her dad are passionately discussing deaths of superheroes and supervillains, and some of those arguments are damn ridiculous. Avanti is torn between liking Devrat a little more and ignoring him, because liking him would mean she liked her dad too.

The pizza slices are disappearing fast. The two men are discussing the near impossibility of a certain Miss Arrow, a woman made of spiders and an enemy of Spiderman, to die because a few birds attacked her in an aviary. The topic is hotly debated and soon books are brought out to corroborate facts.

'She could have just disintegrated into a million spiders and then integrated again,' Dad throws his hands up in protest. 'It was stupid way to die.'

'But Uncle, but what if the birds plucked at the one spider that was her heart? What then? She could never be whole!' argues Devrat.

'It was a chance she should have taken,' frowns her father. Both Devrat and her father collectively mourn Miss Arrow's death—could have been a more able nemesis for Spiderman.

Batman and Spiderman are discussed in explicit details, and

the inconsistencies in the superhero movies are frowned upon. She does like the bit where she gets to know that Mary Jane, Spiderman's love interest, in one of the series died because of Spiderman's radioactive sperm. Avanti hates to admit it but she likes the little camaraderie that the two men/boys have going on.

The conversation dies down when Avanti's father's phone rings and he has to leave.

'There's another cabinet there,' Dad points behind Devrat. 'It has collaborations from major illustrators and story writers. You can have a look.'

Devrat nods excitedly. Her dad's at the door of his study smiling at both Avanti and Devrat, which is both creepy and comforting and leaves Avanti a little confused.

'This. Was. Awesome! Your father is a living legend. He knows every panel by heart. No wonder he's a genius mathematician or whatever you call him,' says Devrat.

'I call him a failed mathematician.'

'Maybe he's just ahead of his time,' says Devrat, still impressed.

Avanti hates to kill his enthusiasm but she has to. 'We had to go out, remember?'

'Oh. Yeah. We have to go,' says Devrat and keeps the comics aside, frowning. 'We can read these brilliant, rare comics later. These awesome comics obviously aren't begging for our attention. They are okay by themselves just sitting in cabinets, unread.'

Avanti can sense the sarcasm in Devrat's voice but she chooses to ignore it. After all, it's *her* father and he can't have a better equation with her father than *her*.

It's as simple as that.

TWENTY

'I feel grossly underdressed,' says Devrat, looking at his worn-out T-shirt and a faded pair of jeans he had worn for his performance last night (though it feels like it happened years ago), and in all other circumstances he wouldn't have given a shit but Avanti looks like she has unmindfully overshot the ramp and is walking with him instead.

'I will take that,' points Devrat to a T-shirt with a graphic of Justice League on it.

'You're a musician, not an illustrator! Shouldn't you take something with a Metallica or an AC/DC graphic on it,' protests Avanti, still a little pissed at Devrat and her father's chemistry over comic books.

'I wish I were both. And I already have T-shirts with everyone I love on them. But I feel like a comic nerd today,' says Devrat and picks up the T-shirt.

'At least try it!'

'Oh. It will fit. Don't worry.'

'Fine,' says Avanti.

It's not that Devrat hasn't noticed Avanti's discomfort since the comic book incident happened with her father, but he doesn't know how to approach that topic. Avanti pays for the T-shirts and the pair of jeans he buys.

'I'm sorry,' says Devrat. They are sitting in a slightly plush restaurant, which doesn't make Devrat feel any better because Avanti is not her usual self—she's all morose and frowning.

'What are you sorry for?'

'For the comic book stuff? For talking to your dad?'

'Why would you say sorry for that?'

Avanti's Thai green curry arrives and she starts to eat with her hands. A little later, her feet are propped up on the couch and she's sitting like one sits on the floor.

'I'm sorry,' says Avanti. 'I can't feel the taste if I don't eat with my hands. It's a compulsion.'

'You can eat whichever way you like.'

'You don't feel embarrassed?'

'Not at all. Well, maybe a little bit. But it's okay because you're pretty enough to pull anything off. You would look great even if you start to lick the gravy that's trickling down to your wrist.'

Avanti does exactly that.

'I know you meant for it to look disgusting but it didn't. If anything, I think that turned me on a little. Do that again,' says Devrat.

Avanti doesn't react. She's looking down at her bowl and scraping mindlessly with her fingers on the plate. Devrat shifts next to her. Avanti looks at him and her eyes have welled up.

'I'm sorry,' mumbles Avanti. 'I don't know why I'm crying. You were just being nice to him. And I just felt very uncomfortable sharing him with you, and it's strange because we, me and my dad, don't really share an equation. I don't know why I am so angry right now at him. And I have never been angry at him.'

Devrat puts his arms around Avanti who dissolves into tears. They eat in silence and leave the restaurant in an hour. The rest of the day is spent ambling aimlessly around the mall. Somewhere in the evening, Devrat finds himself holding her hand, playing with her fingers, and they have not left each other's hands ever since.

'Don't you want to call your dad and tell him that we are going to be late?' asks Devrat.

'Don't you want to tell yours that you're in Delhi?'

There's an awkward silence after which both of them walk in different directions to talk to their parents. It's surprising for Devrat how easily he can talk to his parents (who are mildly surprised that Devrat thought of calling. Though Devrat wants to tell them that he always means to, he feels an immense pressure to please them with every phone call and whenever he didn't have good news to give them, it always kind of holds him back). He wonders if it's the result of the ease with which he could connect with Avanti's father, but then he tries not to dwell on that.

'What did he say?'

'To be safe,' says Avanti. 'He trusts you.'

'He trusts you.'

Devrat finds Avanti looking at her cell phone every few minutes and Devrat asks what it is she's looking at.

'Three minutes,' Avanti says. 'It's my longest phone call with Dad.'

'You want to discuss it?' asks Devrat. No, comes the answer.

They are in a place that's not really a pub, but it isn't really a club either. Everything Devrat had heard about Delhi came true in that 1200-square-foot dimly lit, yet glittering place. The women are overdressed, so much so, that Avanti throws a little tantrum that she wants to leave the place and it takes Devrat five minutes to convince her that she's still the most gorgeous one in the room, and that she doesn't need to be dressed in a shimmery dress to stand out, which is funny because no one really stands out, because everyone is a damn photocopy of the other!

'At least everyone's looking at you,' remarks Devrat.

'They are looking at me because I'm dressed like a housemaid.'

'No, they are looking at you because you look different. And when they look at you, they realize that you look great and they keep looking. Look at that guy. The one near the beer tower? He hasn't taken his eyes off you since you stepped in.'

'I don't care if he is, I care if you are,' says Avanti.

'I haven't taken my eyes off you since I met you.'

They are like five-year-old kids on their first date. Devrat asks if Avanti wants to drink and Avanti shakes her head and tell him that she has an embarrassingly low capacity and she should be off it.

'No, it's okay. I can do without it. Plus I black out pretty easily. And it would kill me to forget this. Besides, you're still scaring me,' says Avanti.

'Why is that?' asks Devrat who finds his hand being caressed by Avanti's.

'You're here, today. Tomorrow, you will be somewhere else, getting drunk with someone else.'

'I am not sure that's going to happen,' says Devrat.

'See. All this is crazy for me. I hope you know that. I have been obsessing over you for years now. I have thought of elaborate scripts in my head of what I would say to you, what

I would do with you, where we will go . . . you know, that kind of stuff? And I thought it's never going to happen, so I was never scared. But now that it's happening, I'm terrified. Not seeing you tomorrow around me would kind of destroy me. I will not be able to think of anything but what I did to push you away. And one of the things that I will count in that list will be this conversation where I'm absolutely freaking you out by telling you that I think you're the cutest, nicest guy I have ever met and if I were even a little bit crazier I would keep you locked in my place and never let you out. Right now, I know you're thinking of darting out of this place and never coming back, but I will hope that you do, even if it means coming back with a girlfriend in tow. But I would still like to have you around.'

Avanti finishes and stares at her feet. It's an embarrassing monologue, cute, but embarrassing nonetheless.

'You're going to run now, aren't you? Change your number? Never call me? Block me? Get a restraining order?' asks Avanti, still looking at her feet.

'No, actually, I expected it to last a little longer. My biggest fan can only fawn over me for forty-five seconds. That's a little embarrassing. I would have expected a few tears but there were none.'

'You're making me cry now.'

'But why is that?'

'Because you're just sitting there, not saying anything to make me feel better. God! You write your own lyrics and you can't put together a single sentence to comfort me. You should be embarrassed about yourself,' complains Avanti.

'Quite frankly, I'm yet to make an opinion about you. And that's a good thing because I don't know what to expect out of you and that's amazing. You're gorgeous and smart and interesting and you know that, and when you look at me and say those things about me, they hardly seem real because everything I am, pales in front of everything you are. Because as far as I'm concerned there's not a thing about you I would change.'

Pause.

'. . .'

'. . .'

'I think I'm going to cry,' says Avanti.

'Oh. Shut up.'

'No. I'm serious. Pass the tissue.'

'Are you okay?'

'I'm sorry for earlier. But if you keep saying things like that to me, you can keep my father and I will not be pissed.'

'Deal.'

The rest of the night passes just like that. People get drunk around them and make out; they collectively make fun of badly dressed women and curse the food and the prices. Devrat gets jealous for Avanti finds the bartender cute, and Avanti gets jealous when Devrat pretends to like someone in the crowd, and places bets on boys who would get lucky tonight.

Devrat doesn't remember the last time he had so much fun, and they haven't even kissed or anything yet. It's not that he's looking forward to that. Okay, that's a lie. Avanti's lips are not ones that you can look at, ignore, and move on. Devrat has had a hard time looking away from them when she's talking and he has wondered about how it would be like to kiss them. Not the carnal I-eat-you-you-eat-me way, but something more tender, that tells her that he likes her but it's not sexual (for the most part). How does one ask to be kissed like that? *I want to kiss you just to see how it feels because I think it will feel great? And don't worry, it won't be sexual. It will be tender and lovely and awesome.*

It's two in the night when they leave the club. It's a different feeling for Devrat. He's not drunk, he's not pukish, he's not cursing that his house is far away, and his breath doesn't smell like a dead rat. They are still holding hands, which is quite a high-school thing to do, but he doesn't want to let go.

'We are looking for an auto, right?' asks Devrat.

'Yes, we are.'

'But we aren't really looking.'

'Because we don't want this walk to end,' says Avanti. It's interesting how she uses to the word 'we', and how correctly she uses it, with the precision of a poet.

'No, we don't. Because if this night ends, it will be another day and another day means I will have to go and *we* don't want that.'

But the Delhi Police wanted the walk to end. They were apprehended and threatened that their parents would be called and when they did call Avanti's dad, they were told that he knew his daughter was with Devrat and was safe with him. The police lets them go.

'See, I told you your father is so chilled out,' remarks Devrat.

'It's very hard to negate anything that comes out of your mouth.'

And talking of mouths, Devrat thinks of the pending kiss again. They take an auto home. Avanti's sleepy by now and Devrat loves how she snuggles next to him, her hands wrapped around his arm, her head on his shoulder, her breath on his neck. Her hair smells of strawberries and she sleeps through the bumps and potholes and Devrat keeps staring at her like a crazy sociopath with binoculars.

'We are here,' says Devrat and wakes Avanti up.

When they enter the apartment, Avanti's father is still awake and he asks if they had a good time and if the police created any trouble.

'No, they didn't, Uncle.'

Avanti's father gives him two mint-editions of Batman comics that he's sure no one else in India has.

'I bought them when I was called to Paris for a convention. I hope you like them,' her father says.

Devrat thanks her father.

'Good night,' her father says to both of them and goes back to his room, smiling.

'I'm sorry I couldn't say no to him.'

'It's okay. I'm not angry,' says Avanti, trying to hide her frown.

'I will give it back to him tomorrow morning.'

'You don't have to. It's just that you make me want to talk to him as well,' frowns Avanti and Devrat instinctively wraps his arms around her. 'Stop hijacking my life. I won't be able to think of a life without you and even as I say these words I feel like a psychopath.'

'But that's all I want to do,' says Devrat.

'Turn me into a psychopath who clings to you and never leaves?'

'Maybe that's your superpower. I approve of that.'

And just like that, she clings to him.

TWENTY-ONE

It's been six months that Avanti and Devrat have been together, and a lot has changed over the last six months, but Devrat's still the lost puppy for Avanti and Avanti's still the intriguing and beautiful girl he had met six months earlier.

It's a sort of long-distance relationship with varying latitudes and longitudes. When Avanti is in Coimbatore, Devrat's performing in a college in Vizag, when Avanti is in Bangalore for a quick training session, Devrat's entertaining a bunch of drunken idiots who know nothing about music in Surat. And yet, they are together.

But today, they are together and the rest of the world doesn't matter. Today, they complete six months.

They are sitting on a quiet corner of a coffee shop in Mumbai. Devrat wanted her to come over because he couldn't bear spending their six-months' anniversary over Skype, and so Avanti took a discounted flight to catch Devrat's performance where he couldn't take his eyes off her the entire time.

There's a half-eaten pastry that Avanti had cut while she sang

'Happy Birthday' because she knew no song for anniversaries, and people looked, and Devrat had blushed, and Avanti had retorted by saying it was his idea to celebrate six months of togetherness.

'You think we shouldn't celebrate it?' asks Devrat. He nibbles at the pastry.

'Obviously I want to. I just want to hear it from you. I'm good with clothes, you're good with words. And that's how it should be. Why do you want to celebrate it?' asks Avanti.

'You look great in that yellow dress.'

'Don't change the topic,' quips Avanti.

'I'm not changing the topic. That was the first line of the little speech I didn't really prepare and if you hadn't interrupted it I would have continued but now I have lost my rhythm and I think we will have to come back to this some time later.'

Avanti shrugs. 'Fine. Don't tell me.'

'I hate it when you get fake-angry at me for it feels so real,' argues Devrat.

'Then you better complete the speech you *didn't* prepare.'

'Ummm . . . earlier I used to look at people celebrating every month of their relationships and think, "that's so wannabe and blah and *ghati* and what not", but now that I'm in love with you, irrevocably and helplessly, I realize that I was just jealous of them. Now that I have you, every day is worth celebrating, let alone weeks, months and years. We haven't celebrated our monthly anniversaries but I need to celebrate this. Six months of us. And if you think that I'm being an over-excited six-year-old girl, then so be it.'

Avanti starts to chuckle.

'See? Now what's funny?'

'You would make a cute, six-year-old girl,' says Avanti and pulls at Devrat's cheek.

'Stop it! People are looking. How did we decide we would talk like when people are looking? That you would talk about how big I'm in my briefs and how good am in bed! You should say that, not this "how sweet and cute you're"! Be a responsible girlfriend and help me with my masculinity and my male ego,' grumbles Devrat.

'Fine. Fine.' And then very dispassionately and loudly, Avanti says, 'Oh! Devrat. You were so good in bed last night. And you're so big. You're the best lover I have had in years. All these people in the café should know how good—'

'SHUT UP! You have to do it naturally. Okay, fine, don't do it,' says Devrat.

The sun is about to set and the waiter comes and lights the little candle on their table.

'Fancy,' says Avanti.

'That was planned.'

'Yeah, right. Are you finished telling me why you're in love with me so much? Am I to believe that you had only ten seconds of appreciative words for me? That's sort of disappointing, Devrat. I'm starting to think that you make someone else write your songs.'

'You're such a brat,' grumbles Devrat.

'It's not my fault that my boyfriend spoils me so much.'

'Why shouldn't he? You're like only the best thing in the world. And I'm sure his life without you would suck. I'm confident, every time he wakes up in the middle of the night and sees you lying next to him, he panics for he thinks of days when you wouldn't be around and he would regret that he didn't celebrate the days you were around to the fullest. And that would majorly suck,' explains Devrat. 'For him.'

'Yes, I know. He's pretty sweet like that. I love him for that.'

'It doesn't end at that. Your boyfriend keeps talking to me about you. He told me he knew after the first conversation that he couldn't let go of you. Believe me, he tried to stay away from you. You sat in a taxi, and he tried not to run after it like a homeless man begging for alms. You boarded a flight, and he tried not to board it, too. His first conversation lasted for three days and he still felt he had a lot to say.'

'Does he love me that much?' asks Avanti, her eyes welled up.

'I think so. He panics every time he leaves you. He wonders if it would happen again, if you would talk to him again, if you would still smile after seeing him; if you would still laugh at his jokes, and ask him to sing your favourite song, if you would still make him hear his own songs, over and over again. He had half a mind to kidnap you, take you to his flat and chain you there. Your boyfriend is a little crazy in his head.'

'And I like him for that,' says Avanti.

'Do you know what happened after your first date with him? The day he surprised you on the aircraft?'

'I don't know. He never told me. Devrat often keeps things to himself. Why don't you tell me? You seem to know everything about him,' says Avanti and rests her chin on her knuckles. Her skin glows from the candle light. *God! She's beautiful.*

'After your first date, he spent hours staring at his phone. The fucking anxiety, the helplessness, the fear, it crippled him during that flight back home and he felt like he would die without you. Like literally die. And he still talks to me about that anxiety. It's there even after six months. I would get him to see a doctor but he says it's incurable. The desperation to hold on to you for that extra few seconds still grips him on every goodbye and doesn't subside till the next time he sees you. It's been six months and he is still not used to your goodbyes. They are still fucking awful.'

'I'm really sorry for him. Devrat is a bit of a clinger. He just never leaves me. If he's such a good friend of yours, why don't you make him understand that I need space too,' lies Avanti and holds Devrat's hand.

'I don't think anyone can make him understand that. Whenever I have tried telling him that Avanti needs space, and that he should back off a little, he reminds me of the time he came to Delhi and both of you had plans to go to Agra and you didn't and you two made a little world for yourselves for those three days stuck in a room,' says Devrat.

'He has told you about that?' asks Avanti.

'Devrat never hides anything from me,' answers Devrat, liking this entire game. He can, at least, tell her freely what he feels about her without sounding too gay to himself. 'He told me about the three days both of you spent in your bed, at your place, with your father in the next room. He doesn't remember how he kissed you during those three days, or how it happened, but he remembers the feeling, the perfection of it all. Although he has to admit, he was shaking in his pants, nervous that he might let you down. He told me you spoilt him by telling him how good a kisser he was. He started liking being told by you that he was a good kisser than actually kissing you.'

'Seems like he's quite in love with me, isn't he? But what if some day I leave him? That can happen, right? Devrat has to be ready for that,' argues Avanti.

'He doesn't believe that will happen. He believes in his love. He told me that Namita got you recommended for flying abroad but you gave it all up since it meant more flying hours and more time away from him. Had you wanted to leave him, you would have left him that very instant. He confessed that he shouted at you for letting go of the opportunity but he was happy that you chose to stick with him instead. Because frankly, he doesn't know what he would do without you. He would be lost.'

'Is that so?'

'Yes. You save him from the world. You came when he was slowly disintegrating. You saved him and he owes everything to you. He was an abandoned puppy who you took care of.'

'He does look like a puppy, doesn't he?'

It's late and the joint is about to close down. The waiter gets them the bill and Devrat clears it. 'Want to go for a walk?'

'If only you keep telling me about what my boyfriend thinks about me,' says Avanti.

'How can I not? You, after all, are the prettiest. You're photoshop-proof and that's saying a lot.'

They are walking through the empty, lit-up streets of Mumbai, turning into random corners, kissing, holding each others' hands and hugging each other just like that.

'Where are you lost?'

'Just thinking.'

'What?' asks Avanti. 'Let's sit. I'm a little tired.' And they sit on the pavement of a deserted in-road in Versova, Mumbai.

Devrat continues, 'How do you make me feel that there's nothing more important than the two of us? Believe you me, I have systematically broken you down in parts and tried figuring out what I'm in love with. Is it that face that constantly beams happiness and warmth right to my heart? Is it that infectious laugh or those distractingly toned legs?'

'I'm glad you noticed. I have been squatting with the world on my shoulders for the last few weeks and it had been insulting that you weren't noticing any change.'

'You're killing my vibe, Avanti. This is the most romantic I have felt since the last Jennifer Lawrence movie came out and you're talking about squatting.'

'I'm sorry. You can continue talking about my toned legs,' says Avanti and pretends to hold her ears.

'This is precisely what I'm talking about. Is this why I like you? Because you're funny, and find me funny as well? The list of questions is endless and the answer to every question is a thumping YES! So I have figured there's no answer to why I really like you. There's growing realization in my heart that you deserve someone better, someone who loves you much more than I do, but I sincerely hope you don't find that someone and have to spend the rest of your life loving me,' says Devrat.

'I don't think I need anything more than you.'

'Not right now, you don't, but what about later? Will you always be in love with me? Arundhati, too, chose the easy way out.'

'Arundhati was a bitch and I'm glad she was one. As for me, there's not one thing I don't love about you, Devrat.' Devrat puts his arm across Avanti who disappears in her embrace. 'Should we start walking to the hotel?'

Just then, Devrat's phone rings and it's his mother. Devrat tells her that he's still in Mumbai and he's with Avanti. Devrat can almost sense his mother smile at the other end of the line. Devrat's never been the perfect son, his career choices have been odd, he's quite uncommunicative, but he has done one thing right—he chose the right girl.

'Ma says "Hi" to you,' says Devrat. Avanti waves at the phone in Devrat's pocket and says, 'Hi Aunty'. 'You have no idea how much my parents dig you. Earlier they used to dread the very idea of coming to my apartment for it looked like a hooker's den, but now they have no such qualms. It's so pretty that it's almost embarrassing to get my friends to visit me.' Of late, little figurines from Orissa, murals from Kerala and flower vases have come to dominate his living space. Every time Avanti visits him, she comes with little souvenirs, she leaves the house a little prettier, as if it's rubbing off her. 'Also, it's safe to say that my mother is absolutely smitten with you. Remember the first time you met her? My mother kept looking at you like you weren't from around here.'

'You're exaggerating now!' Avanti hits Devrat on his arm.

'No, I'm serious. My mother kept telling me that you look Afghani! And then she asked me if you had a boyfriend. Remember that? She even asked you! I think she couldn't wrap her head around the fact that you were dating me. ME. Which is quite strange to me, as well, even after six months.'

'Devrat, all this is so unfair. Why do you always have to say the right things?' Avanti snuggles up to Devrat. They are still a long way from their hotel.

'You deserve nothing less, Avanti.'

'Oh shut up! I'm nothing what you make me out to be. I'm just another vain flight attendant,' argues Avanti. It's something that she does often these days. She derides herself so Devrat could say something sweet and mushy. It's their little game and they never get tired of it. That's what couples do, invent games that are only amusing to them.

'Both of us know that the vain, over-done-up Avanti was what you wanted to project. But the real Avanti inside you is the one who never wants to change from the track pants, the short

T-shirt and one who would rather stay at home, read comics, watch sob movies and sleep for eighteen hours. You love being lazy. I love how you excitedly make a plan, and then as the time comes, you progressively get lazier, start regretting why you made the plan in the first place, and then eventually cancel it. I LOVE THAT ABOUT YOU. ABSOLUTELY LOVE.'

'But I'm sure you have dated better women,' frowns Avanti. The little game is still on, and they have reached the hotel lobby. They sit by the poolside of the in-house restaurant and dip their feet into the cool water. The waiter asks them if they want to order anything, and just so they can sit there, they order lemonade.

'Remember our first time?' asks Devrat.

'It was three months after we first met. I wonder why you waited so long to make a move. You made me really insecure. At points I felt a little unwanted,' says Avanti.

'You think I wanted to wait? Obviously not! But I didn't want you to think why I wanted to be with you was because I wanted to sleep with you or anything. I didn't want to spoil whatever we had on misplaced lust. And I was always a little scared to hurt you, and—'

'I get it,' says Avanti, her memories of being abused now long gone, buried. The fear, somehow, is now gone, and she feels protected in Devrat's arms. She doesn't know how he does it. And when he's down, she just reminds him that he's awesome by sending mails from those twenty accounts from which she used to (they had a big laugh when she told him she was 'them', the fans from Dehradun). They save each other.

'But quite frankly, my memory of our first time is slightly blurred. Not the imagery, but what it felt like.'

'What did it feel like?' asks Avanti. The hotel's restaurant is closing down now. The waiter asks them if they will still be sitting there and Avanti tells him it's their second wedding anniversary, so the waiter lets them stay.

'I don't want to sound all horny, but I clearly remember how you dropped your dress on the floor and slipped into the bed next to me, how you let your fingers slip down to my chest and then lower still till you got to the button of my trousers . . . okay, I think I should stop because I'm turning myself on,' chuckles Devrat.

'Go on,' prods Avanti.

'The point is that I remember the mechanics of it, how we did it, where we did it, the grunts and the moans, and I'm sure it was awesome, but I don't remember what I exactly felt in those moments. What I do remember is that it felt like . . . like I had everything in life, in a very deep, profound and sexy way. It was a little shallow to think, but when I stood tall after you had come, I did feel like such a stud. Like, you know, like I was the shiz or whatever that slang is.'

'I'm listening.'

Devrat continues, 'Though it was a little embarrassing with my paunchy, unfit body. If I were you and I saw it I would have dumped myself. "I like you naked," is what you said after our first time and I was wondering if you had started doing drugs or something. I will never forget that sentence. It was so good for my ego, you have no idea,' laughs Devrat.

'But I do like you naked.'

'God knows how. It's the least flattering image I have ever seen. I would rather see pictures of a crime scene.'

'Because I love you.'

'And I love you. Do you want to go back to the room? And it's not because all this naked talk has suddenly got me horny, but generally, although I have to admit I'm a little horny but you can't blame me for that because it would be an insult to you if I were not. I'm slightly lost in what I really wanted to say, but that's also not new because you do render me speechless quite often, which is strange as well because I should never be out of words, so I will just love you,' says Devrat.

'I got the last part.'

They dry off their feet and start walking to their room.

'Happy six months' anniversary,' says Avanti.

They share a pizza while they watch television, having soaked themselves in a bathtub till their skin shrivelled up. They slip into the fresh, warm blankets and spend the night telling each other how much they love each other. Soon, they are kissing. A little later, spent, Avanti tells Devrat that he's nothing like what she had expected him to be. 'I never thought you would be such a child.'

'You just slept with a child,' quips Devrat.

'Stop killing my vibe, now, Devrat.'

'Fine. Go on.'

'I like how you're this lost boy with an evil mind.'

'That's an oxymoron,' argues Devrat.

'No it's not. Sometimes you're this boy who's totally at sea, not knowing what to do, looking for me. And at others, you're this sly boy who would cancel all movie plans, and make me read your favourite comic books, which I reluctantly read. Just so my father and I have something to talk about.'

'That was an epic move. Another rare moment of extreme "studness",' says Devrat.

'It sure was. I remember how you were quiet at the dinner table that night while my father and I fought about who would win in a battle of Superman vs. Batman. My father kept on insisting that all Batman needed was a water cannon of liquefied Kryptonite and Superman would be done. I don't know who won that discussion but I have never seen my father in the same light ever since. We have conversations. We talk about you. And I can do that because he's not really my father, he's a friend. And there's so much to catch up on. I love you because you gave him to me. You should listen to what Nani says about you. She would get us married if you ever meet her. So, you know, stay away from her.'

'Why would you think I would want to? I would love to get married to you and feel like a stud every night.'

Avanti blushes at this. Soon, they are off to sleep.

In the middle of the night, Devrat wakes up to find Avanti crying, sitting on the ground with her head buried in her knees, crouched. Devrat takes the blanket with him and wraps it around her and sit on the ground next to her. Avanti snuggles up to Devrat, who hums a medley, and she sobs freely. A little later she falls silent.

'You want to talk about it?' whispers Devrat into Avanti's ears.

'No. Just be with me. Save me today.'

'You save me tomorrow.'

Devrat nods and wraps his arms around her.

TWENTY-TWO

Avanti and Devrat complete a year today, and Avanti wants to make it special. Devrat's a shy boy and he doesn't like big parties and celebrations, so Avanti has resorted to what he likes the most—words. For the past one month, she has been trying to write a letter, something that encapsulates the year that passed by. The pages are streaked with corrections, and Avanti lets them be. That's how he must like it, with the imperfections.

She's waiting in a hotel in Mumbai for Devrat's flight to land.

Quite nervous about how Devrat will react to the letter, she hasn't had the courage to call him yet.

Avanti starts to calculate the time it would have taken Devrat to deplane and the time the bus would take from the aircraft to the airport, collecting the baggage and getting here. He should have been here by now, Avanti thinks. But she smiles, thinking that Devrat must have stopped on his way to get something for her. They are completing their first year together, after all. She orders a soup and starts to distract herself. The clock ticks away and she's a little worried now. Avanti calls on Devrat's number but no one's picking up the call. Devrat must have dozed off in the cab to the hotel, Avanti thinks, and starts to brush her hair.

She calls on that number. It still isn't answered. Why hasn't the cab reached yet? She leaves the soup unfinished and switches off the television. She calls again and there's still no answer. She holds her head and is trying to tell herself that maybe he missed his flight, maybe the flight was diverted, maybe he slept in the cab . . . and just then, the doorbell rings. It's like a weight lifted all her shoulders!

'Thank God!' Avanti's eyes tear up.

In those brief moments she had imagined the worst things in the world. She imagined her world end with Devrat. She found herself trading with God, every good memory, every bit of happiness in the future, for Devrat to be at her door, unharmed. She checks herself in the blackness of the television and gets the door. Outside there's a man hidden behind a huge bouquet of flowers. And he's not Devrat.

'This is for you,' the man says. 'Happy Anniversary!' The man places the bouquet of flowers on the table and gives her a card which says, *Can't wait to be with you, Devrat.*

Avanti hugs that bouquet of flowers, and though it might be psychological, she can smell him in those flowers. She reads the little card again. There's something about Devrat's words, even the ones that are seemingly mundane and boring, that stirs Avanti. Smiling, she calls Devrat again, already imagining him bursting through the door, sweeping her off her feet, dropping her on the bed, and kissing her till they are both out of breath. The call is received after five rings and she starts to scream. 'I just got the flowers! They are beautiful. And so is the card. But just the seven words? That's kind of unfair, isn't it? Never mind! Where are you? It's been so long! When you didn't pick up the call, I got so scared. NEVER DO THAT TO ME AGAIN! I'm tired of you keeping your phone on silent. Now, where are you? I'm getting old just waiting for you!'

There's silence on the other side.

'Ma'am.' It's the voice of a woman.

'Who's this?' asks Avanti.

'This is the trauma centre of Eight Hills Hospital. The owner of this phone was severely injured in a road accident.'

Avanti sees her world crumbling. She falls to the ground and she passes out.

TWENTY-THREE

Avanti was the first one to reach the hospital and she was the first one to see Devrat's broken and bleeding body. There was the police and the howling family of the dead driver nearby. Her heart was beating so fast that she thought she would faint soon. There were no answers given to her in the first couple of hours that she went rushing from one place to another, slowly losing her mind. She was the one who had called Devrat's parents and told them about the accident. Her mother had shouted in a voice that echoed a grief that only a mother can feel. Devrat's father, in his broken voice, had told Avanti that they would be there soon. Although Avanti felt like she had killed them already.

She hadn't been able to say a word or even cry until her father flew down to Mumbai, and she broke down in his arms, crying like a hurt animal, crying for hours, remembering Devrat's smashed jaw and his twisted leg and the pool of blood he was in. 'He will be okay . . . he will be okay . . .' she had kept muttering to her father.

Before her father had joined her, she was the next of kin to Devrat, running around, filling forms, trying to make sense of what doctors were trying to tell her and all she could make out were words that spelled doom—fracture, rupture, heart, rib cage, blood loss. She had just nodded, shaking her head in disbelief, just mumbling over and over again if Devrat would be okay, if Devrat would be okay, if Devrat would be okay ...

The pain was physical, and she could feel it in her own body. She had seen Devrat, unconscious, lying on the bed, while they prepared the Operation Theatre. She had seen him bleed, and she had bled with him. Her puppy, her little puppy, was wrapped in blood-soaked sheets and she felt her heart explode and she felt she had just died.

When she saw his broken hand, the same hands she had held for hours, she couldn't breathe. She had fallen to the ground gasping for breath, and she vomited. Those first few moments were of immense trauma and she kept going back to the OT door still thinking that all of this is a dream and Devrat is still out there singing and all the blood, that awful blood, was not Devrat's but someone else's.

For the next three days, Devrat underwent a host of surgeries to save his internal organs. He had already slipped into a coma, a defensive mechanism of the body to save itself from the pain, and all Avanti could think of was her pain, how every part of her wanted to die and never wake up, how she desperately strained her brain to wake up from this awful dream, how she cursed everything and everyone, how she still cried in disbelief that all this was truly happening.

Devrat was in there and they were slowly cutting him apart, making him bleed, putting him back together and the thought always made her sick in the stomach. On the second day itself,

Avanti had fainted and contracted a fever and no matter how hard her father, or Devrat's parents, who themselves were devastated to say the least, tried she refused all medication till the time doctors told them some good news.

Every time the doctors used to come and tell them that they were repairing some or the other organ or tissue or bone, Avanti would want to shout at them for even daring to touch Devrat. Avanti had lashed out against the doctor who had asked if Devrat had signed any organ donation forms; she had tried to hit the doctor and had asked him to shut up and do his fucking job even as her father held her back.

During the first week, she had wanted to barge into the OT and wanted to bellow at the doctors who were nothing but incompetent fools and she would often shout that outside till the time she was threatened to be thrown out. She wouldn't sleep, she wouldn't eat and she wouldn't stop pacing around in the hospital.

Even after the seventh day, there were surgeries every day, there were doctors running to his room and performing emergency tests and operations and every time Avanti read panic on the doctors' faces, she had wanted to go and hold Devrat's hand and tell him not to go, to stay with her. There were times she would start laughing while was crying, still hoping that all this is a dream and she's back in her room in Dehradun, and all this will be gone when she wakes up the next morning.

That day, Avanti was sitting on a corner bench, crying when a senior doctor told Devrat's parents, 'We have done the surgeries. He's stable now. But he's still in a coma. His body has started to heal but he still hasn't gained consciousness. We will have to wait and see when that happens.'

'Wait? What do you mean wait?' asked Avanti angrily.

'You can't tell about these situations, Avanti. It could be today, tomorrow, next week or next month. We can't say conclusively.'

'WHAT do you mean you can't say conclusively?' grumbles Avanti and her father restrains her from standing up and hitting the doctor.

'We are doing the best we can,' said the doctor and asked if he could talk to Devrat's father alone.

Avanti had slumped on the chair, and when everyone was talking to the doctors, she sneaked past them and entered Devrat's room. The room's quietude was punctured by the beeping sounds of the machines that had kept Devrat alive. Devrat was lying on the bed, barely alive, battered and bandaged almost beyond recognition. Avanti's tears kept streaking down her cheek, uninhibited. He had been put together, there were bandages and stitches all over his body, her little puppy was barely in one piece. Quietly, she went and sat beside him and kissed him on his ear, the only part that was not bandaged, and whispered, 'Happy Anniversary, puppy.'

She started to cry.

TWENTY-FOUR

It's been eighteen days and Avanti hasn't stopped crying.

'You should go home,' Avanti's father tells her. 'I will stay here for the night.'

It has been eighteen days since the first anniversary of their relationship and Devrat is yet to wake up from his sleep and wish Avanti. Eighteen nights ago, Devrat's cab was rammed into by a truck moving at a high speed. The driver died on the spot and Devrat's body had to be fetched out from the mangled remains of the car using flame-cutters. His rib cage was shattered, the bones on his right leg were crushed to smithereens and he had multiple fractures in both his arms. The surgery took more than seventy-two hours and a team of doctors working in tandem to save Devrat's, Avanti's puppy's, life. And though he was bandaged and stitched up, he still wasn't awake. Excessive head trauma had sent him into a coma and he's yet to wake up from it. His mind and his body are numb. He's unconscious and he can't feel anything. The doctors haven't told them conclusively about when, if at all, he will wake up, if at all.

She has spent the morning talking to Devrat and he's yet to answer her. 'I have been counting days, Devrat. And I'm angry with you. We are still to celebrate our year end and you're sleeping,' says a crying Avanti. 'I don't know what I did wrong but you need to wake up and listen to me. It's been eighteen days today and I haven't left the hospital yet because I know you will wake up soon and I want to slap you when you do so. Probably I will kiss you before I slap you, but I will slap you, and you're not getting away with this. Why are you doing this to me, Devrat? Please wake up!' She slumps on the bed Devrat's on, heavily bandaged. 'Please don't do this to me, puppy. I love you, please wake up. You have no idea how I have spent these eighteen days. I'm sorry for whatever I might have done wrong, but please forgive me and come back. I got your anniversary card, and also the flowers, but I need to give you my gift as well. You sleeping like this just isn't fair. You not answering is not fair. How can you do this, Devrat? I don't know what I would do without you. Your fans, even the ones in Dehradun, are angry that you're doing this. Please drop the act and please wake up, baby. I swear I will be a good girlfriend and always talk about your masculinity loudly and passionately enough for people to believe me. I swear I will be everything you wanted me to be, but please wake up.' She breaks down in tears and starts to howl when the nurses take her to waiting room.

In the past few days, every time she has seen him, he seemed to be teasing her, smiling in his sleep. Who knows what he's dreaming about? Maybe he's singing songs, or maybe writing long letters to other girlfriends, or enjoying the attention at the bar he's performing—all the things that make Avanti envious. All she wants is to shake Devrat up from his sleep, or be with him in his dreams.

She has lost a lot of weight in the past few days; her eyes are bloodshot for she hasn't slept properly in days. The first day she walked into the hospital, in the tracks she wore for Devrat, she sat crying on a steel bench for the entire time he was in surgery. The doctors had told her and Devrat's parents that his condition was slightly improving. She has barely moved from that bench in the last eighteen days. She thinks it's the key to Devrat's recovery.

'It's been almost three weeks,' says Avanti's father. 'You can come here tomorrow morning? I will get you.'

Avanti shakes her head. 'I can't go home.'

'Yes, shona, you can go home. We will wait here,' Devrat's mother tells her. 'Go and sleep and come here fresh tomorrow morning.'

'She's right. Don't worry. If anything happens, we will call you,' Devrat's father says.

'NO! NO! NO! Stop saying that! Why don't you get it?' howls Avanti. 'I can't move from here. The doctor told us that his health was improving and I was sitting RIGHT HERE! I CAN'T MOVE FROM HERE!' She's crying and bawling and the others in the waiting room look at her. A few nurses come to tell her to be a little quieter. Devrat's father tells the nurse that he will take care of her.

'I can't go, I can't go,' a sobbing Avanti mumbles into her father's shirt.

'You don't have to go,' says her father and wipes the tears and running nose with his shirt, just like he used to when she was a little child.

Devrat's parents are sitting on the bench facing Avanti. Devrat's mother is holding Avanti's hand and is trying not to break down. Avanti has spent most of the time with Devrat's mother. They have taken turns crying on each other's shoulders, while Devrat's father has maintained a stoic demeanour and have done the running around, along with Avanti's father. There have been times when Avanti has seen Devrat's father on his knees, crying, in the dead of the night, in corners of empty corridors, his voice echoing through the still of the night. That's what fatherhood means; to be a hero, no matter how old you are.

'It's cold,' says Avanti, and her father wraps around a shawl around her. 'I will stay here.'

Devrat's mother sits next to Avanti, rubs her hand, and tells her that she can stay if she really wants to be here. Avanti puts her head on Devrat's mother's shoulder and both of them start sobbing softly. Both the fathers leave to check with the doctors.

An hour later, Devrat's mother is sleeping with her head on Avanti's thigh, and Avanti's trying hard to recreate the first anniversary in her head. It should have been so different. If only she had not asked Devrat to come to Mumbai a day earlier, this would never have happened. Devrat would never have got into the cab, the car would have never driven into by the truck, and Devrat wouldn't have been bandaged and lying like a corpse on a hospital bed. It's because of her that this happened. She's the guilty one. She should have been on the bed instead of him, she should have been in that accident, and she should have been the one being fed through tubes.

She should have been sleeping. He should have been the one mourning. She would happily switch places with him for the pain is too much to bear.

She sleeps by Devrat's mother's side. Another day passes by, and she still hasn't heard Devrat talk. Slowly, it's killing her. Her pity for Devrat is turning to anger and irritation. What does he have to lose? He's sleeping like a child, like he always does, unmindful of what he's making others around him go through. It's like he's back to the old Devrat again. The closed, pain-in-the-ass Devrat. Why doesn't he hear his father's cries? Why doesn't he see that his mother is dying every day? Why can't he see what he's making Avanti go through? Why can't he man up and just get up? What would it take for him to do that?

There are times through the day when Avanti breaks down in tears and starts shouting at Devrat's door, and it takes quite a few nurses to restrain her and calm her down. In protest, Avanti mutters that she wouldn't leave the hospital till Devrat wakes up.

And Devrat doesn't wake up for the next sixty-two days.

TWENTY-FIVE

Devrat has shrivelled up in the past twelve weeks that he has been lying in a comatose stage. He has lost over ten kilos. And with him, Avanti has shrivelled. She's a shadow of her earlier self. Though the elders have tried to make her eat, she has become hard to talk to. She's always on the edge, always a little angry, always a little suicidal, always on the verge of tears. Sometimes, she collects herself and acts mature and at others she's howling in the middle of the night.

She has always been an overtly optimistic girl, but nothing about Devrat's condition is optimistic. The frequent checks of the doctors have lessened to a trickle and there's nothing modern medicine can do for Devrat. It's an unending wait for him to wake up. She has spent days talking to Devrat, telling him how much everyone misses him, hoping that somewhere deep inside he's listening. 'I know you're in there somewhere, Devrat. And this trick of yours is really sad. I'm closing my eyes now and the next time I open them, I should see you awake and singing my best song to me. Be the boyfriend this girl needs, not the boyfriend this girl deserves. I know, I know it's a bad rip off of Batman's line, but it's the best I can come up with.'

The crying has now lessened a little, but the hurt hasn't. Instead of a piercing sadness, there's a sense of gloom that has descended over Avanti and Devrat's parents that seems to have changed their DNA. Now it's like they have never been happy. Their faces, their bodies, their hearts, and their spirits have weathered, and they are broken now.

Avanti spends entire days Googling about people who have been in a coma and she knows people have woken up after years. So there's hope, but the wait is slowly draining Avanti of all her strength. It doesn't help to see Devrat treated a like a corpse by the nurses and the doctors. One cursory look, one tick on their papers and they move on; to them Devrat is just a few lines on the monitor of the ventilator.

'He's IN THERE!' she had shouted at a nurse who was trying to flip Devrat on his side. It's done to avoid bed sores but the nurses do it with a disgusted look on their faces and Avanti can't stand it. 'JUST GO! I WILL DO IT! DARE YOU TOUCH HIM WITH THAT SMUG FACE.' Avanti had taken care of Devrat since that day. She doesn't let anyone touch Devrat now. Be it cleaning his sores or massaging him, she's clear that only she or Devrat's mother will do it.

More days pass by. The wait for Devrat to wake up has been endless and unfruitful. Hope has been replaced by a fearful wait. Devrat's condition has been more or less the same in the past three months and eighteen days. Avanti is yet to go home, and even though the doctors have tried to convince her to go home, she's not giving in. She hasn't walked out of the hospital since she came in. Her father has been talking to psychiatrists and other doctors to see if there's anything wrong with her, if the trauma of seeing Devrat slowly die has affected her mental balance. The doctors have talked to her but have found nothing wrong. What could have they found anyway? What would they have diagnosed? That Avanti's in love? Where's the explanation to that? To everyone else, the notion of her sitting there, the girl on that steel bench, counting hours, is stupid. She just knew Devrat for 365 days. And it's been ninety-eight days already that she has been away from him, that he has been sleeping, oblivious to the pain he's causing the ones who are waiting outside.

Today, Karishma and Sumit are in the hospital, and they are sitting next to Devrat's bed. Karishma has been crying for the past hour that she's here. Sumit's trying to maintain a brave front.

'You haven't left the hospital since the time he got admitted?' Sumit asks.

'No,' answers Avanti. 'I can't leave him like this.'

'What do the doctors say?' Sumit asks Avanti.

'They have asked us to wait.'

'Is he in pain?' asks Karishma. Her nose runs, and Avanti passes a tissue box to her.

'No, he can't feel a thing,' answers Avanti.

'This is typical, Devrat.' Sumit's eyes have welled up. 'He puts everyone's life on hold. Every fucking time, this bastard does this.' Tears streak down Sumit's face. 'Keeping us in a limbo, making us wait between hope and sadness, torturing us, making us miss him. Such an asshole.' Sumit breaks down completely. 'Excuse me.' Sumit leaves the room.

'Typical Devrat,' mutters Avanti in her breath and thinks how true it is. 'Sumit is right, Karishma. Remember the time between his first song and the next?'

Karishma shakes her head.

'Fifty-three days.'

Karishma and Sumit spend another couple of hours by Devrat's side. They are going back by that night's flight.

'We have something for you,' says Sumit. And a couple of ward boys come to the room with Devrat's old guitar, the first one he had ever used in a performance. 'This is—'

'I know,' says Avanti. 'This is the first guitar Devrat ever used in a live performance. It was a college in Siliguri, wasn't it?'

Sumit nods. 'It was his first performance. They just paid for his travel and lodging. I went with him and the video you must have seen on his page? I captured it,' says Sumit with pride.

'Thank you,' says Avanti. 'Because that video was one of the million reasons I fell in love with him.'

'I remember how nervous he was before the event. He kept calling me and asking me to pray for him,' adds Karishma.

'He looked so nervous when he went up on the stage,' recalls Avanti. 'He almost stumbled and fell over. No one in the crowd knew who he was and they had started booing him. I could see him sweat. He was SCARED! But then he started to play and the girls started cheering him on. I cried the first time I saw the video.'

'Why did you cry?' asks Karishma.

'He looked so cute and lost on that stage, like a lost puppy,' says Avanti fondly.

Sumit points towards the watch. It's time for them to go. Karishma takes Avanti's hand into hers and tells her, 'Devrat really loves you.' Sumit nods.

'I know that. He's my puppy. He can't do without me. I know he's going to wake up. It's just a long nap.'

Sumit and Karishma ask Avanti to be strong and hang in

there. Karishma kisses Devrat on his cheek and Sumit shakes Devrat's limp hand. Though they are smiling, the sadness in the room is overwhelming. All three of them are thinking about it but no one says it aloud. More than a best of luck wish, the kiss and the hand shake is a last good bye.

They leave the hospital, not with hope, but with the feeling that they might have seen the last of Devrat, their friend, the prodigy, the puppy.

Avanti sees them off at the gate of the building and comes back to Devrat's room. She takes the guitar out of its box and keeps it on her lap. Who says he's dying? She touches the fret board and she feels a certain electricity grip her, the same kind that gripped her every time Devrat touched her.

She sits near Devrat and takes his hand into hers, 'You're still alive, and I know you're listening. So listen to this, I'm going to wait till you wake up and tell me that you love me.'

TWENTY-SIX

It's been 118 days now, and in two days, it will be four months that Devrat would be sleeping, and it will be four months since Avanti stepped out of the hospital.

But with time, she has made quite a few friends in the hospital. The times when Avanti's not crying, or taking care of Devrat, she's talking to people, and she never runs out of words. A hunter will hunt, and Avanti, well, she was born to talk.

'Are you back to adhering to your 10,000 words a day quota?' Avanti's Nani asks over the phone.

'Stop making fun of me, Nani.'

'I'm just saying, shona. The world is a better place when you talk. Remember when you were little and we used to go to birthday parties of your friends? We just used to make you stand in the middle and you used to keep talking and entertaining all of us. God, Avanti, could you talk!'

'Nani,' Avanti blushes. 'I don't talk that much, too.'

'Don't try to fool me now.'

'Okay, fine,' says Avanti.

'Nani? When are you coming?' asks Avanti.

'Soon, beta. You know, naa, how far it is and I can't travel,' sighs Nani.

'. . .'

'How's Devrat?'

'Still the same.'

'Don't worry, Avanti. I'm sure he will wake up soon. No boy can ignore you for so long,' says her Nani and Avanti feels like crying again.

'I will talk to you later, Nani. I miss you.'

'I miss you, too, shona.'

'. . .'

'. . .'

She disconnects the call. Avanti cries a little. It's routine now. Later, she washes Devrat's body with a sponge with the help of Devrat's mother. His mother leaves to take a bath herself, after which she goes for a bath, too, then comes and sits next to Devrat.

'It's going to be four months, Devrat. I don't like this at all,' mumbles Avanti. 'And I know you want me to be strong and wait for you, and I'm trying, but there are days that I think I just can't take it. I'm sorry, Devrat but I have felt suicidal as well, and I would be lying if I say I haven't thought about it. Now, don't be angry about it.' She holds Devrat's hand. 'Who else would I tell this to? Devrat, please be with me. Please. I still need you, puppy. I need you to tell me that you will love me. There are days I still tremble and cry and I miss you. Don't do this to me, Devrat. Please. I'm literally begging you, Devrat. Please come back.' She's sobbing on Devrat's hand. 'Please say something, Devrat. For heaven's sake, please say something.'

After pleading with him and after Devrat doesn't respond,

Avanti leaves for her early morning walk through the premises of the hospital; everyone knows her by now and they wave at her and she waves back at them. Earlier they used to find her a little cuckoo, a girlfriend who lost it after her boyfriend turned into vegetable after an accident, but slowly people have warmed up to her. Their lives light up when Avanti meets them and talks to them for hours at an end. Things they can't tell anyone else, they go and tell Avanti. And though Avanti can't really solve their problems, she does lend an ear to them, and that's often half the solution.

She knows that the ward boy, Ramesh, from the labour room, is in love with a girl who works in the pantry; she's the one who knows that the senior nurse in the paediatrics department is three weeks pregnant with her second child and so on.

'Namaste, didi,' the canteen boy salutes Avanti. He's clearing plates off a table.

'How are you? Still going to school?'

'No, didi. They kicked me out again.'

'So what will you do now?'

'I will sneak in again!' quips the boy, his gap-toothed smile on display.

'That's the spirit.' Avanti winks at him.

She sits on the chair next to the window in the hospital canteen. The canteen boy gets Avanti her early morning chai with two biscuits he knows she won't eat. She pays the boy the money but he refuses it saying that Somraj won't accept it.

'*Somraj ke liye nahi hai, tere liye hai* (It's not for Somraj, it's for you).'

The boy smiles again.

Somraj heads the canteen department of the seven-storey

hospital. 'How are you today?' shouts Somraj from behind the counter.

'Same as yesterday, bhaiya.'

'Okay, okay. Do you want to eat something else?' asks Somraj and Avanti refuses. A few days back, Avanti's father had taught Somraj how to brew a perfect cup of tea, just the way Avanti likes it. And since then, the tea has become a raging favourite amongst the hospital staff.

Somraj gets back to work. She sips on her tea, looking outside, at the cars coming in, patients being walked in, or wheeled in, some in wheelchairs, others on stretchers. She looks away to prevent herself from thinking about Devrat and how he must have been brought in. She wonders if he was in his senses when he was admitted, if he was thinking of her and what it would make her go through, if hers was the last face he saw.

Her love is selfish, it always has been. Devrat has been in a coma for almost four months now and it's getting to a place where it would have a permanent effect on Devrat's brain. He could lose a part or his entire memory. That thought scared Avanti. He would learn to accept his parents as his parents, but would he fall in love with her again? Would he love her as much as he used to before the accident? What if he doesn't? She blocks those thoughts out.

Over time, she has made a scrapbook, slowly and steadily piecing together their twelve months together, with the remnants of what she found—text messages, pictures, mails exchanged, boarding passes, bills of restaurants, recharge coupons, dried flowers . . . she wishes Devrat would look at all that and be hers again.

'Avanti?' someone taps her shoulder.

Avanti jerks up to see who it is. 'Huh?'

It's her grandmother. *What?* She's frailer than Avanti remembers her. For the past four months she has talked to her every day, and she's the only one who hasn't tried to force her to go back home.

'But I just talked to you in the morning and you said you couldn't travel,' Avanti tells her grandmother as she buries herself in her arms. Her grandmother has always had a mortal fear of the railways and airlines, the metro and the like.

'I wanted to see you. And you were with me on the flight. I saw you in the flight attendants. And I know why you wanted to be one,' says her grandmother.

'And why is that?' says Avanti, happy and crying in her grandmother's arms. 'I can't believe you're here. You're actually here. I missed you so much!' She takes her grandmother's wrinkled face in her hands and starts to kiss her everywhere.

'You're kind, Avanti. And your father insisted that I should come and I couldn't say no.'

Avanti's crying in her grandmother's arms. Sitting in the canteen, she talks for hours and then she goes to sleep. When she gets up with a start, it's already afternoon.

'Where am I?'

'It's okay, Avanti. Devrat is still sleeping.'

'We need to go upstairs,' says Avanti.

'Yes, sure,' says her grandmother. Avanti holds her Nani's hand and they start to walk towards the lift lobby. She fills up a small form, never letting go of her grandma's hand, and gets a visitor's pass for Nani who hangs it around her neck. Avanti looks at her grandmother, the same person in whose arms she had grown up, who is now holding on to her like a toddler with a school badge hanging from her neck. 'You look like a nursery student.' Her grandmother flashes her toothless smile.

They walk into a lift. 'I'm excited,' says her grandmother.

Avanti looks at her and her grandmother adds, 'I want to see who you picked. I asked a few kids in the locality to show me his pictures on the computer. He's smart-looking. But I always wanted to see him in real life.' She rubs Avanti's hand, she doesn't know whether to smile at this or cry.

'But he's sleeping,' frowns Avanti.

'I will not disturb him,' her grandmother replies.

They leave the lift behind. Devrat's parents stand up as they see them walking towards them. Rajiv, Avanti's father, touches her grandmother's feet and she hugs him. He introduces her to Devrat's parents and her grandmother tells them that they have a beautiful son. And then she asks Avanti to make her meet Devrat. Her grandmother's smiles and her demeanour are infectious, for she's a little too naughty for her age, but then who knows how old she really is. She could be two hundred for all she knows.

'He's inside,' says Avanti.

'Let's go.'

They open the door. Four months and Avanti has still not become used to the sight of the room, of the drips and the beeping sounds, the white bedsheets, and the metal bed. The room is light brown and white, and it fails in its attempt to be inviting and soothing. It's still a room where people come to die. Seeing Devrat wasting away in his bed, is something she can never get used to. Her grandmother sits on the chair next to bed and runs her wrinkled hand lovingly over his forehead. 'He's gorgeous,' says her grandmother.

'You should have seen him before the accident,' answers Avanti. For the first time in months, she has beamed and been happy.

'Everything will be okay,' says the grandmother and looks in Avanti's direction instead. It's hard for her to stare at Devrat for long, and she doesn't want to cry in front of Avanti. Devrat's weight loss has been drastic and he looks nothing like he used to look in the picture she saw of him.

'You have become so weak,' says her grandmother. 'I made you biryani. It's in my suitcase downstairs. I will ask someone to get it.'

'I'm not hungry, Nanu.'

'If not for yourself, at least eat for his sake. He wouldn't like to see you like that when he wakes up. And moreover, I think he can still feel you around. So by not eating like you should, you're actually hurting him.'

Avanti frowns. 'Now you're being manipulative, Nanu.'

'I'm your nani,' she says. She spots Devrat's guitar lying near his bed.

'It's the guitar from his first performance,' explains Avanti.

'Have you tried playing it?' asks Nani.

'No. It's too painful,' replies Avanti.

'That should be better for the learning, no? Okay, now go and eat, Devrat and I have to talk,' says Nani.

'Are you sure?' asks Avanti.

'Yes, I'm sure. Now move along,' growls her grandmother and sends her away.

Avanti can't tear her eyes away from her grandmother as she takes Devrat's hand into her own and starts talking to him. She doesn't know whether it's beautiful or sad, all she knows is that she won't be able to fall out of love with Devrat, her little puppy.

'So Devrat, my granddaughter is complaining about you and you have a lot of explaining to do—'

Avanti leaves the room. She's in the hallway sharing the biryani with Devrat's parents and her father.

'It's very nice,' says Devrat's mother, but Avanti's distracted.

She's constructing elaborate scenarios of how the doctors will come and announce that he has regained consciousness and that he's okay to go home. How she will be the only one awake and she will run to his room and throw herself on him and scream at him for sleeping too long.

'WHO THE HELL DO YOU THINK YOU ARE?' Avanti will shout.

'I'm sorry—'

'SHUT UP!' Avanti will start hitting him and Devrat will keep apologizing and they both will cry and hug and kiss each other and not stop until forever.

These three months have given Avanti a lot of time to think about death, specifically Devrat's. It's morbid, but Avanti does it intentionally to prepare herself for the pain when it comes. She keeps asking herself more about what will happen when Devrat passes on. The body will be burnt, but what will happen to that smile, that personality, those songs, those feelings? They can't be burnt, right? Where do they go? How can they just vanish from the world? It's believable that they somehow fade away as the person grows old and so when the body dies, everything else does too. But where will Devrat's smile go? It's not something tangible. She felt it. She felt it inside him. Over these conversations with herself, she has realized why people believe in a soul. It's because they have to for they have no other choice. It's hard to bear that all the conversations, all the memories you had with your parents, with your sisters, with the person you loved were burnt or buried, snuffed out of life. So conveniently, people invented the soul, not for the benefit of the deceased, but the loved ones he or she left behind, to make them feel that while they suffer, he or she is watching, and that they equally miss them, like they, too, think of them, and they, too, are watching him.

We can't think of the people we love as bodies buried in caskets or an urn full of ashes, so we think of them as a concentrated mist of nothingness which we call the human soul. No matter how hard we try to make ourselves believe that they are around us, the truth is that they are gone.

Avanti knows this now. She believes her puppy has a soul, and that all her memories will be stored in it, that even if Devrat dies, he will still remember her, and that the songs he wrote about her won't be destroyed in the fire that consumes his body. That's the only way to move on.

Avanti looks at her father. Over the past year, she has sensed the constant restlessness in her father, the constant fidgeting, the looking around, the nervousness, and the guarded smiles. He has noticed that her father is never at ease; it's like he's constantly running from something . . .

She wonders what it must be like for her father. After all, Avanti's mother left him and a month later she died. Does he still blame himself like Avanti blames herself for Devrat? Does he still think that had she not left house she would still be alive? For someone like her father, forging relationships isn't easy, he isn't like Avanti, outwardly positive and kind and gregarious. But like her, he lost someone close to him. Avanti slips her arms around him and buries her face in his chest.

'Do you blame yourself?' asks Avanti.

'For?'

'For what happened to Mom? Do you still blame yourself for that?'

'I used to.'

'Till when?'

'Till very recently,' says her father. 'Till the time you came to live with me.'

'Why?'

Her father pauses, and she feels her chest rise and fall against her face.

'I always thought you and your grandmother still blamed me for what happened. I . . . I had struggled for years not knowing how to ask for forgiveness and then I thought it was too late,' he says. 'I had lost you by then.'

'You haven't lost me.'

'. . .'

'. . .'

'Thank you.'

'You're welcome.'

And at a distance they see her grandmother walking towards them. Avanti's father gets up and helps her to a bench.

'Nanu, you're out of breath,' says Avanti. 'You could have just asked for a wheelchair.'

'A little exercise never hurt anyone and wheelchairs are for old people,' says her grandmother, trying to catch her breath.

'Okay,' says Avanti.

'What were you two talking about?' asks the grandmother.

'I was just telling Dad that I have forgiven him, and that I love him.'

Avanti's father's face reddens, his eyes tear up and he looks at Avanti who just crunches her nose and smiles.

'Is there something you want to tell him too?' asks Avanti.

'What is there for me to tell you?' Avanti's grandmother looks directly at Rajiv. She has always been supportive of her son-in-

law, like she knew what he's like and has always accepted him
as is. Like she always knew that Avanti's father wouldn't be able
to take the death of her wife, like he wouldn't be able to raise a
child or come out of the guilt that his wife would still be alive
if he had not messed up. Nani looks at Avanti's father and says,
'There's nothing to tell you. Except that Avanti's mother loved
you and she told me she loved you and it was her fault, too. She
should have never left you for she knew, too, how you were.'

Tears streak down his cheek and he hugs Avanti tighter as
if to make up for the lost years. Avanti's grandmother closes
her eyes and sits back against the back of the chair like she
has not just said something that has changed Avanti's father's
life forever.

TWENTY-SEVEN

It's been 149 days.

The doctors have given up. No one says this but they have accepted that there will be a day when everyone will rush to Devrat's room and find him dead. Just like that. He will be gone. Avanti's puppy will be dead and gone. Never will she hear him talk again. Devrat's parents have made peace with it, but not Avanti.

She doesn't believe Devrat could leave like this. She staunchly believes he will be back.

When the doctors tell her that Devrat can't hear anything, he can't feel anything, and that his brain, too, is sleeping, she nods her head. But she refuses to believe that. She knows Devrat is listening to everything intently, she knows he misses her, that Devrat is just waiting for his body to respond and, when it will, he will hug Avanti and never leave her.

'I don't believe what the doctors say,' Avanti tells Devrat. It's dead in the night and Devrat's mother is sleeping nearby. 'They all try to tell me that you are gone for good and that you will never be back. But I don't believe anything that they say. You're my puppy, no?' she says and runs her hand over Devrat's emaciated face. She starts to cry a little. Devrat's mother stirs in her sleep. 'How can you die? You're like a six-year-old. I just saw your first performance video. So cute. Baby, please don't die. Please don't. I know you're listening. I'm so sure of that, but I'm on my knees and I'm begging you, please don't die.' Avanti's on the ground, his hand in hers, and she's crying. 'I love you. I love you.' And like many other days, she cries herself to sleep on the ground.

But there are days when she's inclined to believe what the doctors tell her. There are days when she loses it and shouts at Devrat, throws things around in his room, cries and howls and breaks things. There are nights when Devrat's parents and Avanti's father have to restrain her and calm her down. There are times that she thinks she has lost it. There are times she wishes she can open the window of Devrat's room and jump down and end it all . . . but hope stops her.

Today, she's sitting in Devrat's room reading one of his books. Besides comics, Devrat was also into books but they never discussed it, and suddenly, Avanti feels like catching up on her reading. She has been reading Roald Dahl and Ruskin Bond. She's now reading Devrat's favourite young adult authors. She has tried reading the heavier, literary stuff once in a while, but most of them are too slow for her taste.

And when she reads, she can't help but write a little herself. She writes long letters to Devrat which she sometimes reads out to Devrat, and sometimes, just keeps it to herself.

Avanti's writing again, but this time she's writing about other people. Because she figured writing about her wait for Devrat to wake up wouldn't be exciting enough. It's their seventeenth-month anniversary, out of which Avanti and Devrat have spent five months in the hospital.

The dullness, the pain have subsided now. Even Devrat's parents go back to the tiny one-room apartment they have rented close to the hospital. Devrat's father has taken a transfer to Mumbai and doesn't miss office even a single day, in fact works overtime, because the medical bills are mounting and have already eaten through a lot of their savings. Avanti's father has shifted to Mumbai as well. Avanti's flat is slightly bigger than theirs. Her father now teaches in a private university in Mumbai and her grandmother has been staying with them for the last few weeks.

But Avanti doesn't write about these things. She doesn't want him to feel worse knowing that all these people have uprooted their lives to stay in the city he is trapped in. Moreover, she thinks he knows, she thinks he is listening to everything while he's lying there, motionless. The last five months have prepared Avanti for the worst. Now she doesn't imagine miraculous scenarios wherein the doctor would come running and tell them that Devrat is awake. She knows that one day, just like today, the doctor will come and tell them that Devrat passed away in his sleep, and they will be happy for Devrat that he didn't have to go in pain. They will cry, but not as much, for they have been mourning for the last six months. Their hopes are already crushed.

There have been days that Avanti thinks she is losing her sanity, though the psychiatrist she's seeing in the hospital thinks otherwise. She's Dr Bhatt's only patient who pays in lunch. Dr Bhatt and Avanti meet every day during lunch hours and Avanti pays for lunch in return for Dr Bhatt's observations.

'You're my most difficult patient,' says Dr Bhatt.

'I know. I'm incurable.'

'No. It's because you know what's wrong with you,' says

Dr Bhatt and leaves his plate in the sink. 'I need to get back to patients who actually pay.'

Avanti doesn't write about this either. When she reads out the letter tonight, she wants it to sound positive and uplifting. She doesn't want to make him feel bad with the depressing details of her stay, so instead she starts to write the names and genders of all the babies born in the labour ward. She, alone, has suggested and coaxed and managed to convince at least five couples in the past six months to name their baby Devrat. And interestingly enough, whenever she sees a happy parent call their newborn Devrat, she starts to see similarities between the kid and Devrat; the same naughty smile, the wonder in the eyes, and the restlessness. For those few moments, her puppy is alive again, in that restless, crying, lost newborn.

So she writes about that.

She doesn't write about the feeling that she thinks she's slowly going cuckoo, that she's slowly losing it, and what everyone around her says is slowly coming true. It's been six months since she has stepped out of the hospital and now she's scared to do that. 'Devrat, I'm scared,' she would tell Devrat sometimes in the middle of the night. 'What if I have to leave the hospital tomorrow? What am I going to do?' And there would be no answer and she would go back to sleep.

She doesn't want to go out anymore, not for Devrat, but for herself. And it's not just about Devrat anymore, it's about every ward boy, every nurse, every doctor in the hospital. It's like she's the part of the walls now. And people like her here. They know her story. She's loved here. She's the kid of the hospital and everyone loves spending time with her. She doesn't know what she would do out there.

Old doctors treat her like their own daughter and she spends hours talking to them about their old college days. The younger doctors first see her as a slightly maniacal girlfriend who's steadfastly waiting for her boyfriend to wake up, then as a friend and someone they can share everything with, and finally, as someone who makes their relationship troubles look petty.

'So how long have you been here?' asks a medical intern. She has been here for three days now as the part of the group of six new interns that the hospital has hired, and like everyone new, Avanti has been the one making them feel at home. The girl is twenty-two, older than Avanti, but Avanti feels like she has aged years in the past few months.

'We complete six months today. It's like a long date where I'm the only one talking,' says Avanti.

'And you haven't left the hospital in all these months? Like not even once?' asks another intern. The boy's from Jaipur and is a slightly shy guy. Avanti's the only one he really talks to. Only yesterday, he told Avanti how jittery he is to be dealing with patients alone and Avanti had calmed him down.

'No, I haven't.'

'Don't you miss the outside world?' asks another intern.

'Not really. I have everything here. I feel more alive here than I would outside. People say hospitals are depressing, but then truth often is.'

'Truth?'

'No one lies in a hospital. There's only truth, hope, happiness and death. I experience all four of them here every day. I have seen the pain in the couple whose child was stillborn and I have seen the happiness in the eyes of parents whose eight-year-old kid just received a new heart.'

No one says anything.

Avanti chuckles. 'I know, I know. These sound like the words of a godman who is probably a child molester too, but sitting here all day, talking to everyone, mostly old people, you tend to pick up what they think. So sometimes I go all primal on the philosophy part of it.'

'Are we guys done here?' says a voice from behind. It's Dr Anamika Mishra. In her mid-forties, recently divorced, she'd cried on Avanti's shoulders for days after the divorce papers went through.

'I was just telling them that they are lucky to have you as a mentor. Also, I have told the boys that you're single now!' says Avanti.

'AVANTI!' blushes Anamika. 'I'm as old as their moms.'

'But you don't look like that. You can still pass off as a sixteen-year-old. Quite frankly I'm a little jealous. I have seen Devrat's lifeline on the monitor skip a beat when you're around.'

Anamika blushes some more and takes the students with her. Avanti writes about this in the letter which is six pages long now. She reads it again and cuts out lines she thinks are depressing and morose. She checks in on Devrat again. Everything is normal. Well, the new normal, which means he's still breathing, and there are signs of Devrat she knew somewhere hidden in the body that she sees every day. Even after so many days, it somehow feels impossible to her that he's not listening. She knows he is listening, and sometimes at night, she climbs on the bed, puts her arm across him and sleeps there. His parents don't seem to mind at all and she wonders if her heartbeat against him will wake him up. But nothing does.

Today she's reading Devrat a short story by Rabindranath Tagore, a story Devrat's mother told her that he really liked. She finishes just in time for the guitar classes that she takes thrice a week. She's not yet playing on Devrat's guitar because that's the holy grail and she doesn't want to touch it yet.

She has to take the classes on the roof of the hospital because it's not allowed elsewhere, and for now, Avanti thinks she's horrible at it. It looks simple, but it's acrobatics, athletics, X Games all rolled into one for your fingers. Avanti blames it on her little stubby fingers but her guitar teacher says her fingers are good enough. Avanti wants to at least get the hang of the strumming pattern. The class goes as usual. She plays badly, the guitar teacher, Arun, berates her for not practising, she blames the guitar, and they both spend the next one hour listening to Devrat's songs, pointing out mistakes in his imperfect guitar play, yet marvelling at how awesome he is.

She's dropping Arun to the door when the Chairman of the hospital, C.R. Chautala, an old man in his seventies, yet spritely and always busy, calls out from behind. He's flanked by three men, all carrying files. Avanti ignores the call.

'Who's he?' asks Arun at the gate.

'The guy who owns the hospital. He's quite an ass. I don't think he likes me that much. He always looks at me as if I'm going to blow up his hospital or something,' says Avanti.

'Best of luck, then,' says Arun and hugs Avanti. Avanti gives Arun a package and asks him to courier it.

'Who's it for?'

'It's for Namita, a friend of mine. She's getting married in a few days,' says Avanti. Namita had come a few days earlier to invite her (along with her fiancé, nice boy) but Avanti had to turn her down. Namita didn't mind though. The gift card says, *Best Wishes, Devrat and Avanti.*

'Okay. Cool, then,' says Arun.

'Avanti?' the old man says out aloud again. Avanti turns to

face him. Avanti has met him before briefly when Chautala wanted to check if Avanti was not a threat to the security of the hospital. After all, a girl staying for months in a hospital is bound to raise some eyebrows. At that time Chautala had asked the HR people to run a questionnaire amongst the hospital staff to know what they thought of this girl.

The doctors and the ward boys and the nurses described Avanti in the questionnaire that was sent to them as 'polite', 'kind', 'bright spot of my day', 'amazing', 'kindest person ever', 'my patients love her' etc. The HR people reported back to Chautala and they told him that she wasn't a threat, just a girl waiting for her love to come back to life.

But today, Chautala is not talking to her about that. They are in his room, and he's offering her a room next to Devrat.

'When do you plan to leave?' the old man asks. 'You want tea?'

'I don't know. And I really don't need the room. I'm okay in his,' answers Avanti. Chautala's office is warm and homely, and this makes Avanti a little uncomfortable for it doesn't feel like she's in the hospital anymore. By now she's used to the cold, white walls and the marble floor, so here, the brown couch, the small bed on the side, the shiny black table, the coloured curtains, are discomforting.

'I have seen you sleep on the floor for months now.'

'I don't always sleep on the floor. It's only when Devrat's parents stay the night in the hospital.'

'That's why I'm giving the room next to Devrat to you. They have a common door which we will open for you,' says Chautala in a part-businessman, part-grandfatherly tone.

'I'm not sure I will be able to pay for it.'

'I'm not asking you to pay for it. We never run to full capacity,' says Chautala. 'We can spare a room.'

A ward boy brings tea and Chautala pours some for Avanti. It tastes familiar.

'Do you like it?' asks Chautala. Avanti nods. 'It's Somraj's special tea. I heard your father taught him. I'm addicted to it now.' Avanti nods again, this time with pride. 'You can always come over. Drop in a message at my secretary's desk and she will guide you,' says Chautala with a smile.

Avanti appreciates the offer, pours another cup for herself and asks him why he is being so kind to her.

'I wasn't around when my son died . . .' The words, although softly spoken, come down hard like an anvil, crashing on the table that separates them.

'I'm sorry.'

'It was all very sudden,' he says, not meeting Avanti's eyes. 'And I know I couldn't have done anything about it. He would have died anyway.' He sips his tea. 'But I keep thinking about that day, about him, his searching eyes for his loved ones, the last thing he would have said or thought about. It could have been nothing for all I know, and maybe he just went moaning in pain, but I can never stop wondering about it.'

Avanti doesn't have anything to say to that. They finish their tea silently and when they are done, Chautala thanks her for joining him and asks a ward boy to shift all her stuff to the room adjoining Devrat's room. Avanti tries to convince him otherwise but he doesn't listen.

'It's my first date in decades,' says Chautala.

'It's my first in six months,' answers Avanti.

'It will be okay, beta,' Chautala answers and hugs her. 'If you need anything, don't hesitate.'

'I will need a lot of tea.'

Avanti walks out of Chautala's room and into her new

room, which has been tastefully decorated. The steel bed has been replaced with a wooden bed, even the mattress is not the standard but a soft, thick one. There are books on the side-table. Some of them are spanking new, the other are slightly old with broken spines. There's a vase with fresh flowers on the side table as well. Avanti opens the door between the two rooms, and she can see Devrat right in front of her. She takes out the letter and starts to write again, first thanking him for the new room, the anniversary gift, not only the room, but also the spare boyfriend in Chautala.

She writes the last paragraph of the letter:

Chautala told me today why am I here. The question I was battling with, the answer everyone wanted from me. Yes, at first I wanted to be here because I knew you would wake up soon. But then as days passed by, my hopes started to crumble, but I stayed on because even if you flicker an eyelid I want to be around to see that, even if you moan in pain, I want to hear that, even if you move a little finger, I want to be around . . . I don't want to miss a thing. (Reminds me of the Aerosmith song, but it's so true.) Wish I could sing it to you but my guitar isn't that great, and my fingers are small and stubby, and I can't sing. So instead I just want to tell you that I'm waiting. Just give me a sign that you're in there somewhere and I will for another century.

Always yours,

Avanti.

Happy Seventeen Months.

She folds the letter, sprays it in body mist, puts on the tracks she wore the day Devrat met with an accident and sits next to Devrat's bed. She reads the letter aloud. By the time she's done, the letter is wet with her tears.

She starts humming one of Devrat's song, and it reminds her of Devrat's croaky voice . . .

Please wake up.

TWENTY-EIGHT

Today, she completes seven months in the hospital waiting for Devrat to wake up.

Avanti is aware of her insanity, and that makes her less insane, and more acceptable to people for it makes them feel they are better off than her in terms of dealing with grief.

The recent changes in Devrat's body are painful to look at, and he keeps shrinking every day, his muscles are wasting away, the skeletal frame is visible at places, signs that his body has given up and it's only a matter of time that the monitor will show a flat line. But Avanti has decided that she won't leave the hospital without Devrat. She has now become used to the life she leads with Devrat, the silent boyfriend who just listens, never complains, never shouts, and is not interested in any other girl. What more can she ask for? She's used to coming back to him after a long day of work and talking to him about everything that happened during the course of the day. They are so domesticated now that Avanti doesn't feel like writing the letter this time. It's like any other relationship; she has started to take him for granted and she's sorry for it.

She takes out a piece of paper and starts to write down the letter when Ram, the ward boy on her floor calls for Avanti. A patient's relative wants to meet Avanti and she can't turn that down.

Avanti keeps a little busy these days.

It started out as Avanti's inability to stop herself from talking to everyone, but slowly the doctors and the nurses realized it took Avanti just a few conversations to become indispensable to the families she would talk to. Within a few hours she would become a sibling to a girl losing her father, or a daughter to a dying woman whose son is still in the US. People, both patients and relatives, would long for her, and talk to her about her story.

Sometimes a stranger can soothe you more than your own relatives. So now, she spends entire days talking to the patients and their relatives.

Often, the conversation would veer to Avanti's own story and Avanti would tell her story from beginning to end, a story of hope and love and disappointment. She makes everyone meet Devrat.

'This is Devrat,' she would say. 'He's going to wake up soon. It's been months now, but I'm sure he's going to wake up some day and tell me that he loves me.'

And the patient/relative/nurse would just look on, not knowing what to say.

'You're a very strong girl,' they would eventually say and feel a little less worse about their own condition.

The entire hospital now knows Devrat and their love story is quite the legend in the hospital. And whoever new is admitted knows about the story, either from one of the nurses or from

Avanti herself. It doesn't give them courage to face their own situation but it tells them that they aren't alone. They would listen to Avanti's story and Avanti would listen to theirs and there would be tears and hugs and smiles. They would tell each other that it will be okay, and even if it's not okay, it will be okay.

The hospital staff and Chautala noticed how people changed around Avanti and Chautala offered her a position in the payrolls of the hospital. Avanti insisted it would be wrong to charge for it, or treat it like a job, but Chautala reminded that no matter how pious your work is, you still need to get paid for it.

'I do it for selfish reasons,' says Avanti.

'What selfish reasons?'

'It gives me someone to talk to. If I don't, the sadness just crushes me. I force myself to be happy around other people and sometimes I forget that I'm not happy,' says Avanti.

'That's the most unselfish, selfish reason I have ever heard. Moreover, if you don't do it, someone else will, but they wouldn't be as good. I can't let you do it for free for I don't like my employees being underpaid,' Chautala had said and bulldozed her into accepting everything for free at the hospital. She now has a lot of things she doesn't need.

'Dare you call me an employee? I don't want to talk to anyone thinking it's my job!' Avanti had protested.

'Fine, don't. I'm sorry. Now pour me another cup of tea,' Chautala had said.

The new batches of interns have come today and they are waiting for Avanti in Chautala's office. It's kind of a tradition here and Avanti is the mascot of the hospital, the happy face even under distress.

'You're using me,' Avanti had told Chautala on one of their chai dates.

Chautala had frowned. 'No, I'm not. It's like saying NGOs are in a business. You're helping people and I like that. I didn't get into this business thinking I would only earn pots of gold. I wanted to help people but somewhere down the line it got lost. The bottom line, the profits, the shareholders, started to mean everything and then you came along . . .'

'And?'

'I realized one needs great doctors and great facilities to run a hospital, but one also needs people like you, ones who can heal people.'

Avanti hadn't said anything to that. She had just broken down in tears thinking of Devrat.

Today, she's sitting in the middle of a batch of enthusiastic new interns who are all waiting for Avanti to introduce herself.

'I have spent the last five thousand hours in this hospital waiting for someone to wake up. He has been sleeping for seven months now and I haven't had the courage to walk away from him. All of you have chosen a career which doesn't only put you next to God, but also next to a lot of disgruntled devotees. I am one of those devotees. I have blamed God and I have blamed doctors for Devrat's condition and I have a full right to do so. Over the years you will find many like me who would have lost a lot. A stillborn child, a loving father, a nagging mother, a belligerent brother . . . you need to be there for them in their darkest moments. It's hard and I know you will get depressed seeing so many people break down around you and it's something you didn't sign up for, but if you spend those ten extra seconds with the relatives, it will just tell them that you tried your best and you're equally sorry. That's all they need. Just an apology,' says Avanti. And as she says this, every conversation she has had with anyone who had lost someone in the hospital comes rushing to her head and she starts to choke a little.

She has seen sixty people who have died in the past six months. Six of them were newborn children and there's nothing more painful to see a mother holding her stillborn child. It makes you want to curse God and question his ways. It's just cruel.

The cries of their relatives fill up her head and she starts to tear up. She tries to shut those out and think about the happy smiles she brought on the faces of people and narrated those incidents instead.

The three-hour long session ends with smiles and hugs, and the interns thank Avanti for being such an inspiration.

'She's not a doctor but she's better than many,' says Chautala.

'He's just being kind,' says Avanti humbly.

'No, you are,' a girl intern says.

'And you're so beautiful,' another girl says.

The boys are slightly awestruck so they keep quiet. Avanti blushes and tells them that they are getting late for their next session. 'If you ever need me, you have my number. Or I always have my lunch at two in the afternoon at the canteen. Feel free to join me there.'

The students nod and they walk out of there. One girl stays back and asks Avanti, 'Is it tough?'

'I die every day,' mumbles Avanti.

Chautala asks the girl to leave. Avanti sits and pours herself a cup of tea. Chautala sits next to her and takes her hand into his. 'I'm sorry, Avanti.'

'It's okay,' she says. Avanti adds after a long pause. 'I wish

Devrat could just hear me a little and fight a little more inside and wake up.'

'Medically, I don't think Devrat has any idea of what's on going around him. But in the scheme of the universe, it doesn't fit well. Of course he's listening to you,' says Chautala.

Avanti nods.

'Now don't go around breaking stuff in Devrat's room,' says Chautala to Avanti who has a habit of wrecking Devrat's room every few days in anger. There are times she can't take the silence anymore. It's deafening. There are days that a gaggle of nurses have to sit beside her and calm her down.

'I will try not to,' says Avanti.

'You're like the fairy godmother to the staff and the kids,' points out Chautala.

'Oh shut up, sir!' retorts Avanti.

'I'm sure you don't think about it, but I remember seeing you when you first came here. You were nineteen and you behaved your age. Now you are years older than the twenty-three-year olds you just met.'

'Don't make me feel old now,' says Avanti, but she does feel ancient.

'I'm sorry.'

'It's okay,' says Avanti.

Avanti goes back to her room and stares at the empty piece of paper in front of her. She starts to scribble but words elude her. She picks out a book from the shelves around her and writes down the best lines from the books she has read over the last few months. By the time she's finished she has already filled up four pages. She reads them over and over again and thinks she can't do better than that.

She puts the letter in the envelope. A few nurses call Avanti out for lunch and Avanti joins them. It's the usual party at lunch, the time when Avanti is all of nineteen and is the entertainer of the group. She laughs and jokes and asks senior doctors about their love lives, quizzes male gynaecologists about their boredom with vaginas and female doctors about the worst experiences during a hernia examination.

Today, she's taking the case of a young, newly married female doctor.

'So you're telling me you haven't ever been turned on during a hernia examination? Okay, imagine this. If Hrithik Roshan or Ryan Gosling walks into your room in nothing but a gown and he strips it off. His bulging muscles are staring at you, and he somehow has a raging hard-on. What would you do? Now you know that he likes you, because of you know, the hard-on, so what would you do?'

The girl's blushing. 'Don't make me think about it! The next time someone comes for an examination, this is what I will think about, so stop it!'

The group starts to laugh.

The group that started with just a couple of nurses, a few relatives of the people admitted, has now grown to over fifty regulars, some members are transient and they leave the group when the patient they are with recover or die, but newer ones soon join in. Like today, the group of new interns pull chairs and join the conversations.

Avanti's lunch-time table is the great leveller in the hospital. No one asks 'why did it happen to me?' because everyone has a graver story to tell. So everyone laughs and feels good, putting everything that's on their mind behind them and concentrating on that one hour they get to spend with people like them. It's their family for that hour.

The lunch break ends and everyone disperses. It takes Avanti another two hours to get to her room. On the way she meets Mrs Sharma, Mrs Ranjan and a few other young women with children who are suffering from cancer, and plays a round of *seep* and *teen patti* with them, and then plays Uno with the seven kids and loses intentionally. The kids and the mothers in the children's ward love her and she loves them back!

She's helped Arun, a thirteen-year-old with no more than a year to live, compose a text message to his crush, a healthy, gorgeous girl. Arun breaks down twice but Avanti makes him look at the bright side of it.

'There's no bright side to it,' says Arun. 'I'm dying in a year. It sucks.'

'Firstly, we will not talk about that. Dying is no big deal. Everyone dies. You're just getting there faster, which means you need to do everything faster. You should get this girl, fall in true love, and then fall out of it and dump her. And the minute she says anything, protests or cries, just tell her that you're dying! She will not accuse of you anything! If you have to play that sympathy card, don't play it to me, play it to her. Although if you do play it to me, I will be floored and be your girlfriend in a minute!'

'Will you?'

'Yes! You're so handsome. But then again, I'm committed. Yes, he has been sleeping and he wouldn't know if I cheat on him, but let's not do it.'

'But if you break up, will you date me?'

'I will think about it,' says Avanti.

'But I'm dying,' the boy says and starts to laugh.

'Well played,' says Avanti.

Avanti rushes through the rest of the wards and walks back

to her own room. The door of her room is closed. She tries her electronic key but it doesn't work. It happens once every week. The electronic key loses its charge and has to be recharged. At the nurses' counter she gives her key to get it charged and the nurse exchanges it with a red one. Avanti doesn't notice it at first but just when she's about to swipe it, she notices the words on it.

'Happy Eighteenth Anniversary
From everyone whose lives you have changed.'

A big smile shoots across her face and she opens the door to her room. She wants to show it to Devrat and giggle about it. But her room is no longer there. The wall between her room and Devrat's has been brought down. It's just one single room and it has been painted like a little cottage. Her bed is now next to Devrat's and the room's like the inside of a summer house of the rich. It's tastefully done up, there's a little cake on the side, candles have been lit up, and Devrat's ventilator machines are hidden in cute little boxes. You can see the displays but the hideous colourless boxes are out of sight. Avanti's fighting hard to keep back the tears.

'It's not my idea,' says a voice from behind. It's Chautala dressed in an opulent suit and behind him are at least fifty people with big smiles and little gifts in their hands. 'It's their idea. They wanted to do something for you.'

Avanti welcomes them inside, still crying and smiling and thanking everyone. The gifts range from books to little Gummy Bears to cute, little baby-socks (an obsession of Avanti's). She's already quite overwhelmed when Chautala gifts Avanti a gigantic scrapbook.

'What's this now?' asks Avanti. 'You know all this is already a little more than I bargained for.'

'It's just a little something from all of us,' says Chautala.

She opens the scrapbook and flips through it. It takes her a little while to grab what it's about and when she does, her fingers start to tremble. Each page of the scrapbook has pictures from the CCTV cameras of the hospital and it shows Avanti sitting next to Devrat, introducing him to a new friend that she made that day.

'Where did you get this from?'

'I watched on the CCTV every time you got someone to meet Devrat. I watched their grief lessen every time you told them your story. And then you know, they invented screenshots. It wasn't that hard,' explains Chautala.

And beneath each picture is a quote from each of those people who met Devrat. On certain dates there are more than just one picture, and on some, there's a lonely picture of just Avanti and Devrat.

'You have been stalking me,' Avanti tells Chautala.

'It's the best use of the CCTV cameras. These pictures are of love and hope. Not only for me, but for the entire hospital. We wanted to make it special for you. It's to tell you how much we love you.'

Avanti smiles beneath her tears. She starts reading every quote and feels every day of the past year running through her body.

There's a grainy picture of a ten-year-old who had come for an appendicitis operation sitting next to Avanti and Devrat, and beneath that is a quote from the little girl in her sketchy handwriting.

'I remember Avanti di made me listen to Devrat's song while we were in her room. The songs were average, but her love for those songs has made them the best for me.'

She moves to another picture, one of an old woman, who died three months ago at the hospital. Avanti looks at Chautala and Chautala tells her that they have been at this scrapbook for quite some time now. 'It's the least we could do.'

Avanti starts to read again. Chautala asks people to leave the room so that Avanti can go through the scrapbook on her own. Avanti thanks everyone and hugs every one of them before they leave.

She sits on the bed next to Devrat and starts to read loudly. She opens the page to the picture of the old woman who died and is holding Devrat's hand in the picture. Beneath it are her words . . .

'I'm dying and seeing this couple has made my going easier. It reminds of me when I was sixteen and got married. I was in love. So much in love. You make me feel like that, Avanti. And Devrat, you're lucky. You're a lucky, lucky boy. Come back for you're missing the best thing in the world. I wish you get my life, whatever is left of it for I can't see this girl suffer any longer.'

She flips to another page. It's a picture of Chautala and her lunch-time group. She's sitting in the canteen with her small group of nurses, and Chautala and his managers are looking at her from a distance. The picture is from a camera installed on the roof so it's not clear but you can make out the faces if you can see them. Chautala has written . . .

'I didn't like her at first. She was a lunatic waiting for you to wake up. I was angry at her though my staff loved her! And it was irritating for me at first because they kept talking about her. But then I started dating her. We would meet for twenty minutes every day over a cup of tea. And now she's like the daughter I never had. Her capacity to love and accept everyone is almost too good to be true. You can't walk with her from one end of the hospital to the

other end because she has to stop to talk to everyone. It's irritating
because when she's around you feel like a bad, insensitive person.
I felt like that. I felt jealous of the empathy she felt towards others.
And then I started learning from her. Everyone around us did. She
taught us how to be kind. Devrat, I have never talked to you, but I
have listened to your music, and Avanti has forced me to like it, but
I do want to thank you for bringing Avanti into our lives. I wish
the best of luck to both of you.'

Avanti sobs on the scrapbook. She looks at Devrat and says,
'I'm sorry if you feel that I'm a bit self-obsessive reading these
good things about me to you. But I just love it.' She laughs on
her own joke and imagines Devrat laughing with her.

She starts to read again and it's five in the morning by the
time she's done with half of the scrapbook. She's on Devrat's
bed, her hand across his body, her face on his chest, crying.

'If only you could listen to all of this,' mumbles Avanti. 'It's
been eight months Devrat and you have been sleeping. Please,
please wake up. Can't you just listen to me?'

Avanti dissolves into tears, and soon she's angry, and she's
cursing everything in the world and is begging Devrat just to
wake up. Just to give her some sign that he's awake. It's one of
those days when she throws a major fit, and is furious at Devrat.

'PLEASE, DEVRAT! WAKE UP!'

She's pacing around the room, throwing things near Devrat's
bed, and she's shouting at the top of her voice.

'LOOK AT ALL THIS, DEVRAT! PEOPLE LOVE ME!
Can't you see that? Can't you love me enough to at least tell me
that you're inside? That I'm not crazy to talk to you every day
and you don't listen to me! PLEASE TELL ME THAT YOU
DO! PLEASE TELL ME THAT YOU'RE INSIDE. That all
my words, that all my love isn't for waste and you can feel it a

little,' howls Avanti and throws the scrapbook at Devrat. A few pictures spill out.

Avanti's on the ground now, by the foot of Devrat's bed, holding on to it, crying, the cool metal of the bedpost touching against her cheek. She cries and she sobs and she curses and she goes to sleep. As she sleeps, she hopes never to wake up.

A few hours later, Avanti wakes up to a crackling noise in the room but doesn't open her eyes or move. It's the embarrassing day-after of her breakdown. It's not the first time this has happened. Avanti wrecks the room, furious at the unfairness of the world, the rudeness of Devrat for not waking up, for not listening, and the next day Chautala sends a few nurses to put the room back in order.

She doesn't want to open her eyes and face the truth. It's been months now and she has been breaking down every day and, right now, she likes the darkness staring back at her. It's better than the truth that lies behind it.

The crackling noise of the nurse crushing the wrapping papers doesn't stop. Avanti opens her eyes, faking a smile so that she doesn't have to answer the questions about how she is doing today. Avanti looks around but there's no nurse. The room is still in a mess. Lamps are upturned, books lie on the ground, the gifts the staff got last night are strewn across. The sound of the wrapping paper being crushed is still echoing in the room. Avanti looks around for a rat in the room and almost shouts for a nurse to help her in doing that. She starts to collect the strewn portions of wrapping paper, crushes them into a ball and dunks them in to the wastepaper basket. The sound doesn't stop. She looks around and sees a wrapping paper move. It's on the bed on which Devrat is sleeping. It's lying near his hand. Gingerly, she walks over, her heart pumping out of her chest.

She clutches the wrapping paper, tears already damming up behind her eyes and picks it up, hoping that it would be a rat, because she knows she might die if it's what she thinks it is, and she throws the wrapping paper away.

It isn't a rat. It's Devrat's big thumb wiggling.

Avanti falls to the ground, crying and kissing the thumb; she's afraid she might actually die of happiness. She runs to kiss his face and his eyes are moving, they are wet and they are moving. Those puppy eyes are actually moving.

Her puppy just woke up!

TWENTY-NINE

It's been a week and the entire hospital's attention has been focused on the room Devrat is in. Avanti, her father, Devrat's parents have spent hours seeing the doctors doing multiple rounds of nerve conduction tests to check if there are other parts of Devrat's body that can move or feel sensation. For the past week, he has been answering questions by wiggling the thumb and answering in Yes or No. If he wiggles it twice, it means a No, if he wiggles it once, it means a Yes. Devrat has also learnt to do it with his eyes. Blink twice for No and blink once for Yes. The doctors have been assaulting him with questions, and he has been hearing them and answering them in simple Yes or No.

Avanti hasn't been able to tear her eyes off the thumb, like it's a little newborn, who does tricks that are extraordinarily cute and novel; if that isn't creepy enough Avanti has been clicking pictures of the thumb and videos of it wiggling around. The number of selfies she has clicked with Devrat's eyes open run into thousands now.

She hasn't got the time to talk to him much in the past few days, and whenever she has, she has just asked just one question, 'Do you still love me?' And the answer has always come in one wiggle. And she has always replied, 'I love you, too!'

He's learning to talk in Morse code. Avanti has been learning that, too, although Devrat can hear her.

It isn't that difficult to learn. She would hold his hand and he would tap her hand with his thumb. 'A' meant a small tap and then a long one. 'B' meant one long tap and three small taps.

Morse code has tap sequences for every letter.

So 'I love you' means: Two small taps for 'I', one small tap, one long tap, two small taps for 'L' and so on . . .

This is till the time they get him a touchscreen and he can use that. But till then he has to get used to the basics, and so does Avanti. Never had she thought that a wiggling thumb can make her so happy.

She's already making wedding plans and all that. She's thinking she can leave the hospital, with Devrat in a wheelchair, and talk to him all day long. The thought is slight funny in her head, too, but all said and done it's not the thumb that is exciting her, it's the fact that he's alive, truly alive, someone she can talk to, someone whose hand she can hold and feel. It's all going to come back. It feels like the first day of their relationship again! She's nervous of what to say to him, what to ask him; she feels like he's a new person, now that he can communicate. There's so much that she wants to say to him, so much that she wants to hear from him. For the past seven days, she hasn't been able to sleep from the excitement.

The doctors, who had given up, now are hailing it as a small miracle, and are now thinking that there are chances of a full recovery. But Avanti doesn't care about that, and for her, he's already an athlete and she doesn't care how and when he recovers.

On the eighth day, the touchscreen comes in. Avanti's not too happy about it. She liked holding his hand and talking to him; the touchscreen makes it impersonal. That's the thing about technology, the closer you think it brings you, the further it pulls you apart. While Devrat is being trained and doctors are trying to subject him to tests, she's trying to make lists of things that she has to say to him.

It's two weeks by the time the doctors and the therapists leave and hand over Devrat to the family. Devrat's parents are the first ones to talk to Devrat and they talk for an hour. Devrat has a touchscreen pad with his thumb on it and it's kept where he can see it.

Avanti has dressed up today.

She goes and sits next to Devrat. It's like their first date all over again. She sees his pupils train on her and blink. Gingerly, she takes his thumb off the touchpad and takes it in her own palm.

'I like it this way,' says Avanti, tapping on his hand, and talking. 'How are you?'

'Not good,' he answers by tapping on her hand.

'Were you awake all this while?'

'No, just a few days,' taps Devrat.

'Do you remember me?' asks Avanti.

'Clear as day.'

Avanti's crying now; she can die a happy girl now.

'I love you,' says Avanti, and puts her head to his chest. 'I love you so much.'

'More,' comes the answer. 'What have you been doing?'

'Waiting for you to wake up, Devrat,' says Avanti. 'I have

been learning to play your songs on the guitar. Though I'm too scared to use your guitar. Sumit gave me your first performance guitar but I can't use that yet.'

'Play,' taps Devrat on Avanti's hand. 'Use my guitar.'

Avanti gingerly picks the guitar like it's fragile, tunes it, and starts to try strumming some of his songs. She's not that good, she realizes that but Devrat's eyes have welled up and a tear streaks down his cheek. Avanti wipes it clean. Devrat's crying now.

'Am I that bad?' she asks.

'You were imperfect. Like me,' taps Devrat.

'I like your imperfections. Your imperfections fit my perfect love story,' says Avanti.

'Play some more,' taps Devrat. 'And sing.'

'No. You will sing. Not me, I'm not going to sing.'

'I can't talk,' Devrat taps on Avanti's hand.

'But you will.'

And Avanti plays some more. Devrat's eyes are dry of tears and hours pass by like seconds. Avanti then goes on to show him panels of his favourite comics and reads them out, playing different characters with different voices and apologizing for doing the voices really badly. But she doesn't pull back from showing off how much she knows about them now. They also play a brief comic book quiz in which she beats Devrat hands down and Devrat admits in a series of taps that he agrees that the master is now the student.

There are small periods of silences where Avanti lets go of Devrat's hand and wonders why Devrat's not reacting when she sees his hand on the bed, his thumb moving.

Devrat asks Avanti more questions about what she has been doing in the past year or so and Avanti skirts the issue. The doctors have categorically told her and others to try and keep Devrat as positive and upbeat as possible and she doesn't want to depress him with the details of her long stay at the hospital.

Four hours have passed by and it still feels like a blink of an eye. The doctors are at the door waiting for Avanti to leave so that they can resume their battery of tests and therapy on Devrat.

Just before leaving, Avanti asks Devrat, 'Is there anything that you want?'

Devrat's eyes well up and he taps on her hand, 'You.'

'I'm already yours. Is there anything else that you want?'

Devrat doesn't react, but his eyes are wet. He taps on her hand.

'I didn't get it. What did you say?' asks Avanti and gives him the touchscreen.

Avanti is looking at the screen, waiting for words to appear there. Nothing comes up. And then she hears a voice. It's like someone's being strangulated.

She looks at Devrat and his lips are moving. Devrat tries to talk again, his face strained, and the words are more like air whooshing through a punctured piece of cloth, like an old man coughing. She finally makes out what Devrat's trying to say.

'Say it again,' Avanti says, bringing her ears next to his mouth.

'I want to die.'

THIRTY

Avanti's running through the corridors, her fists are clenched, the words she saw on the screen running through her head and in Devrat's voice, her heart wanting to explode. She wants to kill Devrat and herself.

She runs up the six flights of stairs, hoping the exertion would calm her down, but it doesn't, and she's banging at Chautala's door.

'Excuse me?' the man who opens the door asks Avanti.

'Get out of my way or I will smash your head open!' shouts Avanti, tears streaking down her cheeks.

Chautula now notices Avanti at the door and ends the meeting mid-way, sends the people out of the room.

'What's the problem?' he asks, concerned. Avanti's pacing around the room, holding her head, shouting and howling.

'He wants to die.'

'What?'

'HE JUST TOLD ME! HE WANTS TO DIE! HE TALKED AND HE TOLD ME HE WANTS TO DIE!' shouts Avanti.

She catches hold of a plant and throws it along with its pot across the room, and it crashes into a glass cabin.

'Did you ask why?'

'You think I will reason with that? YOU THINK! I WAITED ALL THESE FUCKING MONTHS FOR HIM TO WAKE UP AND THIS IS WHAT HE DOES? HE WANTS TO DIE?' bawls Avanti and trashes Chautala's table, throwing things off the table.

'You need to calm down.'

'You're asking me to calm down? You have seen everything! And still you're asking me to calm down.'

'Does he know you haven't stepped out of the hospital?' asks Chautala.

'What if he doesn't? What if? Now I won't even tell him! Let him die and find out after he's dead about that,' says Avanti. She has slumped on the ground, her face in her palms, crying profusely. 'How can he even say that? How can he just leave me like that? How can he do that to me?' Avanti mumbles between sobs.

Chautala walks up to Avanti and tries calming her down, making her sit on the couch, and tells her that it must be hard for Devrat to wake up one day and find that he's confined to the bed.

'Imagine yourself in his body. He has just woken up and he can't move. He stares at the next thirty years of life like that. Can you imagine the quality of life? He's bound to say that.'

'Are you saying we should kill him? Are you saying that?'

'No, I'm just putting an argument. It's isn't about what we should do because the law says we can't kill him, but you can at least understand why he can want to kill himself,' argues Chautala.

'Why! But why! I can look into his eyes and he can emote and talk with me! That's enough for me! Why kill him? I want nothing from him. I just want him to be around. How's that too much to ask for? This is worse than cheating. And he said he loves me! HOW DARE HE SAY THAT.' Avanti has slipped on the ground and she's bawling, her nose running, her mouth open.

'That's his decision to take, right? It's his life.'

'It's not his life! It's connected to ours. And you can't give a person who's sick the right to choose his treatment. He's sick! What does he know? Oh! Maybe that's why he wants to die? The coma has affected his brain,' retorts Avanti.

'He's not sick, his body is dead. He will have to live with a body that doesn't work for years. He will want to do things and see things and feel things like others do and he wouldn't be able to do that! What's fair in that?' Chautala argues his case. A trolley comes in with their trademark tea and he pours Avanti a cup.

He hands it to her as she's shaking.

'Fair? So you mean just because he longs for something, you will kill him? If someone loses a leg, you will kill him too? There will be longing there too? I cut off your hand and you will miss pouring tea for yourself. Will you kill yourself? Tell me where do you draw the line? Where?'

'That's just ridiculous!' says Chautula in a firm voice. 'You know where the line is. I have been in this hospital business since I was a child. I know the line when I see it.'

'That's a valid argument, isn't it? I can see the line when I see it? And this isn't business . . . this is human life. You're not God! You're not. You can't decide when to kill people. You JUST CAN'T!'

'Oh, please, Avanti, let me explain this to you. I'm not saying this is what we will do, but hear me out.' Chautala holds Avanti's hand. 'Imagine there are so many people like Devrat, confined to bed, wanting to die. Imagine if we give the power to them to die, and they decide to do so, there would be that many more resources for people who die on the streets.'

Avanti jerks her hands off from Chautala's hand. 'You mean you want to kill him and put someone else on his bed! Someone from the streets?' Avanti adds after a pause, her face dug in her palms instead. 'I don't care how insensitive I sound. I just want him to live! And if he doesn't tell me why he can't live with me if he loves me so much, I will kill him with my own hands. I don't care!'

'You do care.'

Avanti's dissolves into tears again. 'But why? If he dies, why can't I ask for death, too? How you can you tell if his pain is more than mine? If everyone starts acting on their own selfish impulses, the world would end, wouldn't it? Tell me? Why would you save me then? I would want to die as well.'

'Why do you make it sound like death is bad thing?'

'Because no one wants to die! That's why! Because we worship life, because we fight for it. We keep even criminals alive. Why not him? He's my Devrat and NOTHING has changed for me. I still look into those eyes and melt. I still feel like wrapping myself around him and hide him from the world. He's still my puppy. He will always be.'

'At the end of the day, it's his body, it's his choice.'

'How can you say that, sir? There are more than a hundred cancer patients in your hospital and all of them would rather die than go through the pain of it. In moments of desperation, they want to die. Do you want Arun to kill himself? He's going to die after a year anyway? But do you want him to die right now? Do you not want him to spend a year with the girl he has a crush on? Do you not? How can you support murder? What about the Hippocratic Oath? That you can't give any patient anything that would kill them?'

'The Hippocratic Oath also said women can't practise medicine and doctors can cut into skin. Do we practise that?' argues Chautala

'I'm sorry. But what about newborns? You get children with problems that they will carry for the rest of their lives? Why don't we give them the choice to kill themselves? We should kill them, too, shouldn't we?'

Chautala doesn't answer that, but Avanti waits for a reply, her eyes stuck on him.

'I have been a part of the debate for too long,' says Chautala. 'And I have been on both sides. Every case is subjective, but when it comes to Devrat, I think he needs to live for you. If he doesn't want to, I would take him to the most selfish person I have ever met.' With this he takes Avanti in his embrace and Avanti cries with her face buried in his chest.

'Does anyone else know yet?' asks Chautala.

'I don't think so.'

'It's all up to you then. If you want to keep him alive, you have to convince him. Put yourself in his shoes and think for a moment. He's powerless. He's staring at a life confined to a bed, helpless, angry and frustrated. If there's anyone who can do this, it's you.'

Avanti nods. She gets up from her chair and walks to the door, zombie-like. Chautala's arguments may have been flimsy but he does make sense. Devrat's trapped in a body that doesn't work, and probably never would.

'What are you going to do?' asks Chautala.

'Maybe I don't want to do anything.'

She leaves Chautala's room and for the next month or so, she doesn't debate Devrat's decision, which is now known to Devrat's parents as well.

Devrat has told them about it. He still can't talk very well for there's a hole cut in his throat so that he can breathe. He takes quite some time to string together a sentence and he gets tired mid-way through the sentence. His voice is nothing like it used to be (his vocal chords are partly paralysed)—now it sounds like someone who's already dead. More than the quality of his voice, it's the defeat in it, which bothers Avanti.

She only sits by his side, loving him, and trying to understand how 'trapped' he is, and how 'difficult' it is for him to live a life with no prospects, no quality, and no dignity and with nothing to look forward to in the future. She has seen Devrat cry incessantly, his eyes straining against his skull, his thumb moving about vigorously, as if he's trying to break out his body, as if his soul is trying to break out. He cries like a newborn, his voice failing him, so he just shouts and keeps shouting. There's no quietening him. He just opens his mouth wide and cries out loud, drooling at the edges of his mouth, and Avanti wipes it clean.

Devrat now doesn't use words, he just wails. But his body speaks more than words can say. It kills her to see him jerk his head on his pillow trying to move, trying to talk, but instead he just ends up crying and making illegible noises.

Avanti has started to feel sorry for him. There are times that she falls asleep and wakes up to find Devrat crying, and when she asks him about how long he has been awake, he answers that he has been up for a few hours and Avanti feels like killing herself instead.

THIRTY-ONE

It's been a month and Devrat has spent countless nights typing out an explanation to everyone on why he wants to die.

When he had first expressed his desire to die, Avanti had thrown a fit, but over the next few days she had seen the point Devrat was trying to make. All she has asked from Devrat is a long letter that she can send to everyone justifying his decision to end his life; something that she can read years later and not feel guilty about her decision. And he has been writing it for the past month, taking out whatever time he can. Everyone he knows and a lot of people he doesn't know have come to meet him. Though all of them have been instructed not to talk about Devrat's decision to kill himself, some of them do broach the topic and Avanti has to ask them to shut up. Today, he has finished the letter.

Devrat would have talked, but talking is a painful and tiring process right now. Hearing his own voice is the most torturous part of his illness, he says. In his own words, he sounds like a baby hyena caught in a hunter's trap, dying. So whatever his explanation to die, he has written it down.

Avanti's has been dreading this moment but there's nowhere to run now. For the past two hours she's been sitting with Chautala talking about the way forward.

'I didn't think you would give up so easily,' says Chautala. 'You waited almost a year. You could have waited longer.'

'I could have held on for an eternity, but I have seen him cry, day in and day out, begging me to release him. What am I to do? Yes, I wanted him to live and I still do, but not like this. Not when he spends every waking moment cursing me and cursing himself, not when he spends day after day in depression, slipping down that slope further as each day passes. The least I owe him is a smiling death. It's going to be hard for me here on. As he says today, he has no hope, I, too, will have none after today. But I have legs, and I have arms, and I think those are what he refers to as hope and those are what we live with. He's right. I can live and he can't. I have everything and he has nothing. He has nothing to live for. And I have a future in front of me. Because I can move my hands. Just great. I'm so lucky, aren't I? That I have these hands and these legs and I can move around even when he's dead.' She's trying hard not to cry here. 'I need to stop being selfish and give him what he wants the most. I owe him this I think. His parents won't have the courage to do it so I have to pull off his breathing support. I'm sorry,' says Avanti and breaks down into tears.

'I will miss you.'

'You're not getting rid of me.'

'I hope not,' says Chautala and hugs Avanti. He slips an injection in Avanti's dress. It's the injection that will put Devrat to sleep.

Avanti leaves the room and makes the long walk towards Devrat's room. The hospital staff looks away from Avanti;

some of them know what Devrat has asked for and they don't have the emotional strength to talk to Avanti about it. Avanti reaches the room and finds Devrat still tapping away on the touchscreen writing the letter.

'Are you done yet?' asks Avanti.

'Yes, almost,' taps Devrat and it shows on the screen. 'The rest, that part, that's for you, I will just say it aloud. If I don't choke that is,' says Devrat. He coughs.

'Can I read it?' grumbles Avanti.

'Why are you so grumpy always?' asks Devrat, his broken voice now totally crushed.

'You're dying, Devrat. What else do you want me to be? Happy?' asks Avanti. 'Now show me the letter.'

Devrat swipes through the screen and reaches the document. It opens on the touchscreen. Avanti starts reading it:

Hey Avanti,

Forgive the typos and the shoddy sentences. Because of you know what.
   On the eighth day.

   It's been eight days, as you have told me, that I have been awake, and every minute is excruciatingly painful. You would imagine that not feeling anything means not having to feel a lot of pain, but it's the other way around. I can feel every second pass by now, and every second is more painful than the last.

   You have no idea the panic I felt the day I finally woke up and got to my senses. I could hear everything, I could smell everything, I could see everything but I couldn't move. I couldn't move, Avanti! Imagine that. I didn't know where I was, all I saw was a ceiling staring down at me. I was crying the entire night, THE ENTIRE NIGHT, before you noticed I could move a thumb. I was trapped in this body and I will forever be. I wanted to shout and scream but I couldn't. I tried to shout, I still try to, I try till my head starts to pain and there's still nothing.

My throat gives away and I can't say a word. I just end up coughing. I'm just stuck. You think it's painful for you to see me go, put yourself in my shoes and then think . . .

I'm already dead, Avanti. I saw pictures of my body. Maa showed me and she cried while she showed them to me. I'm wasted and rotting after eight months of being on this bed. Imagine what will happen after two years, and imagine what will happen after three years . . . Do you think I deserve this? Stuck behind this window from where I see everything, I feel like I'm in a jail, biding my time, waiting to drop dead some day. You think it's easy for me to do this? I see you talking every day, I see everyone talk every day and I want to be a part of those conversations but I can't. But the time I say 'Hi!', the conversation is always over. The eyes that I see are always full of pity and I'm tired of seeing them. I hear the doctors tell you and my parents how lucky you are to get me back. But why don't they talk to me? Whether I feel I'm lucky or not! I'm not, Avanti. I would rather be dead. Regardless of what you or my parents might think, I don't think I want to do this. I want to die. I can't live a life of a brain without a body. I can't live a life of helplessness and frustration. I just can't.

On the eleventh day.

It's eleven days now. And I still want to die. I think sometimes the doctors forget that I can listen. I hear them talk when they say that my waking up was a miracle and further progress would be a miracle, too. Do you think I deserve to live this life on miracles? You keep telling me that there's still so much to live for. What is there to live for? Blinking and moving my thumb around? Trying to talk? I used to sing, and now saying a sentence tires me out. My voice is gone, Avanti. When I try to talk my voice sounds like someone has put a boot on my neck, and it feels that way, too. Is that a way to live? I used to sing, Avanti. That used to be the only thing I used to like, and now, I can't even talk properly. How can someone be expected to not do the only thing he or she wants to do and live a life devoid of it?

Karishma and Sumit came today and they broke down in front of me. I know they both love me. But they love me today, what about tomorrow? I will just be an emotional liability. Do you think they will travel every month and sit beside me waiting for me to type out things that I want to say? I will be reduced to a source of guilt in their lives. They wouldn't come to see me, but they would still feel guilty for not having made it.

Do you think my parents are happy seeing me like this? Their lives were over the day I got into that accident. Now, I'm just making their lives worse by being in this limbo. What happiness can I give them now? I'm just a drain of their wants and needs now. If I go, they can start their lives afresh. They can build a new life without me. But what about me? What do I do? What do you think I do all day? I feel like a decomposing piece of shit. Do you think you will have as much time for me, to sit beside me and talk to me as you have now, all your life? There would come a time when you would have to move on, too. Find something to do other than just staring at a touchscreen, straining your ears to listen to what I'm saying, wiping my drool, and looking after me. Don't you think you deserve better?

On the fifteenth day.

It's been fifteen days now, and I still want to die. Nothing has changed. I met all the patients and the relatives of patients you have made friends with and none of them can change my mind because none of them are in my place and they don't know what I'm going through. Arun came, the little boy, and told me he wants to date you. He's young and dying (lucky him), and hence I didn't feel anything (funny thing because I can't anyway), but what if Arun was a healthy twenty-three year old boy and would have wanted to date you. My insecurities earlier were with me being inadequate sexually or financially, about me being a smaller man, but now, I'm not even human. How can I expect you to be with me? It's just unfair on you and unfair on me. Today, you don't have a job, but tomorrow you will and you will make new friends beyond the ones you have in the hospital. You will go out with them. And I will still be here, waiting, thinking of what you must be doing with them, obsessing about the guys in your group, wallowing in self-pity and inferiority, questioning my existence. Of whatever is left of my life, I don't want to spend it like this. I don't think I can allow myself that.

On the twentieth day.

It's been twenty days now, and I still want to die. I saw my mother coughing today. God forbid that I live to be as old as her, do you have any idea how I would turn out to be? Twenty-five years in this bed? Twenty-five years? I can count seconds, Avanti. Even as I write this, I can hear the second go by on the wall clock and I'm praying to make the clock go faster. Every time I close my eyes I hope that I don't wake up the next time.

And now, it's been twenty-eight days and I still want to die. Nothing is changing. Every day is more frustrating than the other and there's no way this helplessness will ebb. No matter how many therapists this hospital assigns me, I don't think I can live this life. I have nothing to live for. I can't live like a liability, I can't be a burdensome, irritating man for the rest of my life. I want you to say your goodbyes to the guy you know, the guy you were in love with.

Maybe I woke up to say my goodbye to you. So there's nothing more to say now, Avanti. And I want to say my goodbyes. Pull off my breathing support . . .

The letter ends here and Avanti's not looking at Devrat, instead she's looking at the screen, not wanting to cry and hurl abuses at Devrat. Devrat now starts tapping and the words start to appear on the screen . . . but Devrat starts to talk.

He coughs and splutters and gets tired midway through the long monologue and it takes an hour for him to say it, but he soldiers on and still says it. Devrat says, 'I know, Avanti, this is hard for you to take, but I want you to know that if I had a choice of being with you, I would have taken it. I really love you. I still do. And in the past one month I have tried to tell myself that maybe I will tide this through, that maybe I'm strong enough to hold on, but I'm not ... I was happy after I saw you. But seeing you and my parents ecstatic, I knew something was wrong. And then you told me that I was sleeping not for a few days but for eight months. I couldn't share your happiness because for me, in my head, it was just a few days. While you were celebrating and jumping around, I was just here, looking at you, trapped, weighed down by my own body shackling me to the bed. I wanted to hug you and kiss you and I knew in that moment that it would never happen.

'You think I have not thought about the year that we spent together. I have. I remember every minute clear as day, and that those days won't be back again, and that every day that we spend together from here would be harrowing depresses me. Avanti, I want you to know that you were the best thing to have ever happened to me. You found me. I was a little lost newborn in this world and you were this mother to me who found me perfect, no matter how flawed I was, not caring whether I had six fingers or a crooked thumb, you just took me in your arms and loved me like anything. You made me feel loved and wanted and like the luckiest boy in the world. I remember sitting at restaurants and dhabas and fast food counters with plates half-filled because we wouldn't stop talking. And we never ran out of conversations. Every date lasted till we dropped dead of exhaustion, tired, our bodies protesting, our minds dull, and not because I had any intentions to let you out of my sight.

Everyone has a love story to tell, everyone has a relationship to wax eloquent about, but without a doubt, I can assert that ours is better. And I remember we used to talk about how

well we fit together, your exuberance and my shyness, your
dancing and my two left feet, your posed-for smiles and my
drunk laughter . . . I still remember how holding your hand in
public places, even after a year, would still make me feel shy and
mushy, how I had to ask you not to look good lest they think
I got you off escort services. I want all that, Avanti. I want to
be loved . . . I want to be with you. I want to be with you as
much as you want to be with me . . . but I also want you to be
free of me. You have spent the last few months in the hospital.
Yes, I know about that. You think the other patients didn't tell
me about that? And that just makes me feel worse. That makes
me want to kill myself. That I have kept you tied here. What
after this? They will shift me to my parents' house and you will
be there, taking care of me 24/7 for the rest of my life. I don't
want that, Avanti. That's not what you signed up for. That's not
I signed up for.

'I love you. And I don't want to die but I don't know what
to do . . . just kill me. I want to die.'

Devrat's exhausted and tears have started to streak down his
cheek again, wetting the pillow beneath his head.

'I understand Devrat,' says Avanti. From her bag, she takes
out a small injection Chautala had given her that morning. 'I
love you, Devrat.'

'Don't you want to say anything?' coughs Devrat.

'My words would take a lifetime for you to listen.'

Devrat stops crying and starts trying to talk. 'So you will just
let me go like that?'

'I love you, Devrat. You're asking me to kill you. Three minutes
after this injection breaks into your skin, you will be dead and
I will have the dearest thing snatched away from me. What do
you expect?' grumbles Avanti. She loads up the injection just
like she had been asked to by Chautala. Her fingers tremble and

her heart's beating out of her chest; it's taking all her might to not burst into tears and beat Devrat's chest till he reverses his decision, but she knows they are past that.

'I love you, puppy.'

'I love you, too, Avanti,' splutters Devrat. He draws a sad smiley on the screen.

Avanti's shaking now; her body is refusing to do it; killing herself would have been easier.

'I'm sorry,' taps Devrat.

'You will never be sorry enough,' comes the answer. Avanti's still staring at the injection; she has put it in the little orifice that connects the needle to his bloodstream but she doesn't have the heart to empty the syringe.

The tears have come back in Devrat's eyes, and he tries frantically to say something and starts to breathe heavily. Avanti's distracted by the sound of it, and she doesn't push the handle on the syringe.

'Give me two. Let me look at you,' says Devrat.

'Take as much time as you want,' says Avanti and forces a smile, hoping it would make him stay back. Slowly, she feels the life drain out of her.

He's crying and Avanti's crying, too, slumped over his chest, fear grips both of them. It takes a lot more than two minutes. They keep holding hands and looking at each other, trying to soak in the sight of each other before Devrat is lost and Avanti plunges into a life of despair.

'Do it,' says Devrat.

'See you on the other side,' says Avanti and before Devrat can reply to that, she closes her eyes and pushes the syringe all the way. Avanti feels dead inside.

Devrat's eyes close. His body goes numb.

THIRTY-TWO

Dying is a slow process, and Devrat has realized that now. He can't move his thumb, but he's still conscious, and still pretty much alive; he can also hear the monitors beeping, which by his guess should have stopped by now. Two nurses are in his room and they are talking about how they have to keep it low key.

'So when does he die?' asks a nurse.

'It takes a few hours. The body goes numb first and slowly the brain dies, too,' answers the other nurse.

The nurses leave. Devrat's eyes are getting droopy now but he can still see clearly. His parents are nowhere in sight and it makes him wonder what they are up to. Do they know yet that Avanti has pulled the trigger? If they know, why aren't they here yet? Maybe they don't have the courage to see their son die, he thinks. They must be howling and crying in the corridor. Devrat closes his eyes again and hopes he dies before he has to hear and see his mother break down into little tears and howl that all her life is gone now, that she has nothing to live for.

Devrat clearly remembers how he used to find his mother in tears when he used to be late from school. Although he used to get slapped for stopping by an ice-cream vendor and hence being late, he knew his mother had imagined the worst and cried her eyes out. Often he used to find his religious mother hugging a portrait of a god, slumped at the gate of the balcony, looking out at the distance for Devrat.

He has seen his mother wait for his father in the same way as well, with a look of 'all is lost' in her eyes. There have been times Devrat has imagined what his mother's life would be like without him or his father and every time it has been a painful scenario to construct in his mind. When he switches it with his father, imagining what it would be like if he or his mother died, the scenario is comparatively less painful to imagine. At least in the short run.

And this is the time to revisit those scenarios. Now that he's dying. He closes his eyes and imagines their initial shock. The crying will last for a few days, his mother will look at his photographs, his videos and spend entire months in depression. His father will try to be the calming factor, putting up a brave front despite the hurt inside. The house would be in shambles, his parents weak and frail because of the meals they would skip since nothing would taste the same ever again. They would shy away from social gatherings because people would look at them differently and it would only make the situation worse.

But three years after him, their lives will move on.

Even as Devrat says this to himself, he realizes the ridiculousness of it all. His parents will never move on. He can clearly foresee his mother slumped near his bed, back in their hometown with Devrat's things scattered in front of her, crying and cursing the Lord for having snatched him away from them so soon. He knows there wouldn't be a single moment of happiness in the rest of his mother's life. Even after ten years she will walk around like he just died yesterday. She will lose weight, fall sick often, not take medication and not talk for days at end. He knows his mother will die with him, and that he would have killed her with his death. And that's only moments away from now. As he's dying now, he's longing to see her once. But that would also mean his mother seeing him for the last time as well, and that's an image his mother would never forget. The moment in time when she sees her son wilfully dying in front of her and she just standing there, rejected, helpless, asking herself what more she could have done to make her son stay, where had her love fallen short, what could she have said to make her son not kill himself. And he knows that she will talk to herself for years at an end, trying to piece together words into sentences that she could have said to save her son. She would daydream about Devrat getting married, about Devrat having kids and she playing with them, she would imagine Devrat abandoning her for the sake of his future wife and kids, she would imagine how painful it would be to see her young grandchildren not love her . . . she would imagine herself dying and Devrat crying, not the other way around. By him dying, he is snatching every bit of happiness from his mother. These thoughts start to flood Devrat's mind and it starts to hurt. Or maybe it's the injection starting to work now.

Devrat closes his eyes but his father's face flashes in front of him. Devrat hasn't been one of those kids who sits and shares a drink or a smoke with his father. He has always secretly admired his father for his contentment, his niceness and his wry sense of humour, but that's not something a son shares with his father. Instead, they talk about mundane things like politics and cricket. Though that has never meant Devrat or his father loved each other any less. On the days when his mother used to clutch a goddess's picture and pray for his father's well-being, Devrat used to panic, too, and sometimes more than his mother. For him, his father was the quintessential protector and provider of the family. Life without his father would be painful and uncertain.

He remembers he felt strange when he grew taller and stronger than his father, a man he thought would always be around to protect him from the world. It was stranger still when he slowly saw his father grow weaker and older. Every passing year used to show on his father's face in the way of wrinkles, or in a walk which got slower, or on his spine which wasn't straight any longer. Devrat's father has aged a decade in the past year and he knows time's going to go faster for him here on, after Devrat leaves them. Men in offices, in neighbourhoods, in waiting lines to pay bills, in trains, in buses, will discuss about their sons and his father would have nothing to say. Every day he will come back to a depressed wife, an empty house, and an irrepressible urge to end it all. He will spend days and nights asking himself why he needs to live anymore. He would lie in a bed, hoping his heart would give up and he wouldn't wake up to see another day, but then he would look at his wife and undo his wish. Conversation would dry up between his father and his mother. What do you talk about when you have no reason to live?

He's sure his father thinks of the time when he will die, too, and Devrat's mother will be all alone in an empty house, without a son or a husband to talk to, to complain to, live for. He's sure his father wishes that he lives longer than Devrat's mother to spare her the agony of living a life without family, but that doesn't mean he dreads it any less. Devrat tries to check his tears but he can't. He can't help but push images of his mother holding on to a picture of him and his father and lying on the floor. He can't help but think about his seventy-year-old father moaning in pain, alone, confined to his bed, with no one to call his own. There's nothing worse than imagining your old parents without you. The ones who tended to you finding themselves alone in their times of need.

As his eyes get drowsy and he's leaving the world, escaping the pain, he sees the faces of his parents flash in front of his eyes. And behind them, there's Avanti. The girl who was so obsessed with him that she didn't have the courage to meet him. The girl who loved Devrat like a little child, the girl who nurtured him and made him feel awesome about himself. He's abandoning her now. Ever since he has got to know that Avanti has not stepped out of the hospital for eight months, Devrat's been ridden with guilt. He still regrets his first reaction, which was to say, '*Why didn't you leave? You didn't have to stay!*' Avanti hadn't taken offence to that but Devrat would have. Had Devrat been waiting for Avanti to wake up for months, he would have expected her to break down in his arms and tell him that he was the greatest person she has ever met. Devrat did nothing of that. He conveniently overlooked it and jumped to the part where they talked about his pain, about him being shackled, about his horrendous quality of life. Everything was about HIM, HIM, HIM. Except for a few times that they did talk about how Avanti was going to move on after Devrat dies, they hadn't dwelled on it. Because it's Devrat who's going through the pain and not Avanti, isn't it? He realizes he has been blind to her pain, her love for him, her sacrifice. He has just been selfish and he has failed her love in all ways possible. Devrat now wishes he could have had Avanti in his last moments. He wants to apologize for not being worthy of her love. He wants to tell her how sorry he is for making her wait for months and then spoiling it all by wanting to die. He wants to ask her to move on, something he knows might take years. Or forever. Maybe five years down the line, some strapping, successful guy will manage to woo Avanti again and she will be head over heels in love with him. Maybe they will get married soon, have the time of their lives, and have little kids who look like Avanti.

Ten years down the line, he will just be a distant memory in her head, a guy who disappointed her, a guy who couldn't give back as much as she gave to him; he will be an aberration in her life. He cries.

When he leaves, he would leave behind sadness and disappointment, Devrat realizes that now. He's not killing himself, he's destroying three other lives in the wake, lives of people who had only loved him unconditionally. How could he not see that? It's not just him, it's everyone who has ever loved him. His life was not his to take. It was theirs. His pain was not his to take, it was theirs as well.

He's now thinking of how his life would be strapped to a bed if he hadn't killed himself. A month down the line he would be shifted home with all the contraptions that would keep him alive. His mother would spend hours and hours sitting beside him, doing what a mother likes to do the most—talking to him. His father would be a work-shirker at office; he would try to wrap up all the work in the office as soon as possible so that he can go back home to his son and his wife, and see them talk. It's everything that parents want. In an ideal world they don't want their kids to grow up and take care of them. They want their kids to be kids, so that they can keep pampering them and taking care of them and loving them. All they want is that they have the kids all to themselves, something that they get robbed of when their children grow up. He would have been a pampered little 'puppy', as Avanti used to call him. Shackled, as he puts it, to a bed for the next many years, he would have been the best son in the world.

He imagines himself in a bed with the three of them around him. Avanti, in her uniform if she's still flying, his parents and Avanti's father, all looking at him, listening to what he's saying, showering love on him, and still praying that he recovers soon. Suddenly, he's there and he can see their faces, bright with happiness, still discussing that fortunate day when Devrat woke up, talking about how it was a miracle and how it made them so happy. And he's sitting there basking in all the attention, happy that he's alive and he has another chance at life. He sees those smiling faces in his head, and thinks that it's the last time he will ever see them, the people he had loved so dearly, the people who had meant everything to him. He had given up too easily and it's too late now. Tears streak down his cheeks.

He doesn't want to die. He doesn't want to die!

His eyes are drooping. He's slipping away, from Avanti, from his mother, from his father; he's leaving them. He panics and he cries. He tries moving his thumb but it's not responding. He tries harder. He tries to talk but no sound comes out of his mouth . . . he's shouting but his vocal chords can only elicit a faint cry of a dying animal . . .

Avanti and his parents rush in. Their eyes, too, have welled up. They all sit around Devrat. His mother is running her hands through his hair and though he can't feel a thing, he knows how comforting it is. His father is standing at a distance and is smiling under the tears. He's still his superhero. He might have a bent spine and defeated look on his face, but he has still forced a smile. What is he if not a superhero? Avanti has held his hand and it still feels like the first time. Devrat's tears are flowing freely. Devrat's mother is kissing her dying son all over his face, looking at him for one last time. Devrat doesn't want to die. He doesn't want to go away from his parents, and from Avanti. He doesn't want to snatch the thing they love the most away from them. He doesn't want to walk away from what he loves the most.

He musters up the last of his strength and tries to talk. His throat is like it's on fire.

'*I DON'T WANT TO DIE,*' he mumbles.

The three of them burst out crying, hearing what he just said. His mother buries her face in Devrat's chest. Devrat mumbles again.

He's sweating now. Avanti runs a hand over his forehead. She says, 'You are not dying. You're just falling asleep.'

Devrat cries. His eyes close. Darkness. He can hear the howls of his mother. He can hear his father break down. And he cries. And then, all of a sudden, he's gone. He has killed himself and three others. His obituary would read—Devrat survived by a dead girlfriend and his dead parents.

THIRTY-THREE

It's been a year since Avanti injected Devrat and saw the light go out of his eyes. And since then, never have her fingers trembled so much. There are more than fifty people outside, waiting for her to come out and take centre-stage but she's pacing around, wanting to run away.

'You will be great,' says Sumit.

'Shut up! There are people outside, Sumit! There are people waiting outside. I'm so sure I will screw up. I have never played the guitar in front of anyone except you and him.'

Avanti's is now a part of new band, it's called Seven Hills, and it's scratchy and not perfect and they haven't performed anywhere yet. It's just the vocalist and her. She plays the guitar and the vocalist sings. She's not that good. It's been a year that she's been practising, but she doesn't think she's as good.

'There's no way you're backing out now, Avanti. You will be great,' says Sumit, sipping on his Red Bull. He offers some to Avanti who refuses.

'I'm a pile of nerves, Sumit. I can't do this. Look at my

fingers! I can't play with these fingers. Send someone else in,' she says, holding her head, looking outside at the dimly lit stage and the expectant faces.

'It's not for you. It's for Devrat. You think I couldn't get a better guitarist that you? Of course I can! But you have to do this!'

'That's what I'm even more scared of. What if people boo me off stage? What if I snap a string?' asks Avanti.

'None of this is going to happen. Just close your eyes. They are anyway going to concentrate on the vocalist,' says Sumit. And then starts to chuckle.

'What!' snaps Avanti.

'You remind me of Devrat and his first paid performance. He was so anxious that he would disappoint people. He paced around the room just like you're doing right now.'

'How did it go then?' asks Avanti.

'I think it was one of his best performances,' answers Sumit. 'And so is yours going to be. You're good, Avanti. Have faith in yourself.'

Avanti nods.

'And if you still don't think you're confident enough, I recommend a shot of this!' says Sumit and offers her a shot of vodka.

Avanti promptly downs it. 'That was disgusting! But I think that will work.'

Sumit hugs Avanti and tells her that it's going to be great. Avanti nods and tries not to cry. 'It's for Devrat,' says Sumit.

Avanti walks out from the door and sits at the seat designated for the guitarist. The vocalist of the band smiles at her. A few people clap, others are still busy eating. She adjusts the microphone and a piercing static sound fills up the restaurant.

Everyone looks at her. She closes her eyes and waits for the panic to settle down. She strums the guitar to check the levels and mutters 'test' thrice. The nerves have settled down a little.

'Hello,' says Avanti. The crowd mutters a Hello back. She looks at the crowd which is expectantly looking at her and the vocalist who's smiling calmly. She closes her eyes and tries to dam the tears.

'We are here to sing the songs Devrat, the love of my life, used to sing. For years I had obsessed about those songs and always wanted more people to hear them. This is my small attempt to make his songs heard by more people. I'm not a musician. I'm just a girl madly in love.'

The vocalist smiles back at him. Avanti's already crying a little inside.

The crowd claps slowly and at this and Avanti begins strumming the guitar. The vocalist starts to sing the song, and it's not how Avanti remembers it, it's not how Devrat used to sing. But just to hear that song again, fills her up with so much joy that she can't put it down in words.

The crowd asks for an encore and the vocalist sings it again.

'When did you first hear it?' asks a boy in the crowd, not expecting a reply.

Avanti who is re-tuning her guitar to go into the next song, stops midway and answers the questions. 'I was twelve when I first heard the song. It was on his page. Devrat recorded it on his ancient phone and uploaded it. He stopped twice in the middle and said, "Screw it, let's go again" but never did and uploaded the video with its mistakes. I made a lot of my girlfriends hear it but no one really liked it that much. They were into silly white women singing about break-ups. But there was this one female teacher who heard it in class and really liked it! So much so she asked me to send her the list. But then I got jealous and I didn't send it!'

The crowd bursts out laughing at this. The vocalist laughs, too. 'Silly girl,' he mutters.

'But then when Devrat wrote the song, he was in love with a girl who dumped him. She wasn't even pretty or anything. Devrat was way out of her league. But good for me!'

There are giggles all around the room.

And they go on to the next song. And the next. The vocalist screws up almost every song and Avanti's a little pissed at him.

'What the hell are you doing?' Avanti whispers into his ears, mid-way through the performance a few times.

'I don't remember some of the stuff,' answers the vocalist.

'Pay attention!'

There's always someone who wants to know the history of the song. And there were always two versions of the history. One was from Devrat's side and one from Avanti's side. They are as interested in the story as they are interested in the songs.

Avanti tells them the stories behind all the songs Devrat composed just for Avanti. There are boys who put their arms around their girlfriends, suddenly feeling the love in the room, and there are girls who are now choking on their own words. There are more than eighty pairs of eyes stuck on Avanti, hanging on to every word Avanti utters, trying to not break down into little tears.

By the time they are done performing the eighteen songs she had prepared, each of them screwed irreversibly by the vocalist, who couldn't sing them as well as they were first sung by Devrat, the crowd has left everything and is engrossed in Avanti and Devrat's story.

The girls have their mouths covered and are openly crying,

and the boys are repeatedly telling them that they love them. It's been one and half hours and no one has left the restaurant. Not only are the songs repeated, the story is too. The ones who have come in late are being filled up by the people in adjacent tables. 'Devrat was in the hospital for eight months and she didn't leave the hospital for eight months,' the crying girls would whisper to the others coming inside. And then they would have tears in their eyes as well.

The crowd has swelled up to a hundred by the time she's finished. And while she's walking off the stage, the crowd gets up on its feet and applauds the performance. Avanti looks back once, bows to the crowd, and she walks off the stage. The vocalist is swarmed by girls and they are getting pictures clicked with him.

Avanti's pissed. The girls don't even know how good the original songs were. The vocalist just screwed them. *And look how he's enjoying the company of girls throwing themselves on him! Sitting there, basking in all the attentions! Asshole.*

'How did I do?' asks Avanti.

'Are you being sarcastic right now? You were awesome! There were people taking videos, Avanti. This band is so going viral! And you have the perfect manager to take care of that.'

'I don't think so. The vocalist is such an ass. Look how he's getting clicked with all those girls. Just sitting there smiling with his big eyes. I'm not touring with him.'

'Shut up, Avanti. The first thing Devrat told me was that you love to travel! This is your chance. Not only do you get to travel, you get to tell your story to everyone. This is awesome. You can't let go of it!' says Sumit.

'I will think about it,' says Avanti. 'Can we go now?'

'Devrat's parents are here,' answers Sumit.

'Oh! Where are they?'

'They were listening to your band.'

'You're kidding me!' says Avanti. 'That's so embarrassing!'

'Shut up. You guys were great.'

Sumit leads Avanti to where Devrat's parents are sitting. As she makes her way to their table, there are slow claps all around and there are people telling her that she was awesome and they would love to listen to her again. She nods and mutters 'thank you' as she makes her way towards their table.

She hugs Devrat's parents who are in tears.

'You were great,' they tell her. Devrat's mother runs her fingers over her face and tells her that she looks beautiful.

Avanti nods. 'How was it?' Avanti asks her father who's there, too.

'I think you found what you really want to do in life,' says Avanti's father and hugs her. Avanti pulls up a chair and sits near her father. She hears a tapping sound. She looks to her right and a touchscreen is glowing.

'*YOU. WERE. AWESOME,*' says the vocalist who joins them at the table.

'Shut up. You go and get clicked with those girls.'

'Are you jealous?' asks the vocalist.

'Yes, you weren't even that good. Your voice is like one of a toad,' snaps Avanti. 'Go, go, to those girls.'

'I would have, but I'm a little tired.'

Panic takes over Avanti's face. 'Oh? Do you need anything?'

'No,' says Devrat and smiles.

'You shit. You scared me,' says Avanti and then hugs him.

Devrat's sitting in his elaborate wheelchair, all the equipment tucked beneath the seating cushion. Avanti's father worked with Chautala's team to make this chair and it allows Devrat to move around and not be stuck in a bed. Devrat's still paralysed but he can talk and he can sing for a few minutes at least.

'Do you think I really screwed those songs?' asks Devrat.

'A little bit,' says Avanti. 'But you're getting better. So that's okay.' She slips her hand around his arm and keeps her head on his shoulder.

'And actually, I should be the angry one. *Today is the first-year anniversary of when you almost killed me. I could have been dead you know.*'

'I would have never killed you. I could have never killed you.'

'*But you made me believe so. Why would you do so? Why would you make me believe that I was going to die!*'

'There was no other way to make you stay.'

'*Grrrrr!*

'I had to do it. It was Mr Chautala who gave me the idea and he gave me the idea of using the anaesthetic on you. He told me it was the only option to make you want to live! And it worked. You were not going to die. You were going to be asleep for a day. But you thought you were going to die! You have to admit that it was brilliant!'

'*That it was. If you had killed me, my decision would have been the biggest regret of my dead life.*'

Avanti smiles, thinking of the time she made Devrat believe that she had actually given up on him and she would help him die. She made Devrat believe that he had actually died. Everyone in the hospital said it was a big gamble but it paid off. But Avanti knew it wasn't a gamble. She knew Devrat would come around and decide to spend the rest of his life, in whichever condition, with her.

'*I have something for you.*'

'What?' asks Avanti.

'Get your face closer.'

Avanti frowns and gingerly bends over.

Devrat brings his hand up and brushes it briefly against his face before it flops down on his lap again. She looks at her father and Devrat's parents and they are smiling. They know!

'Do it again,' says Avanti.

Devrat tries again and he lifts his hand halfway before it drops again on his lap. 'Do it again,' screams Avanti, crying.

'Okay. Chill.'

'What are you doing, Devrat! You can move! You can move! Oh my God. And you knew?' she looks at her father. 'Why didn't anyone tell me? Can you feel me?' She puts her hand on Devrat's hand and asks him, 'Can you feel my touch?'

Devrat says, 'Yes.'

'Screw you, Devrat! Why didn't you tell me?'

She lunges forward and hugs him.

He mutters, 'You're not the only one with tricks up your sleeve.'

'Shut up.'

'You shut up.'

'Do it again,' says Avanti.

'Shut up.'

'No, seriously. Touch me again.'

'Shut up.'

'No, seriously.'

'Avanti? You need to stop talking. Has someone ever told you that you talk a lot?'

'Sometimes. But it's always—'

'Shut up.'

Hold My Hand

. . . the rest shall follow

Deep, an awkward young man obsessed with libraries and books, has his dream come true when he is sent to Hong Kong on an internship programme. Leaving behind jealous but encouraging friends, a supportive father and a hysterical, overprotective mother, Deep makes his first flight to a foreign land. And then he sees her, Ahana, a stunningly beautiful girl.

But Deep also has to come to terms with another reality: Ahana is blind. Together they explore Hong Kong, Ahana guiding them with the smells and sounds of the wondrous city and Deep bringing to life for her the delightful sights he sees.

They're living a dream, till Aveek, her gorgeous ex-boyfriend comes back into her life.

Hold My Hand is a delightful, young romance with a surprise ending.

Price: Rs 140